Dorothea stretched her hand high to the tempting fruit.

Her smile dissolved into stunned surprise as a strong arm slipped around her waist. The next instant she was being ruthlessly, expertly and very comprehensibly kissed!

Her mind awhirl, senses scorched, she looked up into a dark-browed face. Hazel eyes, distinctly amused, gazed into her own green orbs. Sheer fury erupted within her. She aimed a stinging slap at the laughing face. It never landed.

"No, I don't think I will let you hit me. How was I to know you weren't the blacksmith's daughter?"

understanding, don't you think?"

Stephanie Laurens

Tangled Reins

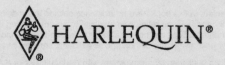

TORONTO • NEW YORK • LONDON
AMSTERDAM • PARIS • SYDNEY • HAMBURG
STOCKHOLM • ATHENS • TOKYO • MILAN • MADRID
PRAGUE • WARSAW • BUDAPEST • AUCKLAND

ISBN 0-373-30312-2

TANGLED REINS

First North American Publication 1998

Printed in U.S.A.

STEPHANIE LAURENS

Born in Sri Lanka, Stephanie Laurens has lived mostly in Australia. After qualifying as a scientist, she and her husband traveled extensively through the Far and Middle East, as well as throughout Europe and England. Four years in London gave her the settings for her Regency romances. Now settled once more in Australia, she lives in a comfortable suburban house with her husband, two young children, a mindless but lovable dog and a cat with a crooked leg.

Chapter One

"Mmmm." Dorothea closed her eyes, savouring the taste of sun-warmed wild blackberry. Surely the most delicious of summer's delights. She surveyed the huge bush. Burgeoning with ripe fruit, it stretched across one side of the small clearing. More than enough to fill tonight's pie, with plenty left over to make jam. She settled her basket on the ground and set to. Working methodically over the bush, she selected the best berries and dropped them into the basket in a fluid stream. While her hands laboured, her mind went tripping. How childlike her sister still was, for all her sixteen years. It was at her suggestion Dorothea was here, deep in the woods of the neighbouring estate. Cecily craved blackberries for supper. So, brown eyes sparkling, golden ringlets dancing, she had begged her elder sister, about to depart for a ramble to gather herbs, to make a detour to the blackberry bush.

Her elder sister sighed. Would London erase that dazzling spontaneity? More importantly, would their projected trip to the capital free Cecily of this humdrum existence? Six months had passed since their mother, Cynthia, Lady Darent, had succumbed to a chill, leaving her two daughters to the guardianship of their cousin, Herbert, Lord Darent. Five interminable months spent at Darent Hall in Northamptonshire while the lawyers picked over the will had convinced Dorothea that no help and much hindrance could be expected from that quarter. Herbert, not to put too fine a point on it, was an indefatigable bore. And Marjorie, his wife, prim, prosy and hopelessly inelegant in every way, was worse than useless. If their grandmother had not appeared, exactly like the proverbial fairy godmother, goodness only knew what they would have done.

Suddenly unable to move, she paused to gaze, unperturbed, at a bramble hooked about the hem of her dress. Just as well it was her old dimity! Despite Aunt Agnes's bleats about mourning clothes, she had insisted on her practice of wearing the outmoded green dress for her foraging expeditions. The square-cut neckline and bodice fitted to the waist belonged to another time; the full skirts, without the support of the voluminous petticoats they were intended to cover, clung to her willowy figure. She examined the tiny tears the briar thorns had left in the material.

As she straightened, the warmth of the clearing, hemmed in by undergrowth and trees and lit by the sun slanting through the high branches, struck her anew. On impulse, her hands went to her hair, hanging heavy in a bun on her neck. With the restricting pins removed, it fell in a cascade of rich mahogany brown to her waist. Cooler, she resumed her picking.

At least she was confident of what lay in store for herself in London. No amount of effort from her grandmother would be sufficient to win *her* a husband! Green flashes ran like emeralds through her huge eyes. Her eyes, of course, were her major, and only, asset. All her other points, innocuous in themselves, were disastrously unfashionable. Her hair was dark, not the favoured blonde; her face pale as alabaster and not peaches and cream like Cecily's. Her nose was well enough but her mouth was too large and her lips too full. Rosebud lips were the craze. And she was too tall and her figure slim against the prevailing trend to voluptuous curves. To cap it all, she was twenty-two, with a strong streak of independence to boot! Hardly the type of female to attract the attention of the fashionable male. With a deep chuckle she popped another ripe berry between her too full lips.

Her relegation to the ranks of the old maids disturbed her not at all. She had enough to live comfortably for the rest of her days and looked forward to years of country pursuits at the Grange with equanimity. She had received considerable attention from the local gentlemen, yet no man had awoken in her the slightest desire to trade her independent existence for the respectable state of matrimony. While her peers plotted and schemed to get that all-important ring on their finger, she saw no reason to follow their lead. Only love, that strange and compelling emotion that, she freely admitted, had yet to touch her heart would, she suspected, be strong enough to tempt her from her comfortable ways. In truth, she had difficulty envisaging the gentleman whose attraction would prove sufficient to seduce her from her established life. For too long now she had been her own mistress. Free to do as she wished, busy and secure—she was content. Cecily was a different matter.

Bright as a button, Cecily yearned for a more glittering lifestyle. Although so young, she had a burning interest in people, and the horizons of the Grange were far too limited for her satisfaction. Sweet, young and fashionably beautiful, she would surely find some elegant and personable young man to give her all her heart desired. Which was the primary reason they were going to London.

Dorothea had been absently regarding a particularly large berry, almost out of her reach. With a sudden smile she stretched one white hand high to the tempting fruit. Her smile dissolved into stunned surprise as a strong arm slipped around her waist. The fact barely registered before a deft movement delivered her into a crushing embrace. She caught a glimpse of a dark face. The next instant she was being ruthlessly, expertly and very comprehensively kissed.

For one long moment her mind remained blank. Then consciousness flooded back. She was not inexperienced. Lack of response would see her released faster than any action. Prosaic and practical, she willed herself to frigidity.

She had seriously misjudged the threat. Despite perfectly clear instructions, her body refused to comply. Horrified, she felt a sudden warmth rush through her, followed by an almost overwhelming urge to lean into that embrace, clearly poised to become even more passionate if she succumbed. No country admirer had dared kiss her like this! The desire to respond to the demanding lips crushing her own grew second by second, beyond her control. Thoroughly unnerved, she tried to break free. Long fingers slid into her hair, holding her head still, and the arm around her waist tightened ruthlessly. The strength of the body she was now crushed against confirmed her helplessness. From a disjointed jumble of thoughts, rapidly becoming less coherent, emerged the conclusion that her captor was neither gypsy nor vagabond. He was certainly no local! That first fleeting glimpse had left an impression of negligent elegance. As she was drawn inexorably beyond thought, senses reeling, a strange turbulence threated to engulf her. Then, abruptly, as if a door were slammed shut, the kiss was skilfully brought to an end.

Her mind awhirl, senses scorched, she looked up into a dark-browed face. Hazel eyes, distinctly amused, gazed into her own green orbs. Sheer fury erupted within her. She aimed a stinging slap at the laughing face. It never landed. Although the action was not betrayed by a flicker of an eyelid, her hand was caught in mid-air in a firm grip and gently drawn down to her side.

Her assailant smiled provokingly, thoroughly appreciative of her beautifully outraged countenance. "No, I don't think I will let you hit me. How was I to know you weren't the blacksmith's daughter?"

The voice was light and gentle, definitely that of an educated man. Recollecting how she must look in her old green dimity with her hair about her shoulders, she bit her lip, feeling ridiculously young as the betraying flush rose to her cheeks.

"So," continued the soft voice, "if not the blacksmith's daughter, who, then?"

At the gently mocking tone, she raised her chin defiantly. "I'm Dorothea Darent. Now will you please release me?"

The arm around her moved not one whit. A slight frown creased her captor's brow. "Ah...Darent. Of the Grange?"

A slight nod was all she could manage. Conversation was a major effort while held so closely against him. Who on earth was he?

"I'm Hazelmere."

A blunt statement of fact. For a moment she thought she had not heard aright. But that face, arrogant amusement deeply etched in the lines about the strong mouth, surely belonged to no one else?

She had heard the rumours. Their old friend, Lady
Moreton, whose estate encompassed these woods, had
died while they were at Darent Hall. Her great-nephew,
the Marquis of Hazelmere, had reputedly inherited Moreton Park. The news had set the district abuzz. In a small
county backwater the possibility that one of the acknowledged leaders of the ton might be the new owner of a
major local estate was, in any circumstances, likely to
generate a certain amount of curiosity. When the person
in question was the Marquis of Hazelmere the curiosity
was frankly rampant.

The rector's wife had primmed up her mouth in a most
disparaging way. ''My dear! Nothing on earth would induce me to acknowledge such a man! Such a shocking
reputation! *So* notorious!'' When Dorothea had, not unnaturally, asked how this reputation had been gained, Mrs
Matthews had suddenly recalled to whom she was speaking and rapidly excused herself on the pretext of passing
around the scones. At Mrs Mannerim's she had heard such
charges as gambling, womanising and general licentiousness laid at the Marquis's door. Although she was inexperienced in wider society, common sense was her forte.
As Lord Hazelmere continued to grace the ton presumably
the gossip, as usual, was exaggerated. Besides, she could
not imagine the eminently respectable Lady Moreton having a licentious great-nephew.

Dragging her mind from contemplation of his mesmeric
hazel eyes and long sculpted lips, she rapidly revised her
opinion of the Marquis of Hazelmere. Put simply, the man
was even more dangerous than his reputation indicated.

Her thoughts had flowed across her face, a clear pro-
cession from initial bewilderment, through dawning realisation, to awed and scandalised comprehension. The hazel eyes glinted. To a palate jaded by an unremitting diet

of society's beauties, on whose simpering faces no trace of genuine emotion was ever permitted, the beautiful and expressive countenance was infinitely attractive.

"Precisely." He said it to see if she would blush so delightfully again and was amply rewarded.

Dorothea indignantly transferred her gaze to contemplation of his left shoulder. She was hardly short, but her topmost curls barely reached his chin. Which left his chest, very close, at eye-level. Nothing in her limited experience had taught her how to deal with a situation like this. She had never felt so helpless in her life!

With her attention elsewhere, she missed the deepening curve of the severe lips which had so recently claimed hers. "And precisely what is Miss Dorothea Darent doing, trespassing in my woods?"

The proprietorial tone brought her head up again, as he had known it would. "Oh! You *have* inherited the Park from Lady Moreton!"

He nodded, reluctantly releasing her and almost imperceptibly moving aside. The hazel eyes did not leave her face.

Relieved of the distracting intimacy, she paused to gather her wits. In a manner as imperious as she could muster she replied, "Lady Moreton always gave her permission for us to gather whatever we wished from her woods. However, now that *you* own the Park—"

"You will, of course," Hazelmere interposed smoothly, "continue to gather whatever you wish, whenever you wish." He smiled. "I will even undertake not to mistake you for the blacksmith's daughter next time."

Dorothea swept him a contemptuous curtsy, green eyes flashing. "Thank you, Lord Hazelmere! I'll be sure to warn Hetty."

The comment stumped him, as she had intended. She

turned to pick up her basket. Still mentally adrift from the
after-effects of that kiss, she hastily concluded that in this
instance retreat was the better part of valour. She had
reckoned without Lord Hazelmere. "And who, exactly, is
Hetty?"

Arrested in the act of ignominious flight, she gathered
together the shreds of her composure to reply acidly,
"Why, the blacksmith's daughter, of course!"

Under her fascinated gaze the striking, almost harsh-
featured face relaxed, the satirical amusement replaced by
genuine delight. Laughing openly, he put out a hand to
grasp the basket, preventing her from leaving. "I think
we're quits, Miss Darent, so don't run away. Your basket
is only half full and there are plenty of berries left on this
bush." The hazel eyes were quizzing her, his smile dis-
arming. Sensing her hesitation, he continued, "Yes, I
know you can't reach them, but I can. If you'll just stand
there, and hold your basket so, we'll soon have it full."

It dawned on Dorothea that her qualifications to deal
with the gentleman before her were inadequate. Unwise
in the ways of the world, she had no idea what she should
do. On the one hand, the rector's wife would expect her
to withdraw immediately; on the other, curiosity urged her
to remain. And, even if she did make up her mind to go,
it was doubtful whether this masterful creature would allow her to leave. Besides, as he had positioned her here
with the basket in her hands and was even now filling it
with the choicest berries from the top of the bush, it would
hardly be polite to walk away. Thus reasoning, she remained where she was, taking the opportunity to more
closely inspect her tormentor.

Her initial impression of quiet elegance owed much,
she decided, to the excellent cut of his shooting jacket.
Honesty then forced her to acknowledge that broad shoul-

ders set atop a lean and muscular frame significantly contributed to the overall effect of masculine power only superficially cloaked. His black hair was cut short in the prevailing mode and curled gently over his brow. The hazel eyes, so appropriate, she thought, in the Marquis of Hazelmere, were disconcertingly direct. The decidedly patrician nose and firm mouth and chin declared that here was a man used to dominating his world. But she had seen both eyes and mouth soften with humour, making him appear much more approachable. In fact, she decided, his smile would be utterly devastating to young ladies more impressionable than herself. Then, too, there was that subtly attractive aura, which fell into the category of subjects no well-bred lady ever discussed. Remembering his reputation, she could find no trace of dissipation. His actions, however, left little doubt of the existence of the fire that had given rise to the smoke.

Correctly guessing most of the jumble of thoughts going through her head, Hazelmere surreptitiously watched her face from the corner of his eyes. What a jewel she was! The classically moulded face framed by luxuriant dark hair was arresting in itself. But those eyes! Like enormous twin emeralds, clear and bright, they mirrored her thoughts in a thoroughly beguiling way. Her lips he had already sampled—soft and yielding, deliciously sensual—and he could readily imagine developing a fascination for them. The rest of the package was equally enticing. Nevertheless, if he was to further their acquaintance he would have to go carefully.

Removing the loaded basket from her hands, he retrieved his hunting rifle from the opposite side of the clearing. Correctly interpreting the question clearly written on her uncertain face, he said, "I'm now going to escort you home, Miss Darent." Inwardly grinning at the

mutinous expression that greeted this calm pronounce-
ment, he continued before she could speak. "No! Don't
argue. In the social circle to which I belong, no young
lady would ever be found out of doors alone."

The pious tone made Dorothea's eyes blaze. Lord Hazelmere's tactics were proving extremely difficult to combat. As she could find no ready answer nor see any way
of altering his resolve, she reluctantly fell into step beside
him as he started down the path.

"Incidentally," he continued conversationally, pursuing a subject guaranteed to keep her on the defensive,
"satisfy my curiosity. Just why *are* you wandering alone
in the woods, without the presence of even a nitwit
maid?"

She had suspected this question might come, precisely
because she had no good answer. The reprehensible creature was undoubtedly teasing her! Swallowing her irritation, she calmly replied, "I'm well known in this neighbourhood, and at my age can hardly be considered a
young miss in need of constant chaperoning." Even to
her ears it sounded lame.

The reprehensible creature chuckled. "My dear child,
you're not *that* old! And quite clearly you do need the
protection of an attendant."

As he had just proved the truth of that, she could hardly
argue the point. But, her temper flying and caution disappearing with it, her unruly tongue marched ahead un-
heeding. "In future, Lord Hazelmere, whenever I'm
tempted to walk *your* woods I'll most certainly take an
attendant!"

"Very wise," he murmured, voice low.

Unattuned to the nuance of his tone, she did not stop
to think before pointing out, in her most reasonable voice,

"But I really can't see the necessity. You said you would not mistake me for a village girl next time."

"Which merely means," he said in tones provocative enough to send a tingling shiver down her spine, "that next time I'll know whose lips I'm kissing."

"Oh!" She gasped and stopped to look up at him, outrage in every line.

Halting beside her, Hazelmere laughed and gently touched her cheek with one long finger, further increasing her ire. "I repeat, Miss Darent—you need an attendant. Don't risk walking in my woods or anywhere else without one. In case the country beaux haven't told you, you're by far too lovely to wander alone, *despite* your advancing years."

The amused hazel eyes held hers throughout this speech. Dorothea, seeing something behind the laughter which made her feel distinctly odd, could find nothing to say in reply. Irritated, furious and light-headed all at once, she turned abruptly and continued along the path, skirts swishing angrily.

Glancing at the troubled face beside him, Hazelmere's smile deepened. He sought for a suitably innocuous topic from the tangle of information poured into his ears by his great-aunt before her death. "I understand you have recently lost your mother, Miss Darent. I believe my great-aunt told me you were staying with relatives in the north."

This promising sally fell wide. Dorothea turned her wide green eyes on him and, ignoring the dictum that ladies should not answer a gentleman's question with another question, asked breathlessly, "Did you see her, then, before she died?"

The marked degree of disbelief, for some reason, stung him. "Believe it or not, Miss Darent, I frequently visited my great-aunt, of whom I was very fond. However, as I

rarely stayed longer than a day, it's hardly surprising that
neither you, nor in all probability the rest of the county,
were aware of that fact. I was with her for the three days
prior to her death and, as I was her heir, she endeavoured
to instruct me in the families of the area.''

This speech, not unnaturally, brought the colour to her
cheeks, but instead of turning away in confusion, as he
expected, she met his eyes unflinchingly. ''You see, we
were such good friends that I was most unhappy not to
have seen her again.''

The hazel eyes held hers for a pregnant second. Then
he relented. ''The end was quite painless. She died in her
sleep and, considering the pain she'd been in over the past
years, that can only be viewed as a relief.''

She nodded, eyes downcast.

In an attempt to lighten the mood he tried again. ''Do
you and your sister plan to remain at the Grange indefi-
nitely?''

This time he had more success. Her face cleared. ''Oh,
no! We're to go to our grandmother, Lady Merion, early
next year.''

Hermione, Lady Merion, previously the Dowager Lady
Darent, had swept through the chilly corridors of Darent
Hall like a summer breeze, warm from the glamour of
London. And had taken undisputed charge. The sisters,
together with Aunt Agnes, the elderly spinster who acted
as their nominal chaperon, had been dispatched home to
the Grange, buried deep in Hampshire, there to wait out
their year of mourning. They were to present themselves
to her ladyship in Cavendish Square in February, six
months from now. And what was to happen from that
point on was, they all had been given to understand, very
definitely in her ladyship's competent hands. Reminiscing,
Dorothea grinned. ''She intends to present us.'' Noticing

the sudden lift of the dark brows, she continued defensively, "Cecily is considered very beautiful and, I believe, should make a good match."

"And yourself?"

Suddenly inexplicably sensitive on this point, she believed she detected a derisive note in the smooth voice. She answered more categorically than she intended. "I am hardly ware for the marriage mart. I intend to enjoy my days in London seeing all the sights, and, if truth be known, watching those about me."

She glanced up and was surprised by the intensity of the hazel gaze fixed unswervingly on her face. Then he smiled in such an enigmatic way that she was unsure whether it was intended for her or was purely introspective. A thought occurred. "Do you know Lady Merion?"

The smile deepened. "I should think all fashionable London knows Lady Merion. However, in my case, she's a particularly close friend of my mother's."

"Please, tell me what she's like?" It was his turn to be surprised. Seeing it, she rushed on, "You see, I've not met her since I was a child, except for the one night she spent at Darent Hall earlier this year, when she came to tell us we were to come to London."

Hazelmere, reflecting that this conversation was undoubtedly the strangest he had ever conducted with a personable young lady, helped her over the stile and into the lane, then fell to considering Lady Merion. "Well, your grandmother has always been a leader of fashion, and is well connected with all the old tabbies who matter in London. She's thick as thieves with Lady Jersey and Princess Esterhazy. Both are patronesses of Almack's, to which you must gain entry if you wish to belong to the ton. In your case, that hurdle will not be a problem. Lady Merion is independently wealthy and lives in a mansion on Cavendish Square, left her by her second husband, George, Lord Merion. She married him some years after your grandfather's death and he died about five years ago, I think. She's something of a tartar, and a high stickler, so I would advise you not to attempt to wander London unattended! On the other hand, she has an excellent sense of humour and is known as being kind and generous to her friends. She's in some ways eccentric and rarely leaves London except to visit friends in the country. All in all, I doubt you could find a lady more capable of launching you and your sister successfully into the ton.''

Dorothea pondered this potted biography, finally remarking in a pensive tone, ''She did seem very fashionable.''

''She is certainly that,'' he agreed.

They had reached a gate in the high stone wall that had bordered the lane for the last hundred yards. Dorothea stopped and reached for the basket. ''These are the gardens of the Grange.''

''Then I'll leave you here,'' Hazelmere promptly replied. He had escorted her home purely to prolong his time in her company but had no wish to be seen with her. He knew too well the gossip and speculation which would inevitably spring from such a sighting. Expertly capturing her hand, he carried it to his lips, enjoying the spark of anger that flared in the green eyes and the blush that rose in response to his understanding smile. ''But remember my warning! If you wish to keep in your grandmama's good graces, don't go about London unattended. Young ladies who venture the London streets alone won't remain alone for long. Farewell, Miss Darent.''

Released, Dorothea opened the gate and made good her escape.

She hurried through the garden, for once unconscious

of the heady scents rising from the rioting flowers. The long shadows cast by the ancient roof of the Grange fell across the path, heralding the end of the day. She stopped in the garden hall; the coolness of the dim, stone-flagged room brought relief to her burning cheeks. The clattering steps of the housemaid sounded in the passageway. Moving to the door, she called her in.

"Take these berries to Cook, please, Doris. And after that you can lay out the meadowsweet on the drying racks." With a wave of her hand she indicated the wooden frames covered with tightly stretched muslin lying on the bench along one side of the room.

As an afterthought, she added, "And please tell my aunt I've gone to lie on my bed until dinner. I think I must have a touch of the sun." More accurately, a touch of the Marquis of Hazelmere! she thought furiously. Successfully negotiating the passageway and stairs undetected, she closed her bedchamber door and sank on to the window-seat.

Gazing over the now deeply shadowed garden, she struggled to bring some order to a mind still seething. Ridiculous! She had left the Grange a serenely confident twenty-two-year-old, entirely secure in her independent world. Yet here she was, a scant hour later, feeling, she suspected, as Cecily might if the Squire's son had made eyes at her! It was not as if she had never been kissed before. It shouldn't make the slightest difference who was doing the kissing. The fact that it had made a great deal of difference exacerbated a temper already tried by a pair of hazel eyes. A pair of all too perceptive hazel eyes. She spent the next ten minutes reading herself a determined lecture on the inadvisability of forming an attachment for a rake.

Fortified, she forced herself to consider the matter in a

more reasoning light. Undoubtedly she should feel outraged, ready to decry the Marquis as a licentious scoun-
drel. Yet, despite her irritation, she was too honest not to
admit that her inappropriate attire was partly to blame.
Moreover, she suspected that the response of a young lady
on finding herself in the arms of the Marquis of Hazelmere should have been quite different from the way she
had behaved. In her defence, she felt it should be noted
that had she swooned in his arms he would have had little
choice but to wait with her until she recovered. Then the
situation would have been, if anything, worse. By following this train of thought, she convinced herself there had
been nothing particularly reprehensible about the proceedings after Lord Hazelmere had released her. In fact, he
had proved a valuable informant on the subject of her
grandmother.

What continued to bother her were the events preceding
her release from that far too familiar embrace. Her fingers
strayed to her lips, which, despite his expertise, were
slightly bruised. The memory of his hard body against
hers was still a physical sensation. The clock on the landing struck the quarter-hour. She determinedly put her
thoughts on the afternoon's events aside, resolutely con-
signing the Marquis and all his works to the remotest
corner of her mind. Nothing was more certain than that
he would forget all about *her* by tomorrow.

Changing out of her old gown and into the freshly
pressed sprigged muslin laid out for the warm evening,
she gauged her chances of unwittingly running into him
again. Well versed in the ways of the local gentry, she
knew it would be all but impossible for him to meet her
socially in the country. And, by his own admission, he
was not in the habit of remaining over-long at Moreton
Park. She told herself she was relieved. To make doubly
sure her relief remained undisturbed, she resolved that, in

future, she would ensure that her reluctant sister joined her on her rambles.

Picking up a brush, she attacked her long tresses vigorously before winding them up in a simple knot. She glanced quickly at her reflection in the mirror perched on her tallboy. Satisfied she had dealt sufficiently with the potential ramifications of the advent of the Marquis of Hazelmere into her life, she went downstairs to her dinner.

A fortnight later, returning to Hazelmere House, his mansion in Cavendish Square, situated almost directly opposite Merion House, the Marquis found a large pile of letters and invitations awaiting him. Sorting through them, he strolled into his library. Extracting an envelope of a particularly virulent shade of purple from the bundle, he held it at arm's length to escape the cloying perfume emanating from it and groped for his quizzing glass. Recognising the flowery script of his latest mistress, a dazzling creature abundantly well endowed for her station in life, his black brows drew together. He opened the letter and scanned the few lines within. The black brows rose. A smile of a kind Dorothea Darent would not have recognised twisted the mobile lips. Throwing both letter and envelope into the fire, he turned to his desk.

The footman who answered the summons of the library bell ten minutes later found his master fixing his seal to a letter. Glancing up as the door opened, Hazelmere waved the envelope to cool the wax, then held it out. ''Deliver this by hand immediately.''

''Yes, m'lord.''

Watching the retreating back of the footman, Hazelmere considered the probable reception of his politely savage missive. Thus ended yet another *affaire*. Stretching his long legs to the fire, he fell to considering the constantly changing parade of his high-flying mistresses.

While providing the ton with a stream of on-dits, he felt that the inevitability of the game was beginning to bore him. After more than ten years on the town, there were few fashionable vices he had not sampled and the pattern of his activities was becoming wearyingly predictable.

Thinking again of the discarded Cerise, he compared her ripe beauty with that of the green-eyed girl whose face had proved disturbingly haunting. His dissatisfaction with his present lot stemmed in large part from that encounter in Moreton Park woods. Entirely his own fault, of course.

Marc St John Ralton Henry, at thirty-one years of age the fifth Marquis of Hazelmere and one of the wealthiest peers of the realm, let his mind wander back to the first time he had heard Miss Darent's name, during a conversation he had had with his great-aunt the night before she died. A remarkably forthright old lady, she had fixed him with a steely look and embarked on an inquisition as to his marital intentions. This had been prefaced by the remark, "I know your mother won't mention this, so I'm takin' advantage of the fact that, as I'm dying, you can't very well tell me to go to the devil!"

Appreciative of the ploy and having admitted he had no present plans in the matter, he had settled down to listen with good grace to the subsequent dissertation, something he would not have done had it been anyone else.

"Can't say I blame you for not wanting to marry any of these namby-pamby misses presented every year," she'd snorted derisively. "Can't abide such ninny-hammers myself! But why not look to wider fields? There's plenty of suitable chits who for one reason or another have never made it to London."

Catching sight of his sceptical face, she had continued, "Oh, you needn't think that just because they're country misses they couldn't handle life in the ton. There's Dorothea Darent, for one. Young, beautiful, well dowered and as well born as yourself. The only reason *she* hasn't been presented is that she's spent the last six years running her widowed mother's household. Cynthia Darent should be *kicked* for not bringing her out years ago!'' Here Great-Aunt Etta had paused, musing on the sins of the late Lady Darent. ''Well, it's too late for that now, 'cause she's dead.''

''Who? The beautiful Dorothea?'' had asked Hazelmere, all at sea.

''No, fool! Cynthia! She died a few months ago and the girls have gone to Darent Hall for a while. Pity. I should have liked to see Dorothea again. No nambypamby miss, that one!''

''How is it that, despite never having been presented, this paragon is not yet wed? Surely the country gentlemen are not such slowtops?''

Great-Aunt Etta had chuckled. ''I rather suspect that's because no gentleman has yet shown her any good reason to marry! Look at it from her point of view. She's got position enough, wealth enough and her independence to boot. Why get married?''

He had grinned back, responding to the laughter in the old lady's eyes. ''I dare say I could make a few suggestions.''

''Yes, I dare say *you* could! But that's neither here nor there, for you're not likely to meet her. Unless Hermione Merion takes an interest. I've written to her, so she may do. There's Cecily too. The younger sister, and another beauty, though of a different style. She'll have to be brought out, too. But Cecily would try the patience of a saint. And, as you definitely ain't one, she won't do for you. But enough of the Darent sisters. I merely give them as examples.'' And so the conversation had moved on.

The idea that Great-Aunt Etta had, in fact, been trying

to make him look at Dorothea Darent as a potential wife had occurred to him shortly after he met that remarkable young lady.

Over the past ten years he had steadfastly refused to seriously consider any of the flighty young females paraded for his approval at Almack's and the *ton* parties. This had caused considerable consternation among other family members, notably his two older sisters, Maria and Susan, who were constantly pushing one or other of their favoured aspirants in his way. His stance had been fully supported by his mother and Great-Aunt Etta, both of whom seemed to understand the almost suffocating boredom he felt within minutes of attempting to converse with the latest simpering and apparently witless offerings. He knew his mother longed for him to marry but had reputedly told an acquaintance that unless they changed the prevailing fashion in débutantes she never expected to see it. As for Great-Aunt Etta, she had never said a word to him on the subject until that night.

Given that Great-Aunt Etta had known him every bit as well as his mother, it was perfectly possible that she had intended to draw his attention to Miss Darent. She would never have been so gauche as to approach the matter directly, knowing that the most likely outcome by that route was polite and chilly refusal to have anything to do with the chit. Instead she had introduced her name in a roundabout fashion, merely telling him that the girl was in every way suitable, but leaving him to make his own ground. *Very* like Great-Aunt Etta! Well, Great-Aunt Etta, he mused with a smile, I've met your Dorothea, and in a more effective way than I think even you would have dreamt of!

Chapter Two

A low moan brought Dorothea's head around sharply to peer through the dim light at her sister, curled in the opposite corner of the carriage. Cecily's eyes were shut but the line between her fair brows showed clearly that she was far from sleep. She moved her head restlessly on the squabs. The coach lurched into a rut as the horses' hoofs skidded on the icy road. Dorothea caught the swinging strap to stop herself from being thrown. As the coach ponderously righted itself and resumed its steady progress she saw that Cecily had drawn herself up into a tight ball and wedged herself firmly into the corner, her face turned away.

Dorothea returned her attention to the dreary landscape, glimpsed fitfully through the bare branches of the trees and hedges lining the road. The grey February afternoon was closing in. The patter of drizzle on the coach windows punctuated the stillness within. Then, rising like a castle through the gathering gloom, standing on a crest surrounded by the dark shadows of its windbreaks, loomed the Three Feathers Inn. As it was just over halfway to London from the Grange, situated on the Bath Road, she had chosen it as their overnight stop. If it had been only herself travelling to London she would have made the journey in a single day. But Cecily was a poor traveller. With luck, their slow pace broken by a night's rest would allow her to arrive in Cavendish Square in a fit state to greet their grandmother.

The only other occupant of the carriage was their middle-aged maid, Betsy, who had tended them from the cradle. She dozed lightly, enveloped in woollen shawls on the seat facing Dorothea. After much consideration, Aunt Agnes had been left behind. There had been nothing specific in Lady Merion's letter summoning them to London, but the discussions at Darent Hall had clearly been on the unspoken understanding that Aunt Agnes would continue to do her duty and escort her charges to Cavendish Square. However, Aunt Agnes's rheumatism was legendary, and Dorothea had no wish to saddle herself with the querulous, though much loved old lady, either on the road to London or once they were arrived, supposedly to enjoy themselves. Furthermore, Aunt Agnes's opinions on men, of whatever station, were dampening in the extreme. Dorothea thought it unlikely that her presence would aid in the push to find Cecily a husband. Nevertheless, her polite note to Lady Merion, informing her of their expected date of arrival, had made no reference whatever to Aunt Agnes.

The coach lumbered on through the steadily thickening mists. It had been overcast all day, but for the most part the rain had held off, much to the relief of their coachman, Lang. The journey to London with the roads only just cleared was always a risky business. Wrapped in his thick frieze coat, he was deeply relieved to turn his team in under the arch of the inn. It was a large establishment, one of the busiest posting houses in the district. The main yard was devoted primarily to travellers changing horses or temporarily halting. The large travelling carriage rumbled through and on under another archway into the coachyard. Ostlers ran to free the steaming horses, and the landlord came forward to assist the sisters into the inn.

Here, however, a problem lay waiting.

While they warmed themselves before the roaring fire in a snug, low-ceilinged parlour Mr Simms apologised profusely. "There's a prize-fight on in the village, miss. We're booked out. I've kept a bedchamber for you, but I'm afraid there's no hope of a private parlour." The rubicund landlord, middle-aged, with daughters of his own, eyed the young ladies anxiously.

Dorothea drew a deep breath. After travelling at a snail's pace all day she did not really care what was going forward in the neighbourhood, as long as she and Cecily were adequately housed for the night. She automatically appraised the neat and spotlessly clean room. At least there would be no danger of damp sheets or poorly cooked food in this house. There was no point in being overly distressed by the lack of a parlour. Drawing herself to her full height, she nodded to the clearly worried Simms. "Very well. I see it can't be helped. Will you please show us to our bedchamber?"

Mr Simms had correctly guessed the Darent sisters' station from Dorothea's letter requesting bedchambers and parlour. While he rarely criticised the ways of his clients, he thought it a crying shame that two such pretty young ladies were travelling escorted only by servants. He led them up to the bedchamber he had had prepared for them. Experience of the goings-on likely to occur within his house before the night was through had led him to house them in the large bedchamber on the north side of the inn. This was the oldest part of the rambling building, isolated from the rest, and reached only by a separate stairway close to his private domain.

Arriving, puffing, on the landing, he threw open a stout door. "I've put you in this bedchamber here, miss, because it's out of the way, like. The inn will soon be fair to burstin' with all the young gentlemen been to see the fight. My missus says to tell ye to stay put in your chamber and lock the door and she'll see to it that only she and my daughter come up with your meals and suchlike. That road, we'll all like as not avoid any unpleasantness. I'll have your bags brought up in a jiffy, miss." With these words Simms bowed and retreated, leaving Dorothea, brows flying, and Cecily, pathetically pale, staring at each other in consternation.

"Oh, my!" said Betsy, sinking down on one of the chairs by the fire, eyes round with dismay. "Maybe we should travel on, Miss Dorothea. I'm sure your grandma wouldn't like you staying at an inn with all these rowdy, boisterous, ramshackle lads, miss!"

"I don't believe there's any other inn near, Betsy. And after all, as the landlord says, if we keep the door locked and stay in our room, surely we'll come to no harm?" Dorothea spoke in her normal calm tones, drawing off her gloves and dropping her travelling cloak over a chair. After her momentary dismay, undoubtedly due to tiredness, she was inclined to dismiss the situation.

"Well, if it's all the same to you, Thea, I would much rather stay here than try to go on," said Cecily.

The thin, reedy voice clearly conveyed to Dorothea just how unwell her sister was feeling. She walked briskly to the bed and turned down the coverlet. The sheets were dry and clean. She plumped up the pillows invitingly. "And so we shall, my love! Why not curl up on the bed until dinner arrives? I must confess, I'm not convinced that removing from here wouldn't land us in a worse pickle than the one we're in at present."

A tentative knock came at the door. "Who is it?" said Betsy, rising.

"It's only me, ma'am. Hannah, the landlord's daughter."

Betsy opened the door to reveal a stout damsel with a mob-cap perched above a comely face. "My mum will have the dinner ready shortly, but she was wanting to know if you needed anything else, ma'am?" Hannah hefted the sisters' bags into the room and stood looking enquiringly at Dorothea.

"Why, yes! We'd like some warm water, and could a truckle-bed be put up in here for our maid? I'd rather she spent the night with us."

The girl nodded. "I'll be back in two shakes, ma'am."

Five minutes later Hannah was back with a jug of steaming water and a truckle-bed in bits. While she and Betsy struggled with this contraption Dorothea and Cecily washed the dust of the road from their faces and felt considerably better. Finally conquering the recalcitrant truckle-bed, Hannah wiped her hands on her apron and addressed Dorothea. "I'll be back in half'n hour with your dinner, miss. Be you sure to lock the door after me."

Dorothea murmured her thanks as the bolts slid to behind the helpful Hannah. Cecily, drowsy, curled up on the bed. Betsy sat by the fire, working on some sewing she had brought with her to while away the time.

Now that her immediate needs were satisfied, Dorothea prowled the room, restless and cramped. After a day spent in the carriage, she longed to get just one breath of fresh air before a night spent within the airless cocoon of the bedchamber. Suddenly she remembered Lang. With Cecily as passenger, they would normally leave mid-morning. However, her limited knowledge of prize-fights and their aftermath suggested that an early departure might be preferable. She looked out of the window, but this faced the back of the inn. She could hear no noise or ruckus to suggest that the audience from the fight had arrived.

Quickly she crossed to Betsy's side. "I'm just going down to see Lang. We should make an early start tomorrow to avoid the crush." She had lowered her voice. "You stay here and watch over Cecily. I'll only be a moment."

Before Betsy could protest she picked up her old travelling cloak and whisked herself out of the door. She paused on the landing to fasten the cloak. Sounds of ribald laughter came, muted, from where she supposed the taproom to be. She made her way quietly down the stairs and along the corridor in the opposite direction, eventually reaching the door giving on to the coaching yard. Here she found a mêlée of ostlers and horses. Pausing in the shadows, she scanned the area, trying to locate Lang. He was nowhere to be seen. Remembering that private grooms often helped the ostlers at times like these, she ventured to the archway and peeked into the main stable-yard.

"My, my! What have we here? A pretty young thing, come to help us celebrate!"

She gasped. The sensation of an arm slipping around her waist made her heart stand still, but instead of hazel eyes lazily regarding her she found herself looking into a vacuous face with cerubic blue eyes that seemed to have trouble focusing. The man holding her had been drinking but he was not altogether drunk.

He dragged her, struggling furiously, around the corner to fetch up within a riotous group of seven semi-drunk gentlemen, intent on a night of carousing, having watched their favourite win the fight. Dorothea realised her mistake too late. The main yard of the inn was full to overflowing. One of the men reached out and flicked her hood back, and the light from the inn's main door fell full on her face. She tried desperately to pull free, but the young man had a good grip on her arm. She winced as it tightened.

Immediately a drawling voice cut through the clamour. "Do let the lady go, Tremlow. She is known to me and I really cannot let you embarrass her further."

Recognising the voice, Dorothea wished the ground would open up and swallow her.

The effect of the statement was instantaneous. The hold on her arm was immediately withdrawn as the dark shadow of the Marquis of Hazelmere materialised at the edge of the group.

"Oh! Sorry, Hazelmere! No idea she was a lady."

This last sentence, uttered *sotto voce*, made Dorothea's cheeks burn. She pulled up her hood as the men in the group peered to see which lady could thus claim Hazelmere's protection.

The Marquis, unhurriedly strolling across the group to her side, largely obscured her from view. Arriving beside her, he turned to the group and continued in the same languid tone, "I feel sure you would all like to offer your apologies for any embarrassment you have, however unwittingly, caused the lady."

A chorus of, "Oh, yes! Definitely! Apologies, ma'am! No offence intended, y'know!" greeted this bald statement.

Simms, having noticed the problem rather late in the day, now hung on the fringe of the group, waiting to render any assistance at all to one of his most valued customers. The Marquis's eye alighted on him. "Ah, Simms! A round of ale for these gentlemen after this slight misunderstanding, don't you think?"

Simms took the hint. "Yes, m'lord! Certainly! If you gentlemen would like to come this way I've a hogshead of a new brew I'd much appreciate your comments on." With this treat on offer, he had little difficulty in herding the group towards the taproom.

As they moved away Anthony, Lord Fanshawe appeared at his friend's side, a questioning lift to his brows. One moment he had been walking across the stableyard beside Hazelmere, heading towards a hot dinner, when Marc had suddenly stopped, uttered one furious oath and then plunged through the crowd towards a small group of revellers near the coachyard. Although nearly as tall as his friend, with Marc ahead of him, he had had no chance to see what had attracted his attention. As he drew closer he heard Marc at his most languid. He assumed there was a lady in it somewhere, but it was only when Hazelmere turned to address some remark behind him that he realised he was effectively protecting her from the eyes of the stableyard.

Hazelmere turned to him. "Check they're all in, will you, Tony? I'll join you in the parlour in a few minutes."

Fanshawe nodded and without a word turned back towards the inn. The languid tones had disappeared entirely, replaced by Hazelmere's normal speech with the consonants somewhat clipped. That single glimpse of his childhood friend's face had confirmed his suspicion. The Marquis of Hazelmere was in a towering rage.

As he had reached her side Hazelmere had unobtrusively taken Dorothea's arm, initially holding her beside him. When the group had made their apologies and moved away he drew her back so that she was shielded by his height and the voluminous driving cloak which hung in many tiers of capes from his broad shoulders. Conscious only of a desperate need to quit the scene, she tried to retreat into the coachyard. He turned but did not release her. With the light behind him, his face was unreadable. "One moment and I'll escort you indoors. I'd like a word with you."

Even to Dorothea, unwise in the ways of the Marquis, the words had an ominous ring. She was furious with herself for falling into this scrape and mortified that, of all men, it should be Hazelmere who had rescued her from it. *And* in such a way!

He turned back to speak briefly with another tall man who came up. Then, much to her relief, as her legs felt strangely weak, he ushered her into the coachyard.

Once in the comparative privacy of the rapidly clearing inner yard, he stopped and drew her around to face him. She almost gasped as the light from the inn door lit his face. The hazel eyes were hard and reflected the light from the inn; his lips were set in an uncompromising line. It was obvious to the meanest intelligence that he was furious, and equally obvious that she was the object of his wrath. "And what, may I ask, were you attempting to accomplish out there?" The sarcastic tones stung like a whip.

Far from being cowed, Dorothea immediately took umbrage. She flung up her head and her eyes snapped back. "I was seeking my coachman, if you must know, to tell him I wish to leave this inn very early tomorrow, to avoid precisely the sort of attention that I was most regrettably unable to avoid tonight!" She was slightly breathless by the end of this speech, but continued to give the odious Marquis back look for look.

His eyes narrowed. After a slight pause he continued in less harsh tones, "It seems very remiss of Simms not to have warned you to keep to your chamber with your door locked."

She had to swallow before she was able to answer, but she managed to return his hard gaze. "He did tell me."

The expression on his face became even stonier. "I can only marvel at your lack of care for your own reputation. I've already warned you that your hoydenish ways will not do in wider society." He had grasped both her arms just above the elbow in a far from gentle grip. For one appalled moment she thought he was going to shake her. Instead, after a pause heavy with tension, he spoke again, his tone a study in suppressed fury. "I can only repeat what I've said before: under no circumstances *whatever* should you venture outside unattended! And add a rider to the effect that if I *ever* find you alone like that again I will personally ensure that you won't sit down for a sennight!"

She gasped, green eyes wide in utter disbelief, whereupon he continued, his tone savage, "Oh, yes! I'm quite capable of doing so."

Looking up into the implacable face, the hazel eyes almost black, she realised that the threat was no bluff. But by now she was every bit as angry as he was. By what right did this imperious man order her around and threaten her? Imperious, arrogant and totally *insufferable!* Normally the most collected of women, she struggled to shackle her anger and direct it specifically towards its source.

But Hazelmere gave her no time to vent her fury. Becoming aware that he was still holding her in full view of the coachyard, thankfully almost deserted, he abruptly turned her towards the inn and, one hand hard at her elbow, swept her indoors. "Which chamber has Simms put you in?"

Unable as yet to command her tongue, Dorothea indicated the door at the top of the small stairway.

"Very wise! That's probably the safest chamber in the inn tonight. You may not have a peaceful night, but with luck it should be free of unwelcome interruptions."

Glancing at her furious white face and over-bright eyes, Hazelmere drew her on to the stairs. On the second step she swung around, thinking to give him a piece of her mind while he was on the lower step and not towering over her. But, correctly guessing her intention, he had slipped past her and continued to draw her upwards on to the small landing.

The landlord suddenly appeared in the corridor, heading for the back of the inn.

"Simms!"

"Yes, m'lord?"

"A glass of your best brandy. At once."

"Yes, m'lord!"

Dorothea thought the request extremely odd, but dismissed it as yet another example of his lordship's vagaries. She was more concerned with giving voice to her frustrations. Turning to face him across the small landing, she was disturbingly aware of his presence so close, and disliked having to look up such a long way to meet his eyes.

"Lord Hazelmere! I must tell you that I find your manner of addressing me quite unacceptable! I do not at all accept your strictures on my conduct. Indeed, I do not know by what right you make them. Tonight was an unfortunate accident, that's all. I'm quite capable of looking after myself—"

"Would you really rather I had left you in the hands of Tremlow and company? You wouldn't have found it entertaining, I assure you." Hazelmere, deciding that she could not be allowed to talk herself into hysterics, broke in smoothly over her diatribe. His words, uttered in a stonily bored tone, acted like a cold douche, effectively stopping her in mid-sentence.

He was again afforded a view of her thoughts as they passed clearly over her face. He watched the realisation that it was, in fact, due to him that she was not at this moment in quite desperate straits finally sink in. He had not thought it possible, but she paled even further. Watching her closely, he saw Simms approaching. He took the proffered glass, dismissing the landlord with a curt nod and the words, "I'll want to speak to you in a few minutes, Simms." Turning, he held out the glass to her. "Drink it."

"No. I don't drink brandy."

"There is always a first time."

When she continued to look rebelliously at him he sighed and explained. "Whether you know it or not, you're exhibiting all the symptoms of shock. You're white as a sheet and your eyes look like green diamonds. Soon you'll start to shake, and feel faint and very cold. The brandy will help. So be a good girl and drink it. If you won't, you know perfectly well I'm quite capable of forcing you to."

The glittering green eyes widened slightly. There had been no change in his tone and she felt no direct menace, as she had before. Then, looking into his eyes, she gave up the unequal struggle. She took the glass and, shivering slightly, raised it to her lips and sipped. Hazelmere waited patiently until she drained the glass, then removed it from her hands and dropped it into one of his cloak pockets.

As she looked up he remembered her unfinished errand. "I take it you're travelling to London?"

She nodded. His face had softened, the harshly arrogant lines of ten minutes before had receded, leaving the charmingly polite mask she suspected he showed the world. She felt as if he had, in some subtle way, withdrawn from her.

"What's the name of your coachman?"

"Lang. I'd thought to leave at eight."

"Very sensible. I'll see he gets the message. I suggest you enter your chamber, lock the door and don't open it to anyone other than the landlord's people." The tone was calm, with no hint of any emotion whatever.

"Yes. Very well." She was completely bemused. Her head was whirling—shock, fury, brandy and the Marquis of Hazelmere combining to make her distinctly befuddled. She pressed the fingers of one hand to her temple, forcing her mind to concentrate on what he was saying.

"Good! Try to get some sleep. And one more thing: tell Lady Merion I'll call on her the day after tomorrow."

She nodded and moved to the door, then turned back. Still angry, she knew she was beholden to him, and pride forbade her to leave without thanking him, however little inclined she was to do so. She drew a deep breath and, head held high, began. "My lord, I must thank you for your help in releasing me from those gentlemen." Lifting her eyes to his, she found that this bland statement had brought the most devastatingly attractive smile to his face.

Wholly appreciative of the effort the words had cost, he replied, his voice light, "Yes, you must, I'm afraid. But never mind. Once you're in London, I'm sure you'll find opportunities aplenty to make me sorry for my subsequent odiously overbearing behaviour." One dark brow rose at the end of this outrageous speech, the hazel eyes, gently and not unkindly, quizzing her. The answering blaze of green fire made him laugh. Hearing voices below, he reached out a finger to caress her cheek gently, saying more pointedly, "Goodnight, Miss Darent!"

Speechless, she whirled away from him and knocked on the door. "Betsy, it's me. Dorothea."

Hazelmere, lips curving in a smile that, had she seen it, would have reduced Dorothea to a state of quivering uncertainty, drew back into the shadows as the door opened with an alacrity which spoke louder than words of the fears of those inside.

"Heavens, miss! Come you in quick; you look white as a sheet, you do!" Dorothea was drawn into the room and the door shut.

Hazelmere waited until he heard the bolts shot home, then made his way, pensively, downstairs. At the back door, he encountered Simms.

"Simms, I have a problem."

"M'lord?"

"I want to make sure those ladies are not disturbed tonight. You don't perchance have a large burly cousin lying about, who could take up sentry duty on that stair?"

Simms grinned as he saw the gold sovereign in his lordship's long fingers. "Well, as it happens, m'lord, my oldest boy has the most dreadful toothache. He's been mooning about in the kitchen all day. I'm sure he could do sentry duty, seeing as you ask."

"Excellent." The coin changed hands. "And Simms?"

"Yes, m'lord?"

"I'd like to be sure those ladies get the very best of treatment."

"Of course, m'lord. My wife's about to take their supper up to them now."

Hazelmere nodded and wandered out to the middle of the coachyard, looking up at the stars, twinkling now that the clouds had cleared. He paused, apparently lost in thought. Jim Hitchin, his groom, stood a few yards away, waiting until his master acknowledged him. He had been

Hazelmere's personal groom ever since the young Lord had required one. Well acquainted with his employer's foibles, he waited patiently. Hazelmere stretched and turned. "Jim?"

"M'lord?"

"I want you to find a coachman staying here, name of Lang, coachman to the Misses Darent. Miss Darent wishes to leave at eight tomorrow, to avoid the inevitable action around here. She obviously cannot deliver the message in person."

"Yes, m'lord."

"And Jim?"

"Yes, m'lord?"

"Tomorrow morning the Darent party is to leave here by eight. If there's any difficulty in achieving that departure I want you to see I'm summoned. Is that clear?"

"Yes, m'lord."

"Wonderful. Goodnight, Jim."

Jim departed, not the least averse to an early morning if it led to a clear sight of this Miss Darent. He had witnessed, distantly, the exchange in the coachyard. To his mind, his lordship was not behaving in his usual manner. Losing his temper with young ladies was definitely not his style. Jim was burning to see what the lady who could throw his master off balance looked like.

Hazelmere, fortunately oblivious to the speculations of his underling, strolled back through the main entrance of the inn and paused outside the open taproom door. Noise, like a cloud, rolled out over the threshold to greet him. Through a bluish haze of tobacco smoke he saw the group of young blades from whom he had rescued Dorothea standing at the end of the bar. It took him longer to locate the last of their number, seated at a small table in the corner, deep in conversation with Sir Barnaby Ruscombe.

After considering the scene for a moment, he walked on to the private parlour he always had when staying at the Feathers. Entering, he saw Fanshawe, feet up on the table, carefully peeling an apple.

Fanshawe looked up with a grin. "Ho! So there you are! I was wondering whether it'd be prudent to come and rescue you."

A ghost of a smile greeted this sally. "I had a few errands to attend to after returning Miss Darent to her room." Hazelmere removed his driving cloak, remembering to extract the glass from the pocket before he threw it on a chair. He moved to the sideboard and poured himself a glass of wine.

"And who the hell is this mysterious Miss Darent?"

The Marquis raised his black brows. "No mystery. She lives at the Grange, which borders Moreton Park. She and her sister are travelling to London to stay with their grandmother, Lady Merion."

"I see. How is it, I ask myself, that I've never heard of the girl, much less set eyes on her?"

"Simple. She's lived all her life in the country and hasn't moved in the circles we frequent."

Fanshawe finished his apple and swung his feet down from the table as the door opened to admit Simms, bearing trays loaded with food. "At last!" he cried. "I'm famished."

Simms placed the platters on the table and, checking that all was in order, turned to Hazelmere.

"Everything's taken care of, m'lord, as you requested."

Hazelmere nodded his thanks, and Simms retired. Fanshawe looked up from heaping his plate, but said nothing.

The friends took their meal in companionable silence. They had quite literally grown up together, being born on neighbouring estates within a month of each other, and had shared their schooldays at Eton and, later, Oxford. During their past ten years on the town the bond between the Lords Hazelmere and Fanshawe had become almost a byword. Over the years there had been few secrets between them, yet, for reasons he did not care to examine, Hazelmere had omitted to mention his acquaintance with Dorothea Darent to his closest friend.

Once the platters were cleared and they had pushed their chairs back from the table, savouring the special claret brought up from the depths of Simms's cellar, Fanshawe, dishevelled brown locks falling picturesquely over his brow, returned to the offensive. "It's all too smoky by half."

Resigned to the inevitable, Hazelmere nevertheless countered with an innocent, "What's too smoky by half?"

"You and this Miss Darent."

"But why?" The clear hazel eyes, apparently guileless, were opened wide, but the thin lips twitched.

Fanshawe frowned direfully but agreed to play the game. "Well, for a start, as she doesn't move in the circles we frequent, tell me how *you* met her."

"We met only once, informally."

"When?"

"Some time last August, when I was at Moreton Park."

The brown eyes narrowed. "But I visited you at Moreton Park last August, and I distinctly remember you telling me such game was very scarce."

"Ah, yes," mused Hazelmere, long fingers caressing the stem of the goblet. "I do recall saying some such thing."

"And I suppose Miss Darent just happened to slip your mind at the time?"

The Marquis smiled provokingly. "As you say, Tony."

"No, dash it all! You can't possibly expect me to swallow that. And if I won't swallow it no one else will either. And, as that fellow Ruscombe's about somewhere, you're going to have to come up with a better explanation. Unless," he concluded sarcastically, "you want all London agog?"

At that the dark brows rose. Hazelmere drew a long breath. "Unfortunately you're quite right." He still seemed absorbed in his study of the goblet. Fanshawe, who knew him better than anyone, waited patiently.

Sir Barnaby Ruscombe was a man tolerated by society's hostesses purely on account of his trade in malicious gossip. There was no chance that he would abstain from telling the story of how Hazelmere had rescued a lady from a prize-fight crowd in an inn yard. The fact that Hazelmere was sure to dislike having his name bandied about in such context would ensure its dissemination throughout the ton. Although not in itself of much import, the story would reveal the interesting fact that the Marquis had some previous acquaintance with Miss Darent. And that, as Fanshawe was so eager to point out, would lead to complications.

After some minutes had passed in silence Hazelmere raised his eyes. "Confessions of a rake, I'm afraid," he said, both voice and features gently self-mocking. Seeing the surprise in Fanshawe's brown eyes, he continued, "This time the truth will definitely not do. The details of my only previous meeting with Miss Darent would keep the scandalmongers in alt for weeks."

Tony Fanshawe was amazed. Whatever he had expected, it was not that. He knew, none better, that, while Hazelmere's *affaires* among the *demi-monde* might be legion, his behaviour with women of his own class was rigidly correct. Then he thought he saw the light. "I take it you mean that when you met her in the country she was unchaperoned?"

The curious smile on Hazelmere's lips deepened. The hazel eyes held Fanshawe's for a moment, before dropping to the goblet once more. "I am, naturally, devastated to contradict you. You're right in assuming we were unchaperoned. But what I meant is, if the truth ever became public property Miss Darent would be hopelessly compromised and I, in all honour, would be forced to marry her."

It was not possible to misinterpret that. "Good lord!" said Fanshawe, thoroughly intrigued. "Whatever did you do?"

Hazelmere, sensing the wild speculations running through his mind, hastened to bring him back to earth. "Control your satyric imaginings! I kissed her, if you must know."

"Oh?" Fanshawe was positively agog.

Feeling horrendously like a schoolboy describing to his more backward friends the details of his first encounter with a wench, Hazelmere regarded him with amusement tinged with irritation. Correctly interpreting the slightly awed expression in the brown eyes, he nodded. "Precisely. *Not* a peck on the cheek."

Fanshawe stared at Hazelmere for a full minute before saying, his voice quavering with suppressed incredulity, "Do you mean to say you kissed her as you would one of your mistresses?" Hazelmere's brows merely rose. "No! Dash it all! You can't go around kissing young ladies as if they were bordello misses!"

"Perfectly true. The fact, however, remains that in Miss Darent's case I did."

Fanshawe blinked. It was on the tip of his tongue to

ask why. But he could not quite bring himself to enquire. Instead he asked, "How long did she take to come out of her faint?"

"Oh, she didn't faint," replied Hazelmere, the smile in his eyes pronounced. "She tried to slap me."

Fanshawe was fascinated. "I must meet this Miss Darent for myself. She sounds a remarkable young lady."

"You can meet her in London shortly. Just remember who met her first."

And that, thought Tony Fanshawe, is a very revealing comment. He sighed, exasperated. "If that's not just like you, to find all the choicest morsels before anyone else has laid eyes on 'em. I don't suppose she has a sister?"

"She does, as it happens. Just turned seventeen and a stunning blonde."

"So there's hope for the rest of us yet." Abruptly eschewing their light banter, he returned to the serious side of the affair. "How are you going to account for your knowing Miss Darent?"

"She's Lady Merion's granddaughter, remember? I'll call at Merion House as soon as we get back to town and, figuratively speaking, throw myself on her ladyship's mercy." He paused to sip his wine. "It shouldn't be beyond us to concoct some believable tale."

"Provided she's willing to overlook your behaviour with her granddaughter," Fanshawe pointed out.

"I rather think," said Hazelmere, his gaze abstracted, "that it's more likely to be a case of Miss Darent being willing to overlook my behaviour."

"You mean, she might try and use it against you?"

The hazel gaze abruptly focused. Then, understanding his reasoning, Hazelmere gave the ghost of a laugh. "No. What I mean is that, although she was furious with me, I'm not sure she'll tell Lady Merion the full story."

Fanshawe mulled this over, then shook his head. "Can't see it, myself. You know what the young ones are like. Paint you in all sorts of romantic shades. The chit will probably have blabbed it all to at least three of her bosom bows before you even get to see Lady Merion!"

The strangely elusive smile that kept appearing on Hazelmere's face was again in evidence. "In this case, I think it unlikely."

A thought struck Fanshawe. "The girl's not an antidote, is she?"

"No. Not beautiful, but she'd be strikingly attractive if properly gowned."

"You mean, she wasn't properly gowned when you met her?"

A soft laugh escaped Hazelmere. "Not exactly."

Reluctantly Fanshawe decided not to pursue it. He was consumed by curiosity but slightly scandalised by the revelations thus far. He had never known Hazelmere in this sort of fix, nor in this sort of mood. For the first time in his life he was sure that Marc was hiding something.

Hazelmere volunteered a few more pieces of the puzzle. "She's twenty-two, and sensible and practical. She didn't faint, nor did she enact me any scenes. If I'd allowed it she would have terminated our interview a great deal sooner. Tonight, instead of falling on my chest and thanking me for deliverance from the hands of Tremlow and company, she very nearly told me to go to the devil. In short, I doubt that Miss Darent is in the least danger of succumbing to the Marquis of Hazelmere's wicked charms."

Fanshawe gaped. "Oh. I see." But he did not see at all.

Unfortunately he had no more time to pursue the matter. A sharp knock on the door heralded the arrival of a group of their friends, come late from the field. More wine was called for and the conversation took a decidedly sporting turn. It was not until much later that Tony Fanshawe recalled his conviction that Marc Henry was concealing something from his childhood friend.

Chapter Three

Early next morning, before the appointed time and without further incident, the Grange party set off from the Three Feathers, watched, appreciatively, by Jim Hitchin.

The day was cool but the thaw had set in. The roads improved as they neared the capital, so the motion of the coach was more even and their progress noticeably more rapid. Dorothea was in a subdued frame of mind. On her return to their chamber the evening before she had been subjected to a barrage of questions from Cecily and Betsy. Her head still swimming, she had let the tide flow over her, knowing from experience that silence would more effectively stop the inquisition than any argument. This time, her normal stratagem had failed. The questions had continued until she lost her temper. "Oh, do stop fussing, both of you! If you must know, I had an encounter with an extremely impertinent gentleman on my way back from the coachyard, and I'm quite vexed!"

Cecily, piqued at her subsequent refusal to recount the incident, had only been diverted by the appearance of their meal. In August, in a moment of ill-judged candour, Dorothea had told her sister of her impromptu meeting with Lord Hazelmere in the woods. The memory of the tortuous explanations she had had to fabricate to conceal from Cecily's avid interest the full tale of that encounter had ensured that this time she easily refrained from blurting out the name of the gentleman involved. In no circumstances could she have endured another such ordeal. Not when she was feeling so unusually exhausted.

She had had little appetite, but to admit this would only have reopened the discussion. So she had forced herself to eat some pigeon pie. After the brandy she had not dared to touch the wine. The meal completed, she had pointedly prepared for bed. Cecily, thankfully without comment, had done likewise.

A light sleeper, Dorothea had found it impossible to even doze until dawn, when the racket in the inn finally abated. She therefore had had ample time to reflect on her second encounter with the Marquis of Hazelmere. His calm assumption of authority irritated her deeply. His arrogant conviction that she would do exactly as he wished irked her beyond measure. The knowledge that, despite this, he possessed a strange attraction for her she resolutely pushed to the furthest corner of her mind. The last thing she felt inclined to do, she had sternly told herself, was to develop a *tendre* for the odious man! In all probability he would spend the night enjoying the favours of some doxy elsewhere in the inn. For some reason she found this thought absurdly depressing and, thoroughly annoyed with herself, had tried to compose her mind for sleep. Even then, when sleep finally came, it was haunted by a pair of hazel eyes.

Once they were under way, the swaying of the chaise quickly lulled her into slumber. She woke when they paused for lunch at a pretty little inn on the banks of the Thames. Only partially refreshed, she forced herself to consider how she was going to handle the coming interview with her grandmother. How, exactly, was she to broach the subject of Hazelmere and his promised visit? Back in the carriage, she dozed fitfully while her problems revolved like clockwork in her mind. She came fully awake when the wheels hit the cobbled streets. Gazing about, she was astonished by the hustle and bustle of life in the capital. As the carriage moved into the areas inhabited by the wealthier citizens the clamour was left behind, and both sisters were soon engaged in examining and pronouncing sentence on the elegant outfits they saw.

After asking directions, Lang finally drew up outside an imposing mansion on one side of a square in what was clearly one of the more fashionable areas. In the centre was an enclosed garden in which children and nursemaids were taking the late-afternoon air. The sun's last rays were gilding the bare branches of the cherry trees there as the sisters were assisted from the carriage by the stately butler who had answered Lang's knock.

Relieved of their cloaks and escorted to the upstairs drawing-room, the sisters made their curtsy to their fashionable grandmother. Lady Merion surged towards them, enveloping them in a mist of gauzes and perfume. Her blonde wig was perfectly set above a face still graced by traces of the pale beauty she had once been. Sharp blue eyes watched her world, set above a long straight nose and a mouth only too ready to laugh at what she saw.

"My dears! I'm so glad to see you safely arrived! Now sit down and let me give you some tea. My chef, Henri, has sent up these delicacies to tempt you after your journey."

Drawing them to sit around the fire, already burning brightly, Lady Merion noted that neither sister was looking her best. "Tonight we'll have a very quiet time. You must both retire immediately after dinner. Tomorrow morning we've an appointment with Celestine, the most fashionable modiste in London. You must have recovered from your journey by then.''

As soon as they had eaten the delicious pastries and drunk their tea, Lady Merion rang the bell. It was answered by Witchett, a tall, angular woman with sparse grey hair whose peculiar talent in life lay in being able to turn out her elderly mistress in the most suitable of the currently fashionable styles. She was burning with curiosity to view the latest challenges to her skill. A quick glance at the Misses Darent told her that Mellow, the butler, had not exaggerated. In spite of their tiredness, their potential was apparent. The younger, properly dressed, would be a hit. And Miss Darent had that certain something that Witchett, a veteran campaigner, instantly recognised. The sisters were therefore favoured with a thin smile.

''Ah, there you are, Witchett. Please conduct Miss Darent and Miss Cecily to their rooms. I suggest, my dears, that you rest before dinner. Witchett will see your things are unpacked, and she'll take charge of your dressing until we can find suitable maids. Off with you, now.'' She dismissed them with a wave of one heavily beringed white hand.

They followed Witchett to two pretty bedchambers, obviously newly refurbished, Dorothea's in a soft pastel green and Cecily's in a delicate blue. Everything was already unpacked, and Witchett helped them undress. ''I'll return to assist you to dress for dinner, Miss Darent.''

Dorothea sank thankfully into the soft feather bed and immediately fell asleep.

Lady Merion had instructed her chef that a light and simple meal was all they required that evening. Consequently there were only three courses, each of some half a dozen dishes. Luckily both Dorothea and Cecily had recovered their appetites and were able to do justice to their first experience of the culinary delights of London.

Their grandmother was pleasantly surprised to find them considerably restored. Throughout dinner she monopolised the conversation. "First and by far the most important task is to have you both suitably gowned. For that, Celestine's is first on our list. She's the best known of Bruton Street's modistes for good reason."

Lady Merion had paid a visit to Celestine as soon as she had decided to launch her granddaughters into the ton. She had made it clear that she required that lady's best efforts. Celestine had built her highly successful business through shrewd assessment of her clients' abilities to display her creations in ton circles. Lady Merion's granddaughters would be paraded at all the most exclusive venues. Having extracted a description of the young ladies, she had graciously agreed to do all possible to ensure their success.

"Celestine's talents are truly stupendous. After that, we'll have to get your hair seen to, and I've organised a dancing master as well. I don't expect you know the waltz?" She paused to help herself to some buttered crab. "Once you're presentable, our first outing will be a drive in the Park. We'll go about three, which at this time of year is the right time to meet people. I'll introduce you to a number of the leaders of the ton, and hopefully we can find some of the younger generation for you to make friends with. In particular, I hope we'll meet Lady Jersey. Her nickname is "Silence", because she chatters all the time. Don't be put out if what she says seems rather odd. Princess Esterhazy should also be there. Both these ladies are patronesses of Almack's. You need vouchers from them to attend. If you're not admitted to Almack's you may as well give up the Season and go home."

"Good heavens!" said Dorothea. "I'd no idea it was that important."

"Well, it is," answered her grandmother with absolute conviction. She continued in this style, pouring forth an abundance of information. Dorothea and Cecily listened avidly. Possessing a fair degree of common sense, they needed no urging to learn all they could of the mores and practices of the fashionable from their experienced grandmama before their first venture into the critical world of the ton.

At nine o'clock, seeing Cecily stifle a yawn, her ladyship brought her lecture to an end. "It's time both of you were in bed. Ring for Witchett, Dorothea. She'll help you change. Go along, now. You've had enough for one day."

As the door shut behind the sleepy girls Lady Merion settled herself more comfortably in the corner of her elegant sofa. She was going to enjoy this Season. Lately, her accustomed routine of fashionable pleasures had been sadly lacking in excitement.

She had not spent over sixty years at the hub of aristocratic life without learning to gauge the qualities of those around her. Every bit as shrewd as she was fashionable, she had been agreeably impressed by her rustic granddaughters when she had met them, for the first time in many years, at Darent Hall. On the basis of one afternoon's reacquaintance she had decided it would be highly diverting to unleash them on the ton. While she had little doubt she would become sincerely fond of them, her main purpose had been purely selfish. Now, having reexamined their fresh faces and charmingly assured manners, she wryly wondered whether she would be able to cope.

Thinking again of the girls, she frowned. Dorothea had seemed strangely preoccupied. Hopefully she had not conceived a *tendre* for some country gentleman. Still, even if she had, the delights of a London Season would soon distract her from her sleepy country past.

Her cogitations were interrupted by a knock on the door. Dorothea, clad in a delicate pink wrapper with her dark hair swirling over her shoulders, put her head around the door. Seeing her grandmother, she entered.

The fair brows over the sharp blue eyes rose to improbable heights. "Why, child, what's the matter?"

"Grandmama, there's something I must tell you."

Ah-ha! thought her ladyship. Now I'm going to find out what's bothering her. She motioned Dorothea to sit next to her.

Sinking gracefully down, Dorothea fixed her eyes on the fire and calmly let fall her bombshell. "Well, for a start I have to tell you that the Marquis of Hazelmere will call on you tomorrow."

"Good gracious!" The exclamation was forced from Lady Merion as she jerked bolt upright, her fascinated blue gaze riveted on her grandchild. "My dear, how on *earth* did you meet a man of Hazelmere's stamp? I didn't know your mother was acquainted with the Henrys."

Hermione was conscious of a dreadful sinking feeling at the mere mention of Hazelmere's name. Drat the boy! He'd been the bane of many a hopeful mother's life, proving so fascinating to their impressionable daughters that there was no doing anything with the silly chits. As he had proved impervious to the charms of all but certain delectable members of the *demi-monde,* careful mothers were wont to advise their daughters that, in spite of his undoubted eligibility, Lord Hazelmere did not feature on their lists of likely suitors. Dorothea's words had started all sorts of hares racing in her mind, but why Hazelmere would want an interview with herself was more than she could imagine. She settled herself so that she had an uninterrupted view of her granddaughter's face. "Start at the beginning, child, or I'll never understand."

Conscious of the steady scrutiny, Dorothea nodded and carefully began. "Well, the first time I met Lord Hazelmere was while I was berrying in Moreton Park woods last August. He had recently inherited the estate from his great-aunt, Lady Moreton."

"Yes, I know about that," said her ladyship. "I knew Etta Moreton quite well. In fact, she wrote to me after your mother's death, urging me to take a hand in your lives."

"Did she?" That was news to Dorothea.

"Mmm. But what happened when you met Hazelmere? I presume he made himself charming, as usual?"

Dorothea reminded herself that she had no idea how charming Hazelmere might be expected to be. She stuck to her edited story. "He introduced himself. Then, because I was unattended, he insisted on walking me home."

Lady Merion, reading into her granddaughter's careful tones rather more than Dorothea would have wished, leapt to a conclusion. "My dear, you needn't be shy about telling me he made love to you shamelessly. He does it all the time. That devil can be utterly undeniable when the mood takes him."

Her gaze wildly incredulous, Dorothea saw the crevasse yawning at her feet only just in time. Lady Merion had used the term "made love' in the sense in which it was used in her heyday, to denote suggestive flirtation. Swallowing the words she had so nearly uttered, she forced her voice to calmness. "Charming? Actually, I found him rather arrogant."

Her ladyship blinked at this cold assessment of one of society's lions.

Dorothea hurried on. "I met Lord Hazelmere again at the inn last night."

Lady Merion would have described herself as being inured to the ways of those around her. It was consequently with some surprise that she realised that her granddaughter, having been in the house for only a few hours, had managed to seriously shake her calm. She repeated weakly, "The Marquis was at the inn last night?"

"Yes. And so were a large number of other gentlemen, because there'd been a prize-fight on near by."

Lady Merion closed her eyes, asking herself what next this outrageous child would reveal. She received Dorothea's carefully censored version of events at the inn in silence. She was, in fact, more than a little puzzled. While Hazelmere had acted most properly in rescuing Dorothea, his subsequent actions were much harder to understand. She could not see why he had been so angry. Highly unlike him to lose his temper at all, let alone with a chit he hardly knew.

Aware that Dorothea was waiting for her verdict, she put the puzzle of Hazelmere's behaviour aside. "Well, my dear, I cannot see anything in your conduct which should cause you undue concern. I would not wish you to go about anywhere unattended, that's true. But I know your life at the Grange lacked the formality it might have had. The happenings at the inn were highly regrettable, but you could not have known how it would be and thankfully Hazelmere was there to rescue you." She paused, suddenly thoughtful. "Do you have any idea why he wishes to see me tomorrow?"

Dorothea had given that particular question a great deal of thought. "I wonder whether it was because of the other gentlemen in the stableyard. He knew them, and they now know he has met me previously. I assume we'll have to agree on some acceptable tale to account for that?"

Lady Merion considered this, then nodded. "Yes, that's a likely explanation." Hazelmere would be well aware of the possible consequences of that public acknowledgement of their acquaintance, and it was quite in character that he should seek to minimise any damage. Whatever else he might be, Hazelmere would always behave as he ought.

Relieved of the nagging worry that she had committed some heinous social sin, Dorothea enjoyed a blissful night's sleep. Cecily, too, slept the sleep of the innocent and was fully recovered from their travelling. Arriving in Bruton Street, they were met by the great Celestine herself. One look sufficed to tell that sharp-witted modiste that in the Misses Darent she had models equal to her talents. Five minutes in their company convinced her that, with their charmingly open manners and that unconscious air of the truly well bred, they were destined to be among the foremost hits of the Season.

The last thing needed to make her throw all her most prized designs at the Darent feet was provided when, on their arrival, Lady Merion took her aside. "My granddaughters' affairs are moving apace, *madame*. Miss Darent has made the acquaintance of one of the unmarried peers. I can't, of course, reveal his name, but he is *most* eligible. Lord H is definitely behaving with very much less than his usual sang-froid. I have every hope to see her creditably established before the Season ends."

No mean player of society's games, Lady Merion was

confident of the response her indiscretion would elicit. At the very least, Hazelmere's intrusion into her granddaughter's life should be put to good use. She had no illusions about her elder granddaughter. Cecily would take very well; she was virtually the epitome of the current craze for blonde beauties. Dorothea was striking, but would, she was sure, pale into insignificance in her sister's company. And, on top of that, she was far too much in command of herself to appeal to any gentleman's chivalrous instincts. Although a brilliant match was wishful thinking, a good match was still well within her reach. Particularly with Celestine's help.

On the matter of style, Celestine, a superbly gowned dark-haired woman of indeterminate age, made her pronouncements with a slight French accent. "Miss Cecily is so young and so fair that she *must* be dressed *à la jeune fille!* For Miss Darent, however, I would recommend a more sophisticated style. With your permission, my lady?" She glanced speculatively at Lady Merion.

"We are entirely in your hands, *madame,*" responded her ladyship.

Celestine nodded. If that was so, she would seize this opportunity with both hands. Dressing the simpering daughters of the ton rarely gave her scope for her genius. To be presented with a client of the quality of Miss Darent was a God-given chance to display her true skill. Good bone-structure, perfect poise, regal deportment, striking and unusual colouring, a truly elegant figure and an arrestingly classical face—what more could a first-class modiste desire in her client? When she had finished with her Dorothea Darent would stand out in any crowd and, thank the lord, had the confidence to carry it off. Her black eyes sparkled. "*Bon!* Miss Darent's colouring is sufficiently unusual. Also her deportment...so much more—how should I say?—elegant, poised. We will use daring colours and severe styling to make best use of what God has created.''

The next two hours were spent in a haze of gauzes and silks, muslins and cambrics as the relative merits of the various designs, materials and finishes were discussed and measurements taken.

After giving an order for a staggering number of gowns, some to be delivered later that evening for their first promenade in the park the next day, Lady Merion triumphantly led her granddaughters back to their carriage.

Returning to their rooms after a light luncheon, the girls found that in their absence Witchett had been shopping too. Opening their drawers, they found them fully stocked with underwear liberally edged with lace, stockings of the finest silk, ribbons of every hue, together with gloves, reticules, scarves, fans—in short, everything else they could possibly need. Witchett, coming up to see if they needed any assistance, found them exclaiming over their finds.

Seeing her at her bedchamber door, Dorothea beamed. "Oh, thank you, Witchett! I'm sure we would have forgotten all these things until we were about to go out!"

Witchett found herself, uncharacteristically, returning the smile. "Well, miss, I'm sure you've got plenty of other things to think about." Really, it was very hard not to fall under the spell of these happy young things. "Now, Miss Cecily! I see you've crushed that pretty dress of yours terribly. You'll have to be more careful with your new London gowns. Betsy can press it while you rest. She's waiting in your chamber to help you undress."

"Oh, but I don't want to rest!"

The querulous tone alerted Dorothea. Cecily could wilt

rapidly when over-tired, and it was only the day before that they had been travelling. Catching Witchett's eye to enjoin her silence, Dorothea, examining a lace collar by the window, calmly said, "If you don't wish to rest then no one shall make you. Of course, we'll have to pay attention this evening while Grandmama teaches us about society's ways, but as long as you're sure you'll be awake I see no point in resting. It's such a beautiful day that I think I'll take a stroll in the park in the square. Why don't you come with me?"

Witchett held herself aloof.

The expression on Cecily's face turned thoughtful. On consideration, she was not so sure she could sustain another evening of dos and don'ts without fortification. "Oh, maybe Witchett's right and I should rest. I always find it so difficult to remember things when I'm tired. Enjoy your walk!" With an airy wave she drifted across the corridor.

Dorothea remained at the window, looking at the cherry trees swelling into bud and the children playing on the lawns underneath. "Witchett, I'm not perfectly sure, but is it acceptable for me to walk in that park?"

"Yes, miss. Provided you have an attendant."

"Who would be an appropriate attendant should I wish to go for a walk now?"

"I'll accompany you, miss, as is right and proper. If you'll wait for me in the hall I'll just get my coat and join you there."

Witchett was as prompt as her word and within five minutes Dorothea was strolling under the cherry trees, enjoying the sensation of sunlight on her face. Her pelisse kept out the cold breeze as she wended her way around the paths past beds of bright daffodils and early crocus. A child's ball suddenly landed at her feet. Stooping to pick it up, she looked around for the owner. A fair lad about six years old stood uncertainly on the lawn on the other side of the daffodil bed. Smiling, she walked around to him, holding out the ball.

"Say thank you, Peter," came a voice from a seat under one of the trees. Dorothea saw a nursemaid rocking a baby in her arms, smiling and nodding at her.

She turned back to find the child bowing from the waist, saying, "Thank you, miss," in a small gruff voice.

Impulsively she asked, "Would you like me to play catch with you for a while? I've just come out to enjoy the sunshine, so why don't we enjoy it together?"

The wide smile that greeted this was answer enough, and, after glancing at his nursemaid to see she approved, young Peter settled down to a game of catch with his new-found acquaintance.

So the Marquis of Hazelmere, strolling around Cavendish Square on his way to Merion House, found the object of his thoughts playing ball in the square. Leaning on the railings surrounding the park, he watched as Dorothea taught Peter to throw. She was facing away from him, some distance away. Suddenly a particularly wild throw of Peter's, greeted with hoots of laughter from the players, sent the ball rolling across the lawn to land in a nearby flower-bed. Dorothea followed. As she bent to pick the ball up Hazelmere couldn't resist asking, "Alone and unattended again, Miss Darent?"

She whirled to face him, an "Oh!" of surprise dying on her lips. For one wild moment his threat to beat her if he found her unattended again took possession of her mind. The appreciative gleam in his eyes left her in little doubt that he had accurately guessed as much. As her equilibrium returned she mustered what dignity she could to reply, "Why, no, Lord Hazelmere! I'm now too ex-

perienced in society's ways to make that mistake, I assure
you.''

One black brow rose. Hazelmere, unused to having
young ladies cross swords with him, noticed Witchett materialising at Dorothea's elbow. ''I'm about to call on
Lady Merion,'' he said. ''I think perhaps, Miss Darent,
you should also be present.''

''Oh, yes. I'd forgotten.''

Unable to see her face as she bent down to take leave
of the boy, Hazelmere could not be certain whether the
comment had been artless or uttered on purpose to deflate
his pretensions. Very little of Miss Darent's conversation
was artless. Well, that was a pleasant game for two to
play, and there were few more skilled in it than he. He
continued his stroll along the railings to the gate, where
he stood, negligently at ease, and openly watched her as
she came towards him.

To herself Dorothea made a firm resolution. Henceforth
she was not going to let the odious Marquis get the better
of her! She was a calm, cool, mature woman—even Celestine had commented on her poise. Why on earth she
fell apart whenever Hazelmere was about was more than
she could comprehend. She was heartily sick of the betraying flush that rose so readily in response to his taunts.
Every second comment he made was designed purely to
throw her into confusion and allow him to manage matters
as he willed. Well, thought the determined Miss Darent,
very conscious of that hazel gaze as she approached the
street, that might work on the London misses but I'm not
going to let him stage-manage me! With the sunniest of
smiles, she met him at the gate.

If Hazelmere entertained any suspicions of this evident
change of heart he kept them to himself. His experienced
eye registered the countrified pelisse and the tangle of her

hair, wind-blown and escaping from its pins. He wondered why such a combination should appear so attractive. In silence they crossed the street and were bowed into Merion House by Mellow. "Lady Merion is expecting you, my lord."

Surrendering her pelisse to Witchett, Dorothea caught sight of her reflection in the hall mirror. Arrested by the picture of her hair in such turmoil, she wondered whether she should keep her grandmother waiting while she set it to rights. She raised her glance to find herself looking into the Marquis's hazel eyes, reflected in the mirror. He smiled in complete comprehension. "Yes, I would if I were you. I'll tell her ladyship you'll join us in a few moments."

Realising she could not continually pull caps with him, particularly when he was being helpful, she confined herself to a curt nod before whisking herself up the stairs, Witchett trailing behind.

Hazelmere paused for a moment to flick a speck of dust from his sleeve before nodding to Mellow. "You may announce me now."

For this interview Lady Merion had arrayed herself in a gown she knew made her look particularly formidable. Instinct born of experience warned her that there was more to the encounters between the Marquis and her granddaughter than she had been told. She was unsure that Dorothea herself knew the full sum. On the other hand, Hazelmere would certainly be aware of every nuance. She was determined to extract a much more detailed explanation from him before she called Dorothea to attend them. As he strolled elegantly across the room to bow over her hand she fixed him with a basilisk stare which in years past had produced confessions from the most hardened of reprobates.

Hazelmere smiled lazily down at her.

With a jolt she realised that there was a large difference between demanding the reason for a cricket ball landing in her drawing-room from a ten-year-old boy and demanding an accounting of his behaviour from a thirty-one-year-old peer, who, aside from being a leader of the ton, was also one of the most dangerously handsome men in the kingdom. And, she fumed, noting the amused understanding in the hazel eyes, the jackanapes knows it!

Baulked, she motioned him to a seat and reluctantly gave her attention to the next item on her agenda. She waited until he was seated, admiring the way his immaculate morning coat sat across his shoulders. His long muscular thighs were encased in skin-tight buff knee-breeches, and his Hessians shone like the proverbial mirror. She might be old, but she still noticed such things. "I understand I must thank you for rescuing my granddaughter, Dorothea, from an unfortunate incident at that inn the other evening."

One well-manicured hand waved dismissively. "Having recognised your granddaughter, even someone with a conscience as faulty as mine could hardly have left her there." The gently mocking tone and the laughter in his face robbed this speech of any impropriety.

Accustomed to the subtleties of social conversation, Lady Merion thawed visibly. "Very well! But why this meeting?"

"Unfortunately the crowd from which I extricated Miss Darent contained at least one member of the ton who cannot be trusted to forget the incident."

"Dorothea mentioned Tremlow."

"Oh, yes. Tremlow was there, and Botherwood and Lords Michaels and Downie. But they are relatively harmless, and, unless I'm much mistaken, would probably not recall the incident unless their memories were jogged, and perhaps not even then. I'm more concerned with Sir Barnaby Ruscombe.''

"Ugh! That repulsive man! He always dabbles in the most *malicious* scandalmongering.'' She paused, then eyed the Marquis speculatively. "I don't suppose there's anything you can do about him?''

"Alas, no. Anyone else, quite probably. But not Ruscombe. Scandal is his trade. Still, given that we can invent a plausible tale to account for my having previously met Miss Darent, I can't see there's any risk of serious damage to her reputation.''

"You're right, of course,'' agreed Lady Merion. "But it would be wise to have her here, I think. Ring that bell, if you will.''

"No need,'' replied Hazelmere, "I met her in the park on my way here. She went upstairs to tidy her hair before joining us.''

As if in answer to the comment, Dorothea entered. Languidly rising, Hazelmere acknowledged her curtsy by taking her hand and, after bowing over it, raised it to his lips, his eyes roaming appreciatively over her.

Lady Merion stiffened. Kissing a lady's hand was not the current practice. What on earth was going on?

Dorothea accepted the salute without a flicker of surprise. Seating herself in a chair on the other side of her grandmother, opposite Hazelmere, she turned an enquiring face to her ladyship.

"We were just discussing, my dear, what story to adopt to account for Lord Hazelmere recognising you at the inn.''

"Maybe Miss Darent has a suggestion?'' put in his lordship, hazel eyes gently quizzing Dorothea.

"As a matter of fact, I do,'' she replied smoothly. "It

would be safest, I imagine, to stick to occurrences no one else could dispute?'' Her delicately arched brows rose as she gazed with unmarred calm into Hazelmere's eyes.

His expressive lips twitched. ''That might be wise,'' he murmured.

Dorothea regally inclined her head. ''For instance, what if, on one of your visits to Lady Moreton, she'd been well enough to be taken for a ride in your curricle—not far, just around the surrounding lanes? I'm sure she would have liked to have done that if she'd been able.''

''You're quite right. My great-aunt did bemoan not being well enough for just such an outing as you propose.''

''Good! Only the outing did occur, and of course you didn't take your groom with you, did you?''

Hazelmere, entering into the spirit of the conversation, promptly replied, ''I feel sure I'd given Jim permission to relax in the kitchens that day.''

Dorothea nodded approvingly. ''Driving down the lane, you met my mother, Cynthia Darent, and myself, returning from paying a visit to...oh, Waverley Park, of course.''

''Your coachman?''

''I was driving the gig. And what could be more natural than that Lady Moreton and my mother should stop to chat? They were old friends, after all. And Lady Moreton presented you to Mama and me. After talking for a few minutes, we went our separate ways.''

''When, exactly, did this meeting occur?'' he asked.

''Well, it would have had to be the summer before last, when both Lady Moreton and Mama were alive.''

''My congratulations, Miss Darent. We now have a most acceptable tale which accounts for our meeting and the only two witnesses who could say us nay are dead. Very neat.''

"Yes, but wait one moment!" interpolated Lady Merion. "Why didn't your mother tell her other friends about this meeting? Surely such a novel encounter would have made an impression in the neighbourhood?"

"But, Grandmama, you know how scatterbrained Mama was. It would be quite possible for her to have forgotten all about it by the time we'd reached home, particularly if something else occurred to distract her on the way."

Reminded of her daughter-in-law's vagueness, Lady Merion grudgingly agreed this was so. "Well, then, why did you yourself not tell any of your friends about it?"

Dorothea opened her large green eyes to their fullest extent and, addressing her grandmother, asked, "But why would I have done so? I've never been in the habit of discussing inconsequential occurrences with anyone."

Lady Merion held her breath. She could not resist glancing at Hazelmere to see how he was taking being classed as "inconsequential". He appeared to be his usual urbane self, but she thought she caught a glint from those hazel eyes, presently fixed on Dorothea's face. Be careful, my girl! she mentally adjured her granddaughter.

"What a wonderfully useful trait, Miss Darent," responded Hazelmere, deciding for the moment to ignore provocation. "So now we have a believable and totally unexceptionable story to account for our previous meeting. Provided we stick to that, I foresee no difficulty in ignoring the inevitable tales of what happened at the Three Feathers." He rose and with effortless grace bent over Lady Merion's hand. "I gather you'll be attending all the ton crushes this Season?"

"Oh, yes," responded her ladyship, reverting to her normal social manner. "We'll be out around town just as soon as Celestine can clothe these children respectably."

He crossed to Dorothea's side and she stood for him to take his leave. Again he raised her hand to his lips. Smiling down at her in a way she found oddly disconcerting, his hazel eyes trapping her own, he said, "Then I will hope to further my acquaintance with you, Miss Darent. I do hope you'll not find me too inconsequential to remember?" The gently mocking tone was back.

Dorothea returned the provocative hazel glance without apparent concern, and, wide-eyed, remarked, "Oh, I shouldn't think I'd forget you now, my lord."

He only just succeeded in controlling his face but his eyes clearly registered the hit. He paused, looking down into her brilliant green eyes, his own brimful of laughter. Forever a sportsman, he could hardly complain, as he had set himself up for that one. Still, he had not expected her to have the courage to fling that back in his face, and with such ease. With one last enigmatic glance, he turned and, bowing again to the sorely afflicted Lady Merion, bid both ladies a good day and left.

As the door shut behind him Lady Merion turned a gaze equally made up of disbelief and conjecture on her granddaughter. However, "Ring for tea, child," was all she said.

Chapter Four

For the Darent sisters, the Season began in earnest the next day. The morning commenced with a visit from Lady Merion's hairdresser. The pert Frenchman no sooner clapped eyes on the girls than his loquacious soul knew no bounds. Celestine had insisted on being present, much to everyone's surprise. It transpired that she had decided to take complete control of the Misses Darents' appearance. Lady Merion was astonished at her unusual condescension and then even more surprised by the transformation wrought in her elder granddaughter. Wearing the first of Celestine's creations, delivered expressly for their promenade in the Park later that day, with her lovely dark hair lightly cropped and arranged in a variation of the fashionable *Sappho,* Dorothea had emerged much as the ugly duckling transformed into a veritable swan. The result, as Celestine confided in a whispered aside to her ladyship, could not be adequately described as beautiful—that was an epithet reserved more correctly for the youthful Cecily. She was attractive, stunning, and trailing a definite aura of sensuality, and the impact of the new Dorothea was unerringly directed at the more mature male.

Lady Merion, with Hazelmere in mind, blinked and rapidly realigned her expectations.

The sisters were next introduced to their dancing master, hired for an hour every morning for a week, to ensure that they would not put a foot wrong in the more conventional dances, as well as to introduce them to the waltz. Both girls were naturally graceful, and country balls had made them familiar with all the current measures, save the waltz.

In the afternoon they set out in Lady Merion's barouche to see and be seen at the Park. The spectacle of the ton taking the air, meeting old acquaintances and making new ones, held both girls enthralled. Lady Merion, her eyes resting for the umpteenth time on the delightful spectacle on the carriage seat opposite, felt happier and more buoyed by expectation than she had in years.

They had barely commenced their first circuit when a tall and angular lady, dressed in the height of fashion and seated in a landau drawn up to the side of the carriageway, waved to Lady Merion, who immediately instructed her coachman to pull up.

"Sally, how delightful! Is Maria back yet?" Without waiting for an answer, Lady Merion continued, "You must let me present my granddaughters. Dorothea, Cecily, this is Lady Jersey."

After exchanging greetings with the girls, Sally Jersey fixed her ladyship with a penetrating stare. "Hermione, you're going to cause a *riot* with these children. You *must* let me send you vouchers for Almack's *at once!* My dear, I had a *dreadful* premonition that the Season was going to be *so dull*, but with two such beauties around I can see there'll be *fireworks!*"

Both Dorothea and Cecily blushed.

Lady Merion remained chatting to Lady Jersey for

some minutes, exchanging information on who had or had not returned to the capital. It became apparent to the two girls that they were attracting considerable attention, from the ogling stares of the soldiers and young bucks, which Lady Merion had instructed them to ignore, to the far more disconcerting stares of other mamas passing by in their carriages with their hopeful young daughters. Under the soporific effect of the drone of their grandmother's conversation, Cecily let her gaze wander to a group of elegant gentlemen chatting to two pretty young ladies on the nearby lawn. Dorothea, similarly abstracted, was abruptly brought back to earth by Lady Jersey. "I hear, my dear, that you are already acquainted with Lord Hazelmere?"

Aware that to show the slightest hesitation would be fatal, Dorothea used her large eyes to great effect, lucently conveying an attitude of complete nonchalance. "Yes. As luck would have it, I met him again recently. He was kind enough to assist me at an inn on our way to London."

Her ladyship's prominent eyes did not waver. "So you had met him before?"

Dorothea's composure held firm. Her brows rose slightly, as if the answer to that question should really be quite obvious. "His great-aunt, Lady Moreton, introduced him to my mother and myself some time ago. She was a neighbour of ours in Hampshire."

"Oh, I see." Lady Jersey was clearly disappointed in this undeniably mundane explanation of Dorothea's acquaintance with one of society's more rakish bachelors. She returned her attention to Lady Merion.

After a further five minutes of acidly social intercourse the coachman was told to move on. As Lady Jersey fell behind, Lady Merion drew a deep breath and bestowed a look of definite approval on her elder granddaughter.

"Very well done, my dear. Now we just have to keep it up."

What she meant by that became rapidly apparent as they engaged in conversation after conversation with dowagers and matrons and occasionally with mothers with unmarried daughters. Without fail, the incident at the inn would somehow find its way into the arena, in one version or another. After her success with Lady Jersey, undoubtedly society's most formidable inquisitor, Lady Merion let Dorothea deal with all these enquiries, only stepping in when some of the younger ladies seemed anxious to lead the description into areas too particular for her ladyship's sense of propriety. Cecily, absorbed in the Park and its patrons and too young for the matrons to waste much time over, largely ignored these conversations.

Almost an hour later they stopped to talk to the Princess Esterhazy. After the introductions were performed, the sweet-faced and distinctly plump Princess smiled sleepily at the girls. "I saw you talking with Sally before, so I'm sure she must have promised you vouchers?"

Lady Merion nodded. "She feels my girls will liven up proceedings."

"Oh, undoubtedly, I should think," agreed Princess Esterhazy.

At this point two elegant young gentlemen detached themselves from a group that had been eyeing the beautiful young things in the Merion carriage and approached. "Your servant, Lady Merion," said the first, raising his hat and sweeping a graceful bow, copied by his companion.

Lady Merion, turning to see who had addressed her, promptly exclaimed, "Oh, Ferdie! Is your mother in town yet?"

Assured that Mrs Acheson-Smythe would be in the capital by the end of the week, Lady Merion introduced her granddaughters to the elegant pair.

Dorothea and Cecily looked down upon two stylishly correct gentlemen, both clearly of the first stare. Neither was tall or broad-shouldered, yet both contrived to give the impression of being well turned out, a perfect fit for whatever niche they occupied in the ton. Mr Acheson-Smythe was slim and fair, his pale face characterised by a pair of frank and guileless blue eyes. Mr Dermont, of similar build, was less confident than his friend, letting the knowledgeable Mr Acheson-Smythe lead the conversation. Knowing that Ferdie Acheson-Smythe could be trusted to keep the line, her ladyship returned to her gossip with the Princess.

Seeing the girls' attention claimed by the young men, Princess Esterhazy took the opportunity to satisfy her curiosity. "But tell me, Hermione. What is the truth of this story that Hazelmere rescued one of these two from a prize-fight crowd at some inn?"

By this time Lady Merion had the answer by rote. "Such a lucky thing he was passing, my dear. Dorothea had gone down to find her coachman, not realising that the gentlemen had already arrived."

"I had not realised your granddaughters were acquainted with Hazelmere."

"Most fortunately, Dorothea had been introduced to him by his great-aunt, Lady Moreton. You must remember, she died last year, and Hazelmere was her heir. The Grange borders Moreton Park, and Cynthia, my daughter-in-law, and Etta Moreton were close friends. Dorothea! Where was it you first met Hazelmere?"

Dorothea, who had been trying to follow two conversations at once, turned to hear her grandmother's question repeated. She answered easily, "Oh, out driving one day.

He was taking Lady Moreton for a ride in his curricle.'' She turned back to Ferdie Acheson-Smythe, as if the details of how she had met the Marquis could not be of any possible consequence to anyone.

Her lack of consciousness convinced Princess Esterhazy that the story was the truth. In her opinion, no young lady who had met Hazelmere in any ineligible way could possibly look as unconcerned as Dorothea Darent.

On their return to Merion House shortly afterwards, Lady Merion led the way upstairs to her private drawing-room. Throwing her elegant hat on a chair, she subsided in a cloud of stylish velvets and breathed a heartfelt sigh. ''Well! We did very well, my dears. That was an excellent start to your Season.'' She settled into her chaise-longue and, supplied with tea by Dorothea, consented to answer their questions.

''Ferdie Acheson-Smythe?'' she said in answer to one of these. ''Ferdie is the only son of the Hertfordshire Acheson-Smythes. Of very good family, first cousin to Hazelmere. Ferdie will have to marry some day, I dare say, but by and large he's not the marrying kind. However, he *is* an acknowledged authority on all matters of etiquette, so if Ferdie drops you a hint on anything to do with your behaviour or dress you'd be well advised to take heed! He's also completely trustworthy; he'll never go beyond the line of what is pleasing. Ferdie is an unexceptionable companion for a young lady, and a very useful cavalier. It wouldn't do you any harm to be seen with him.''

''And Mr Dermont?'' asked Cecily.

''Anyone Ferdie introduces to you as a friend will be much the same style, though Ferdie himself is unquestionably at the head of that class.''

Lady Merion had accepted an invitation to a small party that evening, and both her granddaughters accompanied her. Entirely satisfied with their appearance, she was pleased to see that they mixed easily with the other young people present, although Dorothea, with her stunning appearance and air of calm self-possession, was deferred to as senior to the débutantes and in something of a different category. This was true enough. In a larger gathering, with more mature gentlemen, such as Hazelmere, to claim her attention, her elder granddaughter would not lack for entertaining partners.

Watching Dorothea, she grinned, their words of that afternoon recurring in her head. Cecily had been resting when the rest of Celestine's creations had been delivered; she and Dorothea had been alone in her parlour.

"This is exquisite!" Dorothea had exclaimed, holding up a blue sarcenet ballgown of Cecily's.

"Your own are every bit as alluring," she had returned.

Dorothea had laughed, turning her attention to yet another of Cecily's gowns. "But it's Cecily who needs the husband, not I."

The comment had stunned her to silence. Then, in one revealing instant, she had seen Dorothea through Dorothea's eyes. Despite her common sense and self-confidence, having lived in relative seclusion until now, her granddaughter had little idea how she appeared to others in the fashionable world. To men. Particularly to men like Hazelmere. It was hardly innocence, rather a lack of awareness. After all, she had never been exposed to such gentlemen before. Intrigued, she had folded her hands in her lap and calmly stated, "My dear, if you have visions of becoming an ape-leader, I fear you'll be disappointed."

The green eyes had lifted to hers in genuine surprise. "Whatever do you mean, ma'am? I know I'm too old for the marriage mart and I hardly have the requisite looks for an acknowledged beauty. But I don't repine, I assure you.''

She had snorted her disbelief. "You're two and twenty, girl—hardly at your last prayers! And if you think to be left on the shelf, well! All I can say is, you've another think coming.''

But her stubborn granddaughter had only smiled.

Now, as she saw the small but growing knot of young men around her elder granddaughter, a grin of unholy amusement lit her faded blue eyes. How long would it take for Dorothea to wake up and realise that she was likely to be pursued, if anything, with even more dedication than the vivacious Cecily?

The next morning brought the first of the invitations to the larger gatherings. Initially these arrived in a trickle, but by the end of the week, as Lady Merion's granddaughters became more widely known, the gilt-edged cards left at Merion House assumed the proportions of a flood. As Dorothea and Cecily were only too glad to share the limelight with their less well-endowed sisters, even the most jealous mother saw little reason to exclude them from her guest lists. Moreover, if the Darent sisters were to attend some rival party then half the eligible males would likely be there too.

Lady Merion insisted that they attend as many of the smaller parties held in these first weeks as possible. She was too experienced to discount the considerable advantage social confidence could give. So Dorothea and Cecily obediently promenaded every afternoon and were to be found at a soirée or party or musical evening every night, polishing their social skills and attracting no little interest. Within a short time, both had collected a circle of ardent admirers. While this was no more than her ladyship had

expected, the band around Dorothea gave her endless
amusement. In general not much older than Dorothea herself, these lovesick swains were continually vying one
with the other for their goddess's attention, striking By-
ronesque poses at every turn. It was really too funny for
words. Still, thought the very experienced Lady Merion,
it was serving its turn. Dorothea was being bored witless,
all her social ingenuity being required to keep her temper
with her artless lovers. A very good thing indeed if her
wilful granddaughter could be brought to an appreciative,
not to say receptive, frame of mind before being exposed
to the infinitely more subtle persuasions of Hazelmere and
his set. Luckily these highly eligible but far more dangerous gentlemen were rarely if ever sighted at the pre-
liminary gatherings.

Ferdie Acheson-Smythe was the most constant of Dorothea's cavaliers, rapidly attaining the position of cisis-
beo-in-chief to the dark-haired beauty. His initial approach to Lady Merion's granddaughters had been
prompted by a chance meeting with Hazelmere. His magnificent cousin had suggested that Ferdie might assist in
the squashing of any rumours concerning himself and the
lovely Dorothea. It was the sort of thing Ferdie, an adept
at social intrigue, enjoyed. And, as the favour was asked
by Hazelmere, Ferdie would have thrown himself into the
breach had Dorothea been the most unprepossessing antidote. Finding Miss Darent to be far more attractive than
Hazelmere had indicated, Ferdie took to his task with
alacrity. The result was that within a week a friendship
had been established, close to sibling in quality but without the attendant strains, much to the surprise of both
participants.

It was at a musical evening at Lady Bressington's that
Mr Edward Buchanan made his appearance. A solid coun-

try gentleman of thirty-odd years, he was mildly fair and slightly rotund, his pink face graced by soulful brown eyes at odds with the rest of his robust figure. For reasons Dorothea failed to divine, he made straight for her side, ousting a darkly handsome Romeo by the simple expedient of suggesting that Miss Darent had had enough mindless maunderings for one night.

Miss Darent was slightly stunned. The Romeo, shattered, took himself off, muttering dark and dire threats against unspecified unromantic elders. Mr Buchanan took his place.

"My dear Miss Darent. I hope you'll excuse my approaching you like this. I realise we haven't been properly introduced. My name is Edward Buchanan. My father was a friend of Sir Hugo Clere and I looked in on him on my way to town. He mentioned your name and asked me to convey his regards."

Dorothea sat silent through this speech, delivered in a ponderous baritone. The excuse was hardly substantial; Sir Hugo was a distant neighbour and she could readily imagine the purely formal greetings he would have sent. However, Miss Julia Bressington, a vivacious brunette and one of Cecily's closest confidantes, was about to start singing, accompanied by Cecily herself on the pianoforte, so it was not the time to make even the mildest scene. She inclined her head and pointedly gave her attention to the players.

Mr Buchanan had the sense to remain silent during the performance, but immediately the applause died he monopolised the conversation, determinedly chatting to Dorothea on pastoral issues. This left the majority of her court, most of whom had no knowledge of crops or livestock, stranded. Dorothea herself was utterly bemused by his unstinting eloquence on the subject. But as soon as the last of her admirers had drifted away, defeated by his dogged discourse, he stopped. "Ah-ha! Thought that would do it!" Looking thoroughly pleased with himself, he explained, "I wanted to get rid of them. I knew they wouldn't understand anything of moment. Sir Hugo gave me the fullest description of you, my dear Miss Darent, but he came far from doing justice to your beauty. You clearly outshine all these other young misses, although I must say I find the favoured style of dress for young ladies these days a little too, shall we say, revealing for one of my years to countenance." His eyes had dropped to the swell of her breasts exposed above the scooped neckline of her stylishly simple silk gown. "I dare say you feel that in the circumstances, placed as you are with your grandmother, who, I understand, is a highly fashionable lady, you too must play the part. Still, we can overlook such matters, I'm sure. You would feel far different in country circles, where I'm sure you are much more at home."

Dorothea was rendered speechless by this monologue, which had contrived to progress from over-full compliment to insult in the space of two minutes. Aghast, unable to get a word in edgeways, she was forced to listen to Mr Buchanan's opinions of fashionable practices, which culminated in a description of his widowed mother's belief that, in her exposing her only son to the wicked wiles of London society, he would return to her, corrupted in body and mind. Mr Buchanan assured Miss Darent with jocular familiarity that such an outcome was highly unlikely. Dorothea, incensed and close to losing her temper, bit back an acid rejoinder that if London society could teach Mr Buchanan his manners it would have achieved a laudable goal. Instead she said in frigid tones, "Mr Buchanan, I must thank you for your conversation. If you'll excuse me, I must speak with some friends.'' Which, she reflected, was as close to a verbal cut as made no difference. But even as she rose, and with a cool nod moved to Lady Merion's side, she saw that, far from his taking the hint, the dismissal had not pricked his ego in the least.

By the night of the first of Almack's subscription balls Lady Merion knew she had a major success on her hands. They were fully booked for at least a sennight and the invitations were still rolling in.

She had started preparations for the girls' coming-out ball, for which the ballroom at Merion House would be opened for the first time in years. Squads of cleaning women had already been in, and redecoration would soon begin. The invitations, gold-embossed, had arrived that afternoon, and tomorrow they could start sending them out. She had fixed the date for four weeks hence, at the beginning of April, just before the peak of the Season. By then all her acquaintances would have returned to Town and she could be assured of a full house.

As she watched her granddaughters descend the stairs dressed for their first ball, both apparently unconscious of the positively stunning picture they made, she admonished herself as an old fool. Of course, her ball would be the biggest crush of the Season, but its success would owe far more to these two lovely young things than to anything she herself could do.

Dorothea, a vision in pale sea-green silk, lightly touched with silver filigree work, moved to kiss her on the cheek. ''Grandmama, you look wonderful!''

Hermione unconsciously smoothed her purple satin. ''Well, my dears, you are both an enormous credit to me. I'm sure you'll create a considerable stir tonight!''

Cecily, shimmering in pale blue spangled gauze over a

shift of cornflower-blue satin, impulsively hugged her. "Yes, but do let's go!"

Laughing, Lady Merion called for their cloaks and then led the way to the carriage.

As soon as they entered the plain and unassuming ballroom that was Almack's it was apparent that the Darent sisters' arrival had been eagerly awaited. Within minutes their cards were full, with the exception of the two waltzes. Lady Merion had impressed on them that they were forbidden to waltz until invited by one of the patronesses, who would introduce them to a suitable partner.

The Season was now in full swing and the rooms were crowded with mothers and their marriageable daughters and gentlemen eager to view the new Season's débutantes. Dorothea was thoroughly enjoying herself, being partnered first by Ferdie, with whom she was now on first-name terms, and then by a host of politely attentive gentlemen. Her grandmother, watching over her charges from the gilt-backed chairs arranged around the walls to accommodate the chaperons, noted that Dorothea had attracted far more than her fair share of attention but none of the more undesirable blades had yet sought her company. Talking to Lady Maria Sefton, she watched her elder granddaughter go down the ballroom in the movement of the dance, and then lost sight of her as the music ended and the dancers dispersed.

At the end of the ballroom, on the arm of the charming young man who had been her partner, Dorothea turned to make her way back to her grandmother's side, knowing that the next dance was the first of the forbidden waltzes. A well-remembered voice halted her. "Miss Darent."

Turning to face the Marquis of Hazelmere, Dorothea swept him the curtsy she had been taught was due to his rank and, rising, found that he had taken her hand and was raising it to his lips. The hazel eyes dared her to make a scene, so she accepted the salute in the same unconcerned way she had previously. Then her eyes met his fully, and held.

There followed a curious hiatus in which time seemed suspended. Then Hazelmere, becoming aware of her awkward young cavalier, nodded dismissal to this gentleman. "I'll return Miss Darent to Lady Merion." Faced with a lion, the mouse retreated.

To Dorothea he continued, "There's someone I'd like you to meet, Miss Darent." He placed her hand on his arm and deftly steered her through the crowd.

She had seen him among the throng earlier in the evening. He was dressed, as always, with restrained elegance in the dark blue coat and black knee-breeches currently *de rigueur* for formal occasions, with a large diamond pin winking from the folds of his perfectly tied cravat. She had thought him attractive in his buckskin breeches and shooting jacket, and more so in his morning clothes. In full evening dress he was simply magnificent. She had little difficulty in understanding why he made so many cautious mothers distinctly nervous.

Strolling calmly by his side, her hand resting lightly on his arm, she tried to ignore the light-headedness that had nothing to do with the crowd or the dancing and everything to do with the expression in those hazel eyes. Oh, how very *dangerous* he was!

Their perambulation came to an end by the side of a dark-haired matron. This lady, turning towards them, exclaimed in a cold and bored voice, "There you are, my lord!"

Hazelmere looked down at Dorothea. "Allow me to present you, Miss Darent, to Mrs Drummond-Burrell."

Unexpectedly faced with the most censorious of Almack's patronesses, Dorothea hastily curtsied.

Mrs Drummond-Burrell, on whom her surprise was not lost, was pleased to smile. "I expect Lord Hazelmere did not tell you I wanted to meet you. It seems a vast pity such a lovely young lady should miss even one waltz tonight. So, as he has instructed me, I will give you permission to waltz in Almack's, my dear, and present Lord Hazelmere as a suitable partner."

Although taken aback by the scale of his machinations, Dorothea had been expecting something of the sort since she had first realised he was present. She had sufficient presence of mind to thank Mrs Drummond-Burrell very prettily, bringing an unusually benign expression to that lady's face, before allowing the Marquis to lead her on to the floor as the first strains of the waltz filled the room.

As this was the first waltz of the Season and many débutantes had not yet been given permission to dance, the floor was relatively uncrowded and the assembled company had a clear view of the dancers. The sight of the beautiful Miss Darent in the arms of Lord Hazelmere made something of a stir, and Dorothea, gently twirling down the room, was well aware that many eyes were directed their way. She did not dare allow herself to be distracted, fearing that he would instantly ask her some outrageous question.

As it transpired, she need not have worried. Hazelmere was, uncharacteristically, lost for words. He had thought her quite lovely in an old dimity gown with her hair down her back. Now, in every way perfect in one of Celestine's most elegant creations, she was utterly stunning.

Within seconds of stepping on to the floor Dorothea realised that she was in the arms of an expert, and promptly ceased trying to mark time. She surprised herself by not feeling the least bit awkward at being once again in his arms, and responded to the movements of the dance with a confidence so transparent that it drew even more attention than her beauty.

As they moved gracefully around the ballroom Hazelmere finally remarked, "Does it bother you to be the cynosure of so many eyes, Miss Darent?"

Considering this unexpected question, she looked up into the hazel eyes and with the most complete self-assurance answered, "Not at all, my lord. Should it?"

He smiled and replied, "By no means, my dear. But permit me to tell you that in that you are somewhat unusual."

Misliking where this line of conversation might lead, she rapidly hunted for an alternative. She saw her sister also dancing, in the arms of a man almost as attractive as Hazelmere. "Who is the gentleman dancing with my sister?"

Without glancing at the other couple, he replied, "Anthony, Lord Fanshawe."

Puzzled by a fleeting memory, she finally recognised the man she had glimpsed in the inn yard. Her eyes came back to Hazelmere. "Do you know him?"

He smiled down at her. "Oh, yes." After a pause he added provocatively, "We grew up together, as it happens."

Once again her face gave her away before she guiltily caught herself up. One glance at those amused hazel eyes told her that he had not missed her thoughts, and he promptly confirmed this by remarking, "No, Miss Darent. We are not *that* much alike."

She was pleased that she blushed only slightly.

Hazelmere, seeking to press his advantage, asked, "Are you never thrown into maidenly confusion, Miss Darent? Or is it that, at twenty-two, you no longer feel the need to adopt such missish airs?"

This uncannily accurate reading of her behaviour was, most unfortunately, lost on Dorothea. Instead he came under the concentrated scrutiny of her clear green eyes as she promptly asked, "How do you know my age?"

Mentally castigating himself for not being more careful, he was about to mendaciously attribute this information to his great-aunt. However, under the influence of that steady green gaze, he heard himself reply, "Mr Matthews told me."

"The rector?" Her disbelief was patent.

Highly amused, he could not resist continuing, "He loves to talk, you know. And he knows so much of what is happening in his parish. I've formed the habit of inviting him to dinner whenever I'm at Moreton Park."

Dorothea, knowing full well the rector's failing, immediately saw the implication of these remarks. Her suspicions were immediately confirmed.

"I know all about your visits to Newbury, and Aunt Agnes's rheumatism and the trouble Mrs Warburton had with the parish fair. Incidentally, that reminds me: your Aunt Agnes sends you her love."

The wild incredulity in her face as she imagined his meeting her vague, shy and man-hating maiden aunt sorely tempted him to leave the subject as was. He finally relented sufficiently to add, "Via the rector, you goose!"

Realising that he had accurately read her mind yet again, she found herself returning his smile. She was still smiling as they finished the dance with a flourish not far from her grandmother. Hazelmere drew her hand through his arm and led her back to Lady Merion's side.

Her ladyship had been staggered enough to see Dorothea in Hazelmere's arms, but the sight of Cecily chattering amiably to Lord Fanshawe as she circled the room had made her doubt her senses. It was unheard of for two débutante sisters to stand up with two of the most eligible peers for their first waltz. More importantly, this outcome could only have been achieved by skilful manipulation of the patronesses by the two gentlemen involved. She was not sure she approved of such rapid and direct attack.

However, she was not immune to the glory of the undoubted triumph. Sally Jersey had stopped on her peregrinations about the rooms and, nodding towards Hazelmere and Dorothea, had whispered in her ear, "He'll have her, you know. Never known Hazelmere to stand up for a first waltz before!"

Lady Merion, watching the elegant couple as they drifted past, Dorothea laughing up at Hazelmere, both blithely unaware of the surrounding company, rather fancied that Sally, for once, was right.

Two glowing young ladies were very correctly returned to her side, from where they were claimed by their partners for the next dance. As both Hazelmere and Fanshawe had been acquainted with Lady Merion from birth, neither attempted to disappear without paying their respects. With the sweetly smiling Maria, Lady Sefton sitting at her ladyship's side, the conversation remained on a general plane until Lady Sefton claimed Fanshawe's arm to go in search of her daughter-in-law.

Lady Merion promptly seized the opportunity to remark to Hazelmere, "Well, you certainly don't let the grass grow under your feet!"

He smiled in the thoroughly maddening way he had, then said, "I take it you're not perturbed by my interest?"

"Don't be absurd! You know perfectly well you're one of the biggest prizes on the marriage mart!" His question unsettled her. This was fast going, indeed! "But you must by now know that my granddaughter is highly unlikely to ask my opinion on the matter."

"True. Nevertheless, *I* would be bound to consider your opinion, even if she did not."

"Very pretty talking, indeed!" she responded, not entirely displeased.

Seeing Fanshawe returning, she dismissed them both, adding with a laugh as they both bowed elegantly before her, "I'm sure you can think of more exciting ways to spend your evening."

Towards the end of the ball Mr Edward Buchanan appeared at Dorothea's side. She forced a smile to her lips as he bowed over her hand.

"My dear Miss Darent! A delightful pleasure! I'm afraid, my dear, that I'm not a dancing man. Perhaps you would care to walk about the rooms with me?"

Ferdie, standing beside her, goggled.

With the most heartfelt relief, Dorothea, cool regret in her tone, said, "I'm afraid, Mr Buchanan, that I'm engaged for all the dances this evening."

"Oh?" He was genuinely surprised.

Luckily young Lord Davidson approached at that moment to claim her for the cotillion just forming. With the barest nod to Mr Buchanan, she laid her hand on Lord Davidson's arm and moved away.

Ferdie stared at the strange Mr Buchanan. Feeling the scrutiny, Edward Buchanan blushed slightly. "Friend of a friend, you know. In the country. Dare say Miss Darent could use some hints on how to go on in London. Not up to snuff and too many of these young blades about, y'know. But now I'm here I'll keep an eye on her, never fear."

"Oh?" said the elegant Ferdie Acheson-Smythe in his chilliest voice. With the barest inclination of his fair head he walked away.

Chapter Five

After his waltz with Dorothea, Hazelmere, mindful of the eyes upon him, danced with three other young ladies newly presented to the ton. Of these, two were diamonds of the first water, but both lacked the fire and wit to attract him as the lovely Dorothea did. Feeling the familiar boredom rising, and being debarred by convention from waltzing with Miss Darent again, he looked for Fanshawe. Hearing the music for the second and last waltz of the night start up, he scanned the dancers and easily picked out Miss Darent in the arms of Lord Robert Markham. It was definitely time to leave. Spying his friend in a group by the door, he made his way to him, and together they left for White's.

The small hours of the morning saw them wending their way home through the deserted city streets. They had played Pharoah and Hazelmere had held the bank. Consequently he had risen from the table a cool five hundred guineas richer. However, his thoughts were not concerned with his customary luck with the cards, but with his potential luck with a certain green-eyed young lady. Fanshawe was similarly occupied in wondering which of her numerous qualities was most responsible for making Cecily Darent so attractive. Together they crossed Piccadilly and headed up Bond Street in companionable silence.

Hazelmere finally broke this to say, "Well, Miss Darent appears to have successfully quashed all the rumours."

Fanshawe glanced sideways under his lashes at his friend. "Do you intend to have her?"

Hazelmere checked slightly in his stride. The hazel and brown eyes met for an instant. Then he chuckled. "Is it that obvious?"

"Frankly, yes."

"I suppose, as it's virtually obligatory to play by the rules, given it's the start of the Season, my interest will hardly remain a secret for long."

"No. You're right. We'll have to play by the rules."

"We?" His friend's preoccupation since meeting Cecily Darent had not escaped Hazelmere. "At the inn I mentioned Miss Darent's sister more in jest than design."

"I know that! But she's a deuced taking young thing, all the same. Not in the class of your Dorothea, but attractive none the less."

"Oh, granted! In the absence of Dorothea, Cecily would bear off the palm. But satisfy my curiosity. Does she, like her sister, engage in—er—a conversational style bordering on the improper?"

"Lord, yes! Asked me straight out how I'd jockeyed Countess Lieven into giving her permission to waltz, and then floored me by asking why!"

Entertained by this evidence that a predilection for such conversation was a Darent trait, Hazelmere asked, "And what did you answer?"

"Told her 'twas on account of her beautiful eyes, of course!"

"At which she laughed?"

"Exactly. Lovely sound." After a pause Fanshawe continued, "You know, Marc, I can't understand why all these mamas turn their daughters into such simpering misses you can't exchange two sensible words with. Bores us all to tears and they wonder why. Well—look at the Tremlett girl! Dashed good-looking chit. But as soon as she opens her mouth I'm off! And just look at our set. Besides the two of us, there's Peterborough and Markham, Alvanley, Harcourt, Bassington, Aylsham, Walsingham, Desborough—oh, and a host of others! And they're just our set, let alone the younger ones. All of us are either titled or well connected, independently wealthy, and all of us have got to marry sooner or later. Yet here we all are, over thirty and still unattached, purely because there are so few chits with more wit than hair."

"Which is exactly why," concluded Hazelmere, grasping his erratic friend by the elbow to steer him around the railings of Hanover Square, "we're going to assiduously attend all the ton crushes this Season."

"Good God!" uttered his lordship, much struck by this logic. "You mean they'll all be after the Darent girls?"

"You've just said it yourself. We're all on the lookout for suitable brides and we're all eligible. The Darent sisters are outstanding candidates on any man's terms. You and I, dear boy, have merely stolen a march on the rest. And I'll be much surprised if they don't try and make up lost ground very quickly. I rather think Markham has already made a start."

"Yes, saw that too. And Walsingham was there as well."

"I predict by tomorrow night the whole crew will have gathered. Which, if you're serious about the younger Miss Darent, is going to keep both of us on our toes."

They had come to the corner of Cavendish Square and

paused. "What's on tomorrow night?" asked Fanshawe sleepily.

"The Bedlington rout. Why not come to dinner and we'll go on together?"

"Good idea." He yawned. "See you then." And, with a nod and a wave, he headed off to his rooms in Wigmore Street, leaving Hazelmere to stroll the short distance to his house.

Entering with his latchkey, he made his way upstairs, to be greeted by his very correct gentleman's gentleman, who went by the totally unsuitable name of Murgatroyd. He had never managed to convince Murgatroyd, a dapper and decidedly top-lofty individual, that he need not wait up for him, and that he, Hazelmere, was perfectly capable of getting himself to bed. As by various subtle references Murgatroyd had made it plain that he considered his lordship's clothes required far greater care than his lordship was likely to bestow on them, he had finally capitulated, as in all other ways Murgatroyd suited him very well.

Snuffing out the candle and listening to the footsteps retreating down the carpeted corridor, Hazelmere crossed his arms behind his head and stretched luxuriously, smiling as he thought of a particular pair of brilliant green eyes. Tony had given voice to his own thoughts on their way home. There was going to be heavy competition for those young ladies' favours and most of it from highly experienced players. As things stood, he could certainly not be sure of winning the lady's heart. And, he admitted to himself, for reasons he was not entirely sure of, and quite definitely for the first time in his life, that was something he very much wanted to do.

Lady Bedlington's rout was a gala affair attended by everyone who was anyone. The eccentric hostess was gratified to receive Lords Hazelmere and Fanshawe, as well as a quite astonishing number of their associates. Not only were these gentlemen in attendance, but they also all arrived fairly early.

In the ballroom Hazelmere kept the head of the stairs in view. As Dorothea and Cecily appeared there he adroitly disengaged from the conversation around him and, without the least haste, made his way towards the stairs, his arrival at their foot coinciding with that of Miss Darent.

Seeing him coming towards her, Dorothea smiled and then curtsied as he bowed before her. She resolutely ignored the fluttering nervousness that made breathing strangely difficult.

Raising her hand to his lips, Hazelmere dropped a gentle kiss on her fingers, managing to turn the courtesy into a caress. He did not release her hand but turned it to flip up the dance card hanging from her wrist. These tiny cards with the order of dances listed with a place for each prospective partner to inscribe his name were much in vogue, and all the best hostesses invariably provided the débutantes with a copy, slung on a riband with a tiny silver-encased pencil attached.

"Miss Darent! You appear mysteriously free for all the dances tonight. However, I suppose I shall have to be content with just one waltz—the first, I think?"

As she laughingly assented he duly wrote his name in the appropriate spot, then, releasing her hand and turning to survey the descending multitudes of her admirers, continued in a voice lowered so that only she could hear, "And, as a reward for being so early, I really think I should be allowed to escort you to supper, don't you?"

Dorothea did not reply, but her eyes met his in amused enquiry.

Correctly interpreting the glance, he answered, "Quite proper, I assure you." With a smile he moved away to make room for the hordes of gentlemen wishful of securing a dance with the lovely Miss Darent.

As he did so he noticed, as he had predicted, Markham, Peterborough, Alvanley and Desborough among the throng. In the crowd around Cecily Darent he could make out Lords Harcourt and Bassington, as well as Fanshawe, who had executed a similar tactic to his. This was not a matter for surprise; they had discussed it over dinner. Satisfied with their success, they both moved away to claim their partners for the first dance.

Dorothea had no chance to ponder the wiles of the Marquis, being claimed for every dance and attended assiduously by a coterie of admirers. She was thoroughly enjoying herself and consequently looked radiant in a bronze silk dress covered by transparently fine tissue faille, shimmering whenever she moved. The high-waisted style suited her slender figure, making her appear more startlingly beautiful than ever. More than one furious mama wondered why Celestine never suggested such designs for their daughters.

Unaware of this sartorial jealousy, Dorothea noticed a distinct and disturbing change in the quality of her partners. At Almack's, with the exception of the Marquis and Lord Markham, these had been charming young lads not much older than herself, who were in awe of the beautiful and self-possessed young lady and entirely amenable to allowing her to control both conversation and action. Tonight the majority of her partners were older, of the same vintage as Hazelmere, and with that came a great deal more difficulty. Some, like the gentle Alvanley, were no problem, and she quickly came to regard them as friends. Others, like wild Lord Peterborough and the rakish Walsingham, she was much more wary of. When, more than midway through the evening, Hazelmere came to claim her for the first waltz, rescuing her from Lord Walsingham's side, she went into his arms with a sensation much akin to relief.

Thoroughly appreciative of the situation, he could not resist remarking, "Rather heavier weather tonight, Miss Darent?"

For an instant the hazel and green eyes met. Then Dorothea, in a voice every bit as languid as his, replied, "Why, no, my lord! I find it all most entertaining."

"Trying it on just a little too thick, my child," he murmured.

Dorothea hit back, wide-eyed innocence writ large on her face. "My lord! Such cant terms. How improper!"

Hazelmere laughed, then immediately returned to the attack. "If we're to discuss impropriety, my dear, why is it that, try as I might, I cannot recall a conversation with you that has not been improper?"

She caught that up easily, murmuring with complete self-assurance, "I should have thought the reason for that was obvious, Lord Hazelmere."

As their glances once more caught and held, Hazelmere saw complete enjoyment of the moment reflected in her eyes. That was the second time he had walked himself into a trap with her. He must be slipping. Nevertheless, there was hay to be made yet. Trying for a sterner tone, he said, "I'll have you know, my dear Miss Darent, that I'm not in the habit of conducting improper conversations with well-behaved young ladies."

Not seeing where this was headed, she could do no more than show a politely surprised face. "Oh?"

As the last strains of the waltz drifted across the ballroom, he whirled her to a halt. Smiling down into those glorious green eyes, he replied, "Only with you."

Eyes blazing in mock indignation, she could not keep a straight face. With a gurgle of laughter she allowed him to draw her hand through his arm and lead her back to Lady Merion's side. "As I said, Lord Hazelmere, you are most improper."

He promptly corrected her, raising her hand to his lips, his eyes fully on hers, "We are both most improper, Miss Darent."

Later he escorted her to supper, extricating her from the figurative clutches of Lord Peterborough. As he was well practised in the art of detaching young women from the attentions of his close acquaintances, these otherwise difficult tasks were accomplished with a minimum of fuss. They shared a supper table with Cecily and Lord Fanshawe and Julia Bressington, who had the punctilious Lord Harcourt in tow. The conversation was general and decidedly hilarious. Fanshawe, with Cecily interpolating the occasional observation, described the singular scene they had just witnessed between old Lady Melchett and Lord Walsingham, when that irascible old dame had taken his lordship to task for not dancing with her niece.

Realising that, with her limited experience of the ton, Dorothea could not be appreciating the half of the story, Hazelmere spent a pleasant five minutes filling in her knowledge, his head close to hers so as not to disturb the rest of the table.

For Dorothea and Cecily, the Bedlington rout was to provide a blueprint for the behaviour of the Marquis and Lord Fanshawe. Present at almost every major gathering they attended, their lordships were always among the first to write their names in the dance cards, usually for a waltz, and more often than not squired them to supper.

While considerable attention was initially focused on them, as the days lengthened to weeks the ton became accustomed to the sight of Miss Darent in Lord Hazelmere's arms and Cecily Darent in Lord Fanshawe's. Their lordships put up with a considerable degree of ribbing regarding their habit of being in everything together. This they bore with equanimity, surprising their associates and convincing those gentlemen that the affairs were indeed serious. By the first week of April, three weeks into the Season and the week preceding the girls' coming-out ball, the knowledgeable among the ton spoke of an understanding between the Darent girls and Lords Hazelmere and Fanshawe. Once this point was reached, their lordships knew that a far greater degree of licence would be permitted them in their dealings with their chosen ladies.

During those first weeks both were careful not to overstep the line at any point. Hazelmere realised that Dorothea, for all her vaunted independence, turned to his arms as to a safe harbour, knowing that there she was protected from the likes of Lords Peterborough and Walsingham. Recognising the sterling service that these gentlemen were, however unwittingly, rendering him, he did not attempt to dissuade them from trying to cut him out. He found it ironic that in avoiding what she considered their dangerous attentions she should choose to seek shelter with him, where, had she but known it, she was in far greater danger.

He watched her carefully over the weeks of balls and parties and saw no sign of partiality for any other gentleman's company. He knew she enjoyed being with him; her eyes told him so every time he thought to gaze into them, which was often. What he did not know was whether she was in love with him. There was an elusive quality about her that for all his wide experience he had never before encountered.

Still, there was plenty of time. The rush of the coming-out balls would occur in the next few weeks. Afterwards the activities of the ton normally settled to a more comfortable pace, and such matters as marriage could be concluded in a more restful atmosphere.

As the Season progressed, Dorothea found herself in a curious quandary. Lord Hazelmere was the most fascinating man she had met. He was always attentive in a subtly understated manner that she appreciated far more than the suffocating endeavours of her younger admirers. He was, quite frankly, the only man she had ever, in the remotest recesses of her mind in the darkest hours of the night, considered marrying.

It had not needed Lady Merion's none too subtle hints to make her realise that the Marquis had singled her out, his continuing attentions making it clear that he was seriously courting her. But he had done nothing to further his interests beyond the tentative stage. She had a sneaking suspicion that, because she had not appeared to succumb to his quite considerable charm, he was laying siege to her susceptibilities, holding her tantalisingly at a distance until she acknowledged his attraction. She was a challenge and, as such, had to be conquered. Then his arrogant pride and imperious manner would, she felt, be quite insupportable.

There were even rumours of a bet being placed on the outcome of their contest of wills. Unwise in the ways of betting, she had no idea if this could be so, but she rather felt it rang true of the scandalous Marquis.

However, the questions that increasingly occupied her mind were concerned with his reasons for choosing her.

They were starting to disturb her sleep. He had to marry some time, that much was obvious. But why her? Was he in love with her or was she merely convenient? How did he see her? A challenge to be overcome, a suitable connection, the granddaughter of one of his mother's closest friends, a woman of common sense, not so beautiful as to require constant vigilance? Or did he see something more? By all the tenets of her class, it should not matter one jot. But to her it mattered a great deal. She was in the enviable position of not having to wed unless she wished it. But, if their relationship continued to develop along its present course, refusing him if and when he offered might prove difficult. But when it came to ascertaining Hazelmere's motives she faced a problem—how could she tell? He was a man of considerable experience and ready charm. If he merely wanted a conformable wife, one who would interfere little with his established pursuits, then it would be, she reasoned, entirely in character for his arrogant lordship to choose, as the easiest route, to make a country miss fall in love with him and so more readily accept his suit.

Her inability to divine his motives was frustrating. Still, as things stood, there was little she could do. The reins were at present very much in his hands. With little scope for manoeuvre, the best she could do was enjoy his company and leave all difficult questions until they demanded an answer.

Chapter Six

The Saturday before the Darent sisters' coming-out ball saw them riding in the Park, a daily treat organised by the enterprising Ferdie. He was now firmly established as their chief mentor and guide through the shoals of the Season, and had reached the position of being regarded by Dorothea, Cecily and even Lady Merion as part of their household.

The previous week he had decided that the Misses Darent would look well on horseback and had presented himself at Merion House with horses especially for them. Dorothea loved riding and even Cecily enjoyed a gentle canter, so he had not been disappointed with their reception of his idea. Within ten minutes both girls had changed into the elegant riding dresses Celestine had concocted and were on their way to the Park, escorted by the proud Ferdie and his shadow, Mr Dermont.

Attired in a severe sage-green outfit that showed off her figure to admiration, her glossy curls topped by a soft felt cloche with a beautiful peacock plume curling around her head, Dorothea had easily controlled a frisky bay mare. Cecily, quite happy with her docile palfrey, had been a picture, turned out in a pale blue tunic with fur trimming over a darker blue skirt with a matching fur hat. Their first excursion had been a resounding success.

This afternoon, riding easily beside Ferdie, Dorothea heard herself addressed in a familiar, gently mocking voice.

"What a very accomplished young lady you are, Miss Darent."

Turning to meet the frankly admiring gaze of the Marquis of Hazelmere, Dorothea felt herself blushing. But, setting eyes on the beautiful black gelding he was riding, she involuntarily exclaimed, "Oh! What a magnificent animal!"

The magnificent animal took exception to her tone but was effortlessly held. "And with good taste, too! Which is more than can be said of this brute at present. He's not been out for three days and is in an evil temper." The hazel eyes were fixed on her face. "Why don't you come for a gallop, Miss Darent?"

Sorely tempted, she glanced around for her mentor, to find that Ferdie had unaccountably vanished.

"Afraid?" came that mocking voice again.

Dorothea threw caution to the winds. "Very well. But which way?"

"Follow me." The black leapt forward down a wide ride reaching into the depths of the Park. Although the gelding was the superior animal, Hazelmere rode a great deal heavier than Dorothea. She was an accomplished rider and so was not far behind as he drew up in a wide arc in the clearing at the end of the ride. Not as strong, she pulled up in a wider arc, closer to the trees. A low branch swept her hat from her head.

Both were laughing with exhilaration as Hazelmere rode to where her hat lay and dismounted to retrieve it. She rode back and waited as he picked it up and dusted off the plume. Curling the feather in his hand, he walked to her side, but instead of handing the hat to her he reached up to place his hands about her waist.

"Come down, Miss Darent."

She considered refusing but had no idea how to without sounding missish or, worse, coquettish. Feeling the strength in the hands resting lightly at her waist and finding the hazel eyes amused as ever, she decided that boldness was her only answer. She slipped her feet free of her stirrups, and without effort he lifted her down to stand in front of him.

"Stand still," he commanded and, freeing the long hat pin, expertly inserted it through her coiled hair to secure the hat in place. He ran his hand over the plume to settle it back around her face.

Dorothea found that she was looking into eyes which no longer laughed but glinted strangely. Mesmerised, she felt her own thoughts scatter to the four winds. She was acutely aware of the man before her and little else. She wondered for one moment if he was going to kiss her. But the next instant the mocking look returned and she was lifted back on to the mare.

"At least I'll return you to Ferdie in every way as immaculate as when I inveigled you away from his side." The cynical tone sounded odd to her ears.

Deflatingly bewildered, she felt a spurt of anger that he should tantalise her, only to withdraw at the last moment. She frowned and then nearly gasped as the indelicacy of her thoughts struck her. She wheeled her mount, horrified that he would see her blushing and guess the cause.

Hazelmere remounted, and without comment they moved back along the ride, soon falling into an easy canter. He had seen her delicate brows draw together but attributed the response to anger at his actions rather than frustration at his reticence.

They emerged from the trees and by unspoken consent turned up a slight rise and halted, looking for the others. The rest of the party was not far distant. Lord Fanshawe had joined the group and was deep in conversation with Cecily. Even from her present distance, Dorothea could see that her sister was entirely captivated. Ferdie and Mr Dermont had been joined by two cronies and all four were aimlessly wandering further and further from the dallying couple. It suddenly dawned on her that Ferdie's judgement might not be infallible.

Assailed by sudden guilt, she realised that she, too, had been remiss. It would not be easy to explain why she had been alone with the Marquis of Hazelmere in a deserted ride. Thankfully she did not think they had been seen. But to leave Cecily virtually alone with Fanshawe in the middle of the Park! Really! Where had Ferdie's wits gone begging?

A deep chuckle from beside her brought her green eyes back to Hazelmere's face. The mocking gaze held hers steadily. "You really can't blame Ferdie, you know. He would be as protective as you could wish were any others involved. But he would never see Fanshawe or myself as potentially threatening."

She threw him an exasperated glance and headed off towards her sister. As she approached, Fanshawe looked up in surprise and lifted an enquiring eyebrow at Hazelmere, close behind. Dorothea did not need to see his answering laughing grimace to realise that, as far as her sister and herself were concerned, if Lords Hazelmere and Fanshawe were present the "safety in numbers' maxim was unlikely to apply.

Seeing her quick frown, Cecily smiled sunnily, not the

least bit discomfited, but she willingly brought her mount alongside as Dorothea turned towards the gate.

At that moment they were joined by Edward Buchanan, mounted on a showy cob. Hearing the news that the Darent sisters rode every day in the Park, he had conceived the happy notion that, while he might not shine in the ballroom, Miss Darent could not fail to be impressed by the vision of himself on a mettlesome steed. Unfortunately for him, his mettlesome steed, hired from a commercial stable, was far from elegant, being too long in the back and with a noticeable tendency to throw one leg.

Pulling up beside the group, he bowed to Dorothea. "Well met, Miss Darent."

Dorothea inclined her head, an action she managed to infuse with an arctic iciness. "Mr Buchanan. I'm afraid we were on the point of returning to Cavendish Square." Hazelmere's lips twitched.

"No matter, dear lady," said Edward Buchanan, airily gesturing. "I'll be only too happy to join your escort."

Dorothea nearly choked. Short of refusing him point-blank, there was nothing she could do. Her face a mask, she was forced to introduce him to her companions. The Marquis merely raised one black brow in acknowledgement, and Lord Fanshawe was similarly reticent. Neither showed any inclination to surrender their positions flanking the Darent sisters to Mr Buchanan. Dorothea almost sighed in relief, then tensed as she saw the gleam in Edward Buchanan's eye. As they walked their horses towards the gate he launched into a discussion of harvesting techniques.

This time he had badly misjudged his victims. Hazelmere, brought up from infancy to the management of the vast Henry family estates, and Fanshawe, not yet come into his patrimony but already involved in running the

Eglemont acres, both knew more about that topic than he did. Between them they efficiently rolled up the subject, then turned an inquisitorial light on Mr Buchanan himself. Under a subtle pressure he had no defence against, he found himself admitting that he possessed a country holding in Dorset. No, not particulary large. How large? Well, actually, quite small. Livestock? Not a great number. No, he had not yet launched into breeding.

Her side aching from suppressed laughter, Dorothea glanced back at Ferdie, just behind, surprising a beatific grin on the guileless face. Mr Dermont, too, appeared strangely entertained. And Cecily, who had not previously encountered Mr Buchanan, was ecstatic. Her grin left no doubt that she understood their lordships' tactics. Dorothea returned to her sphinx-like contemplation of Mr Buchanan's difficulties, presently being added to by Fanshawe. Her eyes strayed to Hazelmere's face and, as if sensing her gaze, he looked down at her. The expression of unbridled hilarity that glowed for a moment in his eyes very nearly overset her.

Then Mr Buchanan, desperately seeking to change the subject, and by now conscious that his mettlesome mount could not hold a candle to any of the others in this group, said, "I'm most impressed with the quality of your horses, Miss Darent. I take it they're hired?"

"Why, yes. Ferdie gets them for us." She turned to Ferdie as she spoke and was surprised to see a peculiarly blank, not to say wooden, expression on his face.

"Ah. And which stable do they come from, Mr Acheson-Smythe, if I may make so bold as to enquire?" asked Edward Buchanan.

"You use the Titchfield Street stables, don't you, Ferdie?" said Hazelmere.

Ferdie started. "Oh! That is, yes! Titchfield Street!"

Dorothea wondered what on earth was the matter with him.

Hazelmere, well aware that there were no stables in Titchfield Street, and further, that, as far as he knew, there was no Titchfield Street in the metropolis, smiled amiably on Mr Buchanan as they reached the gate.

Mr Buchanan, seeing the smile, decided that he had borne enough in the interests of his future for one day. Suddenly recalling a pressing engagement, he regretfully took his leave of the party.

His departure left them in stricken silence, which lasted until he was out of sight. Then they all dissolved into laughter.

Finally, still flanked by Lords Hazelmere and Fanshawe and with Ferdie and Mr Dermont bringing up the rear, the Misses Darent returned to Cavendish Square. On the way their lordships maintained a steady flow of general conversation, including both young ladies impartially. Dorothea suspected that this evidence of impeccable behaviour was a ploy to convince her there had been no impropriety in their actions in the Park. With a reasonable idea of what she and Cecily could expect on future rides, she realised that they would have to make plans to at least minimise the opportunities for such manoeuvres. She was not optimistic of their chances of eliminating such occurrences altogether; their lordships were simply too experienced in such matters.

Arriving in Cavendish Square, she moved to dismount but was forestalled by Hazelmere, who lifted her down. Holding her for a moment between his hands, he looked down at her lovely face, serious for once. The hazel eyes glinted, then Cecily laughed and the moment was gone. Releasing her, he swept her a bow and, with his usual amused air, said, "*Au revoir,* Miss Darent. I dare say we'll meet again tonight."

Brought back to reality, Dorothea smiled her goodbyes and, finding Cecily at her elbow, entered Merion House.

Once inside, Mellow informed them that Lady Merion was resting before the ball and had insisted that her granddaughters do likewise. The Duchess of Richmond was entertaining tonight and her ball was one of the highlights of the Season. Held on the first Saturday of April, this was followed by all the coming-out balls. Traditionally the most important of these were held on the Wednesdays and Saturdays during the rest of April, sometimes stretching into May. While there were a number of lesser gatherings scheduled for the next Sunday, Monday and Tuesday, there was only one ball on the following Wednesday night—at Merion House. A few other mothers had originally planned to hold their daughters' balls on that night too, but, having taken stock of the Darent sisters, these ladies had wisely decided to change their dates. Better to be a bit thinner of company than to have no company at all.

Her interlude with Hazelmere had given Dorothea food for thought, so, thinking her grandmother's advice very timely, she and Cecily retired to their respective chambers, supposedly to rest.

Trimmer, her new maid, was waiting to help her change. Lady Merion and Witchett had decided that Betsy should stay with Cecily, as she was familiar with that young lady's occasional indispositions. Dorothea's style was more demanding of the attentions of a first-class dresser. When asked if she knew of any suitable candidate Witchett had eventually produced her niece, Trimmer. Luckily she and Dorothea had got on well, and Trimmer had, as her aunt before her, fallen under the spell of her lovely young mistress.

Pausing in the middle of the room to draw out the hat pin the Marquis had placed in her hair, Dorothea wished that Trimmer would go away, but did not have the heart to summarily dismiss her. She patiently waited while the attentive maid divested her of her outdoor clothes and left her enveloped in a green silk wrapper before letting her mind shut out the rest of the world and concentrate on the question of what she was to do about the Marquis of Hazelmere.

Sitting at her dressing-table, she loosened her hair and absent-mindedly brushed the gleaming tresses, staring unseeingly at her reflection in the mirror. From the moment she had first met him Hazelmere had made serious inroads against her heart's defences. That much, she admitted, was incontrovertible fact. But up until now she had avoided considering the natural outcome of that situation.

Staring intently into her own green eyes, reflected in the highly polished surface, she sighed. It had taken her some time to understand the novel emotions he aroused in her. But after today she could no longer delude herself. Alone with him in the clearing in the Park, she had been quite sure he would kiss her. And she had wanted him to. Preferably as he had before by the blackberry bush. Scandalous it might have been, but she had been wishing for weeks that he would repeat the performance.

She laid the brush down and carefully rewound her hair. She knew she looked forward to meeting him wherever they went, and she derived much pleasure from his company, despite his high-handed ways, which still on occasion infuriated her. The disconcerting habit he had of reading her mind merely added spice to their encounters, and she thoroughly enjoyed their highly irregular conversations. When he was not with her, alternately mocking or provoking her, with that certain amused expression in his hazel eyes, she felt sadly flat and found little to please her. The inescapable conclusion was that he had captured her heart. That admitted, what exactly was she to do about it?

Rising to cross the room, she lay on her bed, idly playing with the tassels of the bedcurtain cord. While she was now sure of her feelings, what had she learnt of his? He certainly seemed genuinely attracted to her. But he was of an age when he would be expected to marry. Maybe he had simply, in his customary high-handed way, decided that she would do. Surely, if that was the case, and his interest in her was illusory, she would be able to tell? But he was a master at this game and she was a novice. In the normal way of things, it seemed certain that he would, at some point, offer for her hand. And, by the same agreed code of behaviour, she would accept him. The trouble was, she loved him. Did he love her?

She pondered that question for half an hour. Despite his ability to guess most of her thoughts, she felt sure that she had not yet betrayed the depth of her interest in him. It seemed prudent to shield her heart until he gave her some indication of his regard.

However, the present stage of innocuous dalliance could not last; this afternoon's events proved that. Perhaps, during one of their numerous interludes, she could find a way of encouraging him to declare himself? The idea of encouraging such a man as Hazelmere brought a grin of amusement to her face. That, at least, should not prove too difficult. Feeling, for no particular reason, more confident, she placed her head on her pillow and, worn out by her cogitations, slept until Trimmer came to dress her for the Duchess of Richmond's ball.

* * *

If she had looked out of her window instead of into her mirror Dorothea would have seen Hazelmere, Fanshawe and Ferdie entering Hazelmere House. They left their mounts in the mews behind the mansion and walked back to the front door, deep in discussion of horseflesh. Hazelmere opened the door with his key and crossed the threshold, only to come to an immediate halt. Ferdie, following, cannoned into him and, peering around his shoulders, remarked in wonder, "Good lord!"

Hazelmere brought his quizzing glass to bear on the piles of band-boxes and trunks strewn about his hall. Seeing his butler attempting to approach through the welter of luggage, he enquired in a deceptively sweet voice, "Mytton, what exactly is all this?"

Mytton, knowing that tone, promptly replied, "Her ladyship has arrived, m'lord."

"Which ladyship?" pursued Hazelmere, assailed by a sudden and revolting thought.

"Why, the Dowager, m'lord!" replied Mytton, at a loss to understand the strange question.

"Oh, of course!" said Hazelmere, relieved as enlightenment dawned. "For one horrible moment I thought Maria and Susan had come back."

This explanation made all clear to the assembled company. Hazelmere's antipathy towards his elder sisters was common knowledge. This stemmed from an attempt made some years previously by those rigid ladies to manage his matrimonial affairs for him. Their inevitable and ignoble defeat had culminated in their being *persona non grata* in his various establishments. As they were both married to men well able to provide for them, Hazelmere saw no reason for them to be cluttering up his houses with their meddling, strait-laced ways.

Absorbed in his own affairs, he had entirely forgotten

that his mother, Anthea Henry, the Dowager Marchioness of Hazelmere, always came to town for a few weeks of the Season, and invariably attended the Duchess of Richmond's ball. Again surveying the scene, he asked, "How is her ladyship, Mytton?"

"She has retired to rest, m'lord, but said she would join you for dinner."

Hazelmere nodded absently and led the way in between the various trunks and boxes, down the corridor and through the double doors into the beautifully appointed library. Ferdie followed, with Fanshawe bringing up the rear. Closing the doors behind them, Fanshawe turned with a grin. "They all seem to move with mountains of luggage, don't they? Can't think your mama will need the half of it, but mine's exactly the same."

Hazelmere ruefully agreed. Realising that to dine alone with his sharp-eyed parent might not be all that soothing to his temper, already under strain, he decided to call in reinforcements. "Tony, you'll come to dinner? And you too, Ferdie?"

Fanshawe nodded his acceptance, but Ferdie replied, "Pleased to, but don't forget I'm to escort the Merion party to the ball, so I'll have to leave at seven."

"Well, if you're leaving at seven we'll have to leave earlier," said Fanshawe. "Don't you dare leave Merion House until the carriage is away from this door!"

Hazelmere crossed to the bell pull and, when Mytton appeared, gave his orders. "And my respects to her ladyship, but we dine at five and are to leave for the ball at seven. See that the carriage is waiting no later than seven."

Mytton retreated to convey this unwelcome news to the culinary wizard downstairs. Hazelmere poured glasses of wine and, having handed these around, sank into one of the wing chairs gathered around the marble fireplace. Fan-shawe had taken the chair opposite, and Ferdie was ele-gantly disposed on the chaise. Now that they were com-fortably settled, a companionable silence descended. This was broken by Fanshawe. "What on earth made you come back from that ride so quickly?"

Without looking up from his contemplation of the unlit fire, Hazelmere replied, "Temptation."

"What?"

With a sigh he explained. "Remember we agreed we'd have to play by the rules?" Fanshawe nodded. "Well, if we'd stayed any longer in that ride the rules would have flown with the wind. So we came back."

Fanshawe nodded sympathetically. "All this is turning out a dashed sight more complicated than I'd imagined."

That brought Hazelmere's gaze to his face, but it was Ferdie, all at sea, who spoke. "But why is it all so com-plicated? Would've thought it was all pretty much plain sailing, myself, especially for you two. Simply roll up and ask the girls' guardian, the horrible Herbert, for their hands. Simple! No problem at all."

Seeing the expression of amused tolerance this speech elicited, Ferdie realised that he had missed some vital point and waited patiently to be set right. Hazelmere, eyes fixed on the delicate wine glass held in one white hand, eventually explained, "The difficulty, Ferdie, lies in di-vining the true state of the Misses Darents' affections. To whit, I can't tell if Miss Darent is merely playing the game or whether her heart is at all engaged by your humble servant."

Ferdie regarded him with absolute disbelief, utterly be-reft of words. Finally regaining the use of his tongue, he exclaimed, "No! Hang it all, Marc! Can't be true. You, of all people. Must be able to tell."

"How?"

Ferdie opened his mouth to answer and then shut it again. He turned to Fanshawe. "You too?"

Fanshawe, head sunk on his chest, merely nodded.

After a pause while he digested this astonishing intelligence, Ferdie said, "But they both seem to enjoy your company."

"Oh, we know that," agreed Hazelmere dismissively. "But beyond that, I, for one, can't tell."

"True," Fanshawe confirmed. "Only need to look into those eyes to see they like having us around. Like to talk to us, dance with us. Well, why wouldn't they, all things considered? Fact of the matter, Ferdie, m'lad, is it's a very long hop from that to love."

The dilemma they were in was now clear to Ferdie. He was considering the possibility of helping them out, when he suddenly found himself the object of the Marquis's hazel gaze.

"Ferdie," said Hazelmere softly, "if you so much as breathe a word of this conversation outside this room—"

"We'll both make your life entirely unbearable," finished Fanshawe. This was a standard threat between the three, and Ferdie made haste to assure them that such an idea had never entered his head. He faltered slightly under Hazelmere's sceptical gaze.

A dismal silence settled over them, until Fanshawe glanced at the clock on the mantelshelf and stirred. "I'd best be off to change. Coming, Ferdie?"

All three rose. After seeing them out, Hazelmere went upstairs to find Murgatroyd already awaiting him. As Tony had said, it had become a lot more complicated than anticipated.

Over the light meal they sat down to before the Richmond House ball, Dorothea, prompted by Hazelmere's comments in the Park, drew out Lady Merion on the relationship between the Marquis, Lord Fanshawe and Ferdie Acheson-Smythe.

Lady Merion, thinking this a sensible question in the circumstances, was happy to describe the situation as fully as she could. "Well, the principal seats of the Hazelmere and Eglemont peerages, held by the Henry and Fanshawe families respectively, lie in Surrey and adjoin each other. The families have always been close allies and friends. Hazelmere and Fanshawe were born only a few weeks apart; Hazelmere is the elder. Both have two older sisters and Hazelmere has a younger sister, too, but neither has any brothers. Consequently it was only natural that the boys grew up together. They went to Eton and Oxford together and have been on the town for…oh, over ten years now. The bond between them is very strong— stronger than if they had in fact been brothers, I suspect."

"What about Ferdie?" asked Cecily.

"Ferdie is the son of Hazelmere's mother's sister, and so a first cousin to Hazelmere. He is about five years younger than Marc, but he was sent to spend most of his childhood summers at Hazelmere. I don't quite understand why, for in temperament they seem very dissimilar, and there's the age difference too, but Ferdie and Hazelmere and Tony Fanshawe are very firm friends indeed. They always help each other out and used to cover up for each other when they were younger and got into scrapes. Ferdie is very sincerely attached to the Marquis and Lord Fanshawe, and they always seem very protective and tolerant of him."

By this time they had finished their meal and Lady Merion, glancing at the clock, shooed them off to put the finishing touches to their *toilettes,* saying, "You know Ferdie will not be late and he hates to be kept waiting!"

Lady Merion was quite correct in telling her grand-daughters that the bond between Ferdie and their lordships ran deep. It dated from Ferdie's first visit to Hazelmere, when, on his first morning there, the shy eleven-year-old had seen his magnificent sixteen-year-old cousin and his friend leave the stableyard for an early-morning ride. He had been in his bedchamber at the time, and had hurriedly dressed and gone down to the stables, thinking to get a horse and catch up with them. Instead, he had fallen victim to two young stable-lads, who, for a joke, had set him on a half-broken Arab stallion. The horse, very fresh, had broken away, Ferdie clinging for dear life to its back. Luckily it had headed in the direction taken by the older boys. In the ensuing chase, Marc and Tony Fanshawe had worked with Ferdie to save both him and the stallion. Sheer good luck and a deal of courage from them all had pulled it off. From that day onwards the three were, as far as their disparate ages and interests allowed, insepa-rable. Whenever other children had tried to bully Ferdie, they had very quickly learned they had to answer to either Tony or the even more formidable Marc.

Habits formed in childhood ran deep, and when Ferdie had got into trouble in the petticoat line at Oxford, it was to Marc, rather than to his own scholarly and eccentric father, that he had turned. And Marc had very efficiently sorted the problem out. On his coming on the town, those who belonged to the better of the gentlemen's clubs had quickly realised that if Ferdie Acheson-Smythe was threatened then Lord Fanshawe and the Marquis of Ha-zelmere had a habit of materialising behind him. When Ferdie got involved in controversy over another gentleman's efforts at fuzzing the cards and was challenged to a duel, illegal though that practice then was, it was Hazelmere who stepped in and ruthlessly put a stop to it.

In return, it must be said, their lordships had found that Ferdie possessed a rare talent: he was so very trustworthy that women tended to pour all their secrets into his ear. Thus Ferdie had proved more than useful to them over the past five years. However, as Hazelmere had truthfully told Dorothea, it was quite impossible for Ferdie to view either himself or Tony Fanshawe askance.

The Dowager Marchioness of Hazelmere descended the stairs of Hazelmere House, thinking how pleasant it would be to have a new Lady Hazelmere to make use of its beautifully proportioned salons. She had come up from Surrey, as was her custom, but this year she had much higher expectations of the Season.

At just over fifty, she was still a striking woman, tall and willowy, her abundant chestnut hair still retaining much of its glory, and the years had not robbed her face of its piquancy. She had contracted a bronchial complaint some years before and, as this was exacerbated by the fumes of the city, she usually spent only a week or so in London. Her expectations had been fuelled by the extraordinary intelligence conveyed to her by her London correspondents. As well as the carefully worded missive from Hermione Merion, detailing the history of her son's involvement with Dorothea Darent, she had received no less than six letters from other close friends, all comprehensively describing Hazelmere's infatuation with Miss Darent. Of these, the most informative had been the most recent, from the Countess of Eglemont. Tony's parents had returned to London a week earlier and Amelia Fanshawe had dutifully reported how things stood between both her son and Cecily Darent and Hazelmere and Miss Darent. More than anyone else, she would trust Amelia to correctly interpret Marc's behaviour. And what Amelia had written had been intriguing. Consequently she had been amused rather than surprised to find that her usually cool son had moved dinner forward so he could arrive at the ball ahead of his inamorata.

Entering the drawing-room, she was taken aback to find Tony Fanshawe and Ferdie in attendance. As her elegant son strolled across the room to plant an affectionate kiss on her cheek her eyes openly quizzed him. He was as immaculate as ever, in a perfectly cut black coat that looked as if it had been moulded to his broad shoulders, skin-tight knee-breeches encasing his powerful thighs. Diamonds winked amid the snowy folds of his cravat.

"Welcome to town, Mama! As always, you look quite ravishing."

His eyes returned her regard with a bland and innocent air, which deceived her not at all. While Tony and Ferdie made their bows Mytton entered to announce dinner.

Throughout the meal Hazelmere, ably seconded by her nephew and Tony Fanshawe, kept her entertained, describing all that had occurred thus far in the Season, with two notable omissions. Amused by their strategy, she was even more entertained than they intended.

After the servants withdrew she seized the initiative. She fixed both her son and Fanshawe with a look that from long experience they knew meant that she intended to get to the bottom of whatever had excited her attention. "Yes, that's all very well," she said, breaking into yet another of Ferdie's anecdotes, "but what I really want to know is why none of you has yet seen fit to mention Hermione Merion's granddaughters. From everything I hear, you have all been somewhat preoccupied with them, have you not?"

She found herself looking into her son's hazel eyes as he gently explained, "But, Mama, you already know all about them, and more, from all the letters you've been sent. We didn't want to bore you."

With the ground cut so masterfully from under her feet, she could think of nothing to say. Instead she raised her glass in mock salute. "I trust they will be present tonight?"

"Most assuredly. Ferdie is to escort them there."

"Then you must both promise to introduce them to me and I'll promise to be silent on the subject all the way there."

"And back?" asked Fanshawe, used to the Hazelmere conversations.

She laughed. "All right. *And* back."

"Under those conditions, I promise," answered Hazelmere with a grin.

"And I," echoed Fanshawe.

"Good heavens!" ejaculated Ferdie, surprising them all. "I'll have to dash or I'll be late. Never do to keep them waiting!"

Amid laughter, he departed for the other side of Cavendish Square, urging them to make haste if they wanted to get to Richmond first.

Arriving on the doorstep of Merion House as the Merion carriage rounded the corner, Ferdie had the forethought to ask Mellow not to announce it until the Hazelmere carriage, already standing outside Hazelmere House and clearly visible across the square, had departed. Mellow, accepting the golden *douceur* Ferdie slipped him, understood perfectly.

Inside the drawing-room, Ferdie caught his breath at the visions of loveliness that met his eyes. Even he had started to wonder for how much longer the Darent sisters could dazzle in elegant gowns that were quite unique.

Dorothea, standing by the marble mantel, was a stunning picture in ivory satin, overlaid with lace around the neckline and in a broad sweep down one side of the skirt. The pearls at her throat shone warmly in the firelight, and her hair appeared burnished by the flames. The simplicity of the gown was breathtaking. Thinking of the effect this creation would have on Hazelmere in his present mood, Ferdie almost felt sorry for the Marquis.

Cecily was adorned in pure white, with trimming of aquamarine ribbon set with tiny seed-pearls criss-crossed over the bodice and looped around her skirt. Again the effect was unique and quite lovely.

Lady Merion, satisfied with the effect her granddaughters' gowns had had on Ferdie, spoke up, telling him that they were now ready to depart.

Ferdie gulped and asked innocently, "Oh, has Mellow announced the carriage?"

"No, Ferdie, he hasn't," said Dorothea, suddenly suspicious.

"I don't know what's keeping them, then," muttered her ladyship. "We called for the carriage long ago."

"Er—yes." Ferdie decided that Lady Merion was the safest of the three to address. "Just came from dinner at Hazelmere House. Lady Hazelmere was there, ma'am, and sent her regards. Said she'd see you at the ball."

At this juncture, with Ferdie fervently searching for some topic to distract his three ladies, Mellow entered and solved the problem by announcing the carriage.

Chapter Seven

After an uneventful drive, the Merion carriage joined the long queue of coaches lining up to disgorge their fair burdens on the torch-lit steps of Richmond House. There had been little conversation on the journey, and Ferdie had had time to ponder what lay between the Darent sisters and his friends.

He recalled the look in Dorothea's eye that afternoon when he had hurried to catch up with them as they left the Park. He had been unable to interpret it at the time, imagining that the four of them had been together the whole time. But now, from what Marc and Tony themselves had said, it was clear that had not been the case. Ferdie's mind boggled when he tried to imagine what exactly had happened between Dorothea and Marc. And this while the Misses Darent were, after a fashion, in his care! If such a thing ever got out, his carefully nurtured reputation as a trustworthy ladies' companion would be ruined!

The carriage drew up and he helped his ladies to alight. Soon they were following the glittering line of arrivals up the grand staircase. At the top, they were greeted by the Duchess, and moved on into the ballroom as their names were proclaimed in stentorian accents by two massive footmen flanking the door.

Dorothea had only taken a few steps when she found Hazelmere at her elbow. Smiling up at him, she saw that his eyes were not laughing, but glinting at her in a way that made her heart stand still. All the other symptoms she now associated with his presence—breathlessness, confusion and a certain anticipation—immediately came to the fore. Then he smiled and the intense look dissolved into his usual warmly amused expression, dispelling her unease. His lips lightly brushed her gloved fingertips before he drew her hand through his arm.

"Come with me, Miss Darent; there's someone I'd like you to meet."

"Oh? Who, pray tell?"

"Me."

She chuckled. She was drawn out of the mainstream of the arriving guests, a tactic that confused the small army of gentlemen waiting patiently to greet her further along the ballroom. Hazelmere led her towards a corner, into the camouflage of earlier arrivals. He moved automatically through the crowd, not seeing them, not hearing them. His mind was awhirl with a heady sensation he had never experienced before. Whatever it was, it was exciting and uncomfortable at the same time, and its cause was the unutterably lovely creature walking so calmly beside him. The sight of her, encased in ivory, had taken his breath away. Then she had smiled at him with such open affection that he had had to fight an impulse to kiss her in the middle of the Duchess of Richmond's ballroom.

The temptation to continue their ambling stroll into the adjoining rooms was strong. He knew Richmond House fairly well. He was sure he could find a deserted ante-room where Miss Darent and he could analyse his strange response to her presence in more depth. He sighed inwardly. Unfortunately such intimate discussions were not listed among the acceptable ways of wooing young ladies during the Season.

Reluctantly pausing, he looked down at her again, drinking in the flawless symmetry of her face, drowning in her emerald eyes. He saw them widen, first in amused enquiry and then, as he remained silent, in increasing bewilderment. "I'll have you know, Miss Darent, that I'm rapidly running out of ideas of how to whisk you away before your devoted admirers surround you."

Smiling in response, Dorothea hoped that he couldn't hear the thudding of her heart. She was no longer sure of her ability to keep him from guessing her feelings—as he stood before her, magnificent as ever, the spell he cast was too potent. He had developed a certain way of looking at her, which made her feel deliciously warm and tingly and led her unruly thoughts into fields they had no business straying into. Well-brought-up young ladies weren't supposed to know of such things, let alone weave fantasies about them. Thinking that she could quite happily bask in that hazel gaze for the rest of forever, she forced herself to try for their usual conversational mode. "Well, you seem to have succeeded to admiration this evening. I feel utterly deserted!"

"Do you, indeed?" he murmured, adding in a provocative undertone, "Would that you were, my dear."

In spite of her intentions, she was finding it harder and harder to meet his eyes with her customary cool unconcern.

Hazelmere finally looked down to examine her dance card. "I don't suppose I should tell you that Lord Markham is presently making a cake of himself, searching through the place for you? No! Don't look around or he might see you. And the only reason Alvanley, Peterborough and Walsingham ain't doing the same is that they're watching Robert do it for them. Miss Darent, I notice there's a waltz immediately preceding supper, which is a very sensible innovation. I must remember to compliment the Duchess on her good sense. Will you do me the honour, my dear Miss Darent, of waltzing with me and then allowing me to take you into supper?''

Dorothea had managed to gain a firmer hold on her composure during this speech and was able to serenely reply, "That will be delightful, Lord Hazelmere."

One black brow rose. "Will it?"

But she refused to be drawn with such an unanswerable question and simply smiled sweetly back. Hazelmere laughed and raised one finger to her cheek. "Promise me you'll never put a rein on your tongue, my dear. Life would become so dull if you did."

The caress and the even more provocative tones brought a familiar flash to her large green eyes.

"Ah! Miss Darent! Lord Hazelmere. Your servant, sir." Sir Barnaby Ruscombe materialised at Hazelmere's elbow. Hazelmere suavely inclined his head, and Dorothea drummed up her best social smile for London's most notorious rattle. Sir Barnaby, beaming as if delighted by these mild acknowledgements, waved his hand towards the figure on his arm, a sharp-featured woman of indeterminate years, dressed entirely in a quite hideous shade of puce, clashing outrageously with her improbable auburn locks. "Permit me to introduce you. Miss Darent, Lord Hazelmere. Mrs Dimchurch."

The exchange of curtsies and bows was purely perfunctory. "But I'm sure Miss Darent remembers me from the assemblies at Newbury," gushed Mrs Dimchurch. Hazelmere felt Dorothea stiffen. "So sad about your dear mama! Lady Cynthia and I always enjoyed a comfortable cose while we watched over our daughters.'' Her sharp eyes were fixed on the Marquis. ''I must say, I was surprised to hear Lady Cynthia had made your acquaintance, my lord. She never mentioned it. Strange, don't you think?''

As an attempt to throw Hazelmere, it was so crude that Dorothea only just managed to retain her composure.

His lordship, used to stiffer competition, made short work of it. Regarding the offending Mrs Dimchurch with a coldly gentle smile, he softly said, ''I very much doubt, my dear ma'am, that Lady Darent was the type of lady who would presume, on the basis of a single chance introduction, to claim acquaintance with anyone. Don't you agree?''

Mrs Dimchurch turned brick-red, rendering her *toilette* even more hideous.

Without waiting for a reply, Hazelmere nodded to Sir Barnaby and, bestowing a devilish smile on the unfortunate Mrs Dimchurch, drew Dorothea's hand once more through his arm and strolled back towards the milling crowds in the centre of the large room.

Once out of earshot of the importunate couple, Hazelmere glanced down. ''My dear Miss Darent, how many such mushrooms have you had to endure?'' He sounded distinctly guilty.

She chuckled, then answered airily, ''Oh, hardly any since the first week.'' She looked up, confidently expecting him to laugh with her and was surprised to see the hazel eyes reflecting real concern. Before she could do more than register the fact they were spotted by her prospective partners.

The rooms were filled to overflowing and more people were arriving. Finding any lady in the crush was extremely difficult. Having totally lost Miss Darent, one of the crowd looking for her had asked if anyone had seen Hazelmere, as, knowing his lordship, Miss Darent was probably with him. This had led to a search for the Marquis who, because of his height, was a great deal easier to spot than Dorothea. With various comments, mostly in an uncomplimentary vein, being thrown at his head, Hazelmere good-humouredly surrendered Dorothea to her swains and was swallowed up in the crowds.

Dorothea was amazed that anyone could find anyone else in the throng of people filling the ballroom and spreading into the adjoining salons. She had no idea where her grandmother or Cecily were, but with so many acquaintances among the ton she was not in the least put out. Somehow her partners seemed to find her for their respective dances, when the ballroom would miraculously clear as the music began. As each dance finished, the floor would fill again with a shifting sea of gorgeously clad ladies, the gentlemen in their more sober clothes providing stark contrast. The evening passed in a whirl of conversation and dancing, and she had no time to ponder the subtle change she had detected in the Marquis.

The only cloud on her horizon was the persistent Mr Buchanan. He seemed to dog her erratic footsteps, continually appearing as if by some malignant magic wherever she chose to pause. Finally she appealed to Ferdie for advice. "How on earth can I get rid of him?" she wailed as they trailed and dipped through a cotillion.

Although highly sympathetic, having already endured too much of Mr Buchanan's company and lacking Hazelmere's acid capacity to silence at will, Ferdie could find no magic formula to rid his protégée of this unexpected encumbrance. "Hate to say it, but he's the sort who never takes the hint. You'll just have to be patient

until he slopes off.'' Then he was seized with inspiration.
''Why not ask Hazelmere to have a word with him?''

''Lord Hazelmere would probably laugh himself into
stitches at the idea of Mr Buchanan pursuing me! He'd
be more likely to encourage him!'' returned Dorothea.
They were separated by the movement of the dance, so
she failed to see the effect her answer had on Ferdie.
Retrieving his dropped jaw, he shook his head. Personally,
he could not imagine Hazelmere encouraging anyone to
pursue Dorothea, much less the importunate Mr Buchanan, who, unless he missed his guess, was a fortune-
hunter of the most inept variety. Clearly a word in his
cousin's ear would not go amiss.

No longer feeling the need to dance with other young
ladies as a cover for his pursuit of Dorothea, Hazelmere
spent much of the evening talking to friends, acquaintances and a not inconsiderable number of his relatives.
He was not pleased when, turning in response to a tap on
his arm, he looked down into the severe countenance of
his eldest sister, Lady Maria Setford. Knowing that she
would have heard of his interest in Dorothea, he persist-
ently misunderstood every quizzing remark she made on
that subject. Exasperated, she finally recommended he
look out for his other older sister, Lady Susan Wilmot,
who, she informed him, was also somewhere in the rooms
and desirous of speech with him.

Her brother merely looked at her with an expression
that very luckily she was incapable of interpreting, before
excusing himself on the score of having seen their mother,
with whom he required a few words.

He did, in fact, pass by Lady Hazelmere, deep in conversation with Sally Jersey, and paused to whisper,
''Mama, I know you've always sworn you were faithful

to my father, but how on earth do you account for Maria and Susan?''

Lady Jersey, overhearing, burst into her twittering laugh. Lady Hazelmere made a face at him before asking, ''You don't mean they've started sermonising already?''

''I'm sure they would like to, only they haven't decided whether it's worthwhile yet,'' returned her undutiful son, winking at her as he moved on.

Like Ferdie, Hazelmere had spent the journey to Richmond House sunk in thought. A despondent mood had overtaken him earlier in the day, when he had had to deny himself the pleasure of kissing Dorothea in the glade in the Park and had realised that would be his lot for some time to come. Since he was naturally autocratic and, as Dorothea had surmised, used to getting his own way in most things, the need to keep his passions on a very tight rein did not appeal in the least. He had already decided that he could not ask her to marry him until much later in the Season. This was not because he thought he needed more time to win her, nor that he feared to put his luck to the test. Rather it was because he, unlike Dorothea, was well versed in the ways of the ton. He could not be entirely sure of her answer, so he had to consider the possibility that she would refuse him. As their courtship had been carried out in full view of all the gossips and scandalmongers, such an outcome at the height of the Season would place them both in an intolerable situation. In addition, Lady Merion, Fanshawe and Cecily, and Ferdie too would be made to feel highly uncomfortable.

His mood had lightened when he learned that Fanshawe was in a similar position. A much more easygoing individual than himself, Tony would not find the enforced restrictions quite as hard to bear. Cecily, too, was as yet too young to do other than enjoy every moment as it came. Dorothea was another matter. While she never in any way encouraged him, she nevertheless accepted with complete self-assurance every attention he bestowed upon her. He shrewdly guessed that, being older, more mature and definitely more independent than the general run of débutantes, she was more ready and more able to savour the delights of sophisticated lovemaking, to which he was only too willing to introduce her. Her passionate nature, which he wryly suspected she did not yet realise she possessed, was not going to help matters. It was at this point in his mental ramblings that his sense of humour had come to his rescue. How very ironic it all was!

He had quit their carriage in a much lighter mood than he had entered it, and the last shreds of despondency had been wafted away when he had seen Dorothea enter the ballroom.

Moving through the salons, he saw Lady Merion ensconced in a corner, chatting amiably with Lady Bressington. He stopped to audaciously compliment them both on their dashing new *toilettes* and stayed to exchange the usual pleasantries.

Suddenly becoming aware they had been approached by some others, he turned to view the newcomers, surprising a look of annoyance on Lady Merion's face as he did so. The cause of this was immediately clear: the couple who approached were none other than Herbert and Marjorie, Lord and Lady Darent.

Hazelmere had been introduced to Herbert Darent years ago when that sober young man had first come on the town. Two years younger than the Marquis, Herbert was also a full head shorter and, in his ill-fitting coat, cut a poor figure in comparison.

After two minutes' conversation Hazelmere fully appreciated Lady Merion's decision to take the Darent girls under her wing. The idea that two such pearls could have made their début under the auspices of the present Lord and Lady Darent was too awful to contemplate. What a mess they would have made of it. To his experienced eye, Marjorie Darent lacked any degree of style or charm, and her austere observations on modern social customs, delivered for the benefit of the company without any invitation whatever, simply appalled him.

Lady Merion was so thunderstruck that she was literally speechless. When Herbert tried to engage Hazelmere in a discussion of rural commodities she was even more incensed. However, as she listened to Herbert, who had little real idea of what he was discussing, lecturing Hazelmere, who, as one of the major landowners in the country, had a more than academic interest in such matters, her sense of humour got the better of her. She rapidly hid her face behind her fan.

Looking up, her eyes met Hazelmere's, full of heartfelt sympathy as he adroitly extricated both himself and Lady Bressington, on the pretext of taking her ladyship to find her errant daughter.

As she moved off on his arm Augusta Bressington heaved a sigh of relief. "Thank you, Marc. If you hadn't rescued me I would have been stuck. Poor Hermione! What a dreadful couple!"

"Definitely not one of the hits of the Season," he agreed.

"And to think Herbert comes from the same stable as those two lovely girls," she continued, quite forgetting his interest. As this came to mind, she blushed, but, glancing up at him, found he was laughing.

"Oh, no! I feel sure Herbert's mother must have played his father false, don't you?"

Lady Bressington gasped and then burst out laughing

too. Drawing her hand from his arm, she bade him take himself off, adding that she now saw why all the girls fell to mooning over him.

Hearing the strains of the Roger de Clovely drifting from the ballroom and knowing it to be the dance before the supper waltz, Hazelmere accepted his dismissal with easy grace and moved back to the ballroom to find Dorothea. He had little difficulty in picking her out, whirling down the dance with Peterborough. Pausing for a moment to catch the tune and work out where they were likely to finish, he stationed himself near the end of the ballroom. As the dance concluded, Peterborough whirled Dorothea to a halt a few paces away. He strolled towards them. "How obliging of you, Gerry, to bring Miss Darent to me."

Peterborough whirled around, an entirely unacceptable oath on his lips. "Hazelmere!" he groaned. "I might have known!" As the Marquis possessed himself of Dorothea's hand he continued, "I suppose you have the supper waltz?"

"Precisely," said Hazelmere, his amused glance clearly baiting his friend.

Lord Peterborough turned to Dorothea and in a serious tone, belied by the expression on his face, said, "I shouldn't have anything to do with Hazelmere if I were you, Miss Darent. Don't know if anyone's told you, but he's far too dangerous for young ladies to deal with. Much better to let me take you away."

Dorothea laughed at this graceless speech. But Hazelmere's voice again drew Peterborough's attention. "Oh, Miss Darent knows just how dangerous I am, Gerry." At this outrageous statement Dorothea's eyes blazed. Looking up, she found the hazel eyes quizzing her as he continued smoothly, "But she has agreed to overlook my dangerous tendencies. Haven't you, Miss Darent?"

Aware that to answer this provocative question in any way at all would be highly improper, Dorothea threw him a fulminating glance.

Smiling, he turned back to Peterborough and said, quite simply, "Goodbye, Gerry."

"Oh, I'm off, never fear. Take care, Miss Darent!" he added insouciantly as, sketching a bow to her, he disappeared into the crowd.

Turning to Dorothea, Hazelmere saw she had opened her fan. "You're flushed, Miss Darent. Now I wonder if that's due to these overheated rooms, the Roger de Clovely, Peterborough's remarks or mine?"

Smiling up at him, she calmly answered, "Why, a combination of all four, I should think."

"Then, instead of waiting for the next dance, why don't we repair to the terrace, where I see quite a few others have already gone to enjoy the cool of the evening?"

Looking in the direction he indicated, Dorothea saw that the long windows at the end of the ballroom giving out on to the terrace had been thrown open. A number of couples were strolling in the moonlight. She had definite misgivings of the wisdom of venturing into such a fairy-tale scene at Hazelmere's side, but she was certainly feeling overly warm and the cool night air beckoned invitingly.

Hazelmere, correctly guessing her thoughts, made her decision for her by taking her arm. Together they strolled through the windows. Dorothea exclaimed at the sight of the formal gardens touched with moonlight. A few adventuresome couples had descended to the parterre below, where they appeared as pixie-like characters in the soft light. Without breaking the spell, Hazelmere strolled by her side to the far end of the terrace. He had a very good memory. There was an orangery built along the side of the house below the ballroom which could only be reached from the terrace. Knowing the Duchess of Richmond was a considerate hostess, he felt the orangery would be open. Coming to the end of the terrace and turning, he found that his confidence in the Duchess had not been misplaced.

"There's an orangery down these steps, which, if memory serves, gives on to the fountain court. Shall we investigate?"

The question was merely a formality. Dorothea was literally enthralled by the silvery beauty about her and, without thought, went down the steps by his side.

Inside the orangery, deserted save for themselves, they found the doors giving on to the fountain court thrown wide. Hearing the music of the fountains, Dorothea drew her hand from his arm and, looking very like a fairy queen, drifted to the open door to look out on the magical scene. The three fountains in the court were playing and the moonlight glistened and sparkled on each drop of water thrown up in the still night air to fall back with a silvery tinkle into the large marble bowls. She stood in the doorway, rapt in the beauty of the scene.

Silently Hazelmere shut the doors from the terrace and, coming up behind her, gently drew her back to lean against him. Feeling his hands about her waist, she allowed her head to rest against his shoulder. For some moments they were as still as the statues in the fountains. Then, prompted by her own particular devil, Dorothea turned her head to smile up at him. There was, after all, one certain way to precipitate matters.

His response was all she could have wished. Turning her slightly, Hazelmere swiftly bent his head to drop the

gentlest of delicate kisses on her lips. As he raised his
head her eyes opened wide. For one long moment they
remained perfectly still, the hazel and green gazes fusing
in the moonlight. Then, slowly, he turned her fully and
deliberately drew her into his arms. She lifted her face
and his lips found hers in a kiss that possessed her senses
with gentle certainty. With infinite care he started her sensual education, his caresses deepening by imperceptible
degrees so that her senses were never overwhelmed, but
taught, step by steady step, to savour the exquisite delight
he created. His control was absolute and Dorothea, en-
folded in his care, for the first time in her life, willingly
let go of the reins.

She lost all track of time, gently led down paths where
joy, as exquisite as dew on a buttercup, lay waiting to
greet her. The sensual landscape conjured forth by his
touch was a new frontier in which each discovery brought
its own thrill. When, finally, he drew her back to reality
she was dazed and breathless and exquisitely happy.

Then they were waltzing in the moonlit orangery to the
music wafting through the open windows of the ballroom
above. In no mood to protest, she gave herself up to the
enjoyment of the moment. Hazelmere, looking down at
her lovely face, serene and untroubled in the starlight, did
likewise.

As the last chord sounded and they glided to a halt he
firmly drew her arm through his and made for the door
and the steps back to the terrace.

"Do we have to leave?" she asked, hanging back. "It's
so very lovely here."

"Yes," he replied uncompromisingly. If they stayed in
this isolated spot a moment longer he knew very well
what would happen. Which would all be very pleasant,
except he had no idea what would happen next. After that

little interlude he was no longer sure how far he could trust himself with her, and he had a shrewd suspicion that, innocent though she was, she was no more enamoured of the rules restricting their conduct than he was. It was bad enough that he had to exercise restraint for the both of them, as he was magnanimously doing at present, but if she started pulling in the opposite direction the temptation to capitulate might become too great. He groaned inwardly and closed his eyes to rid his mind of the intoxicating possibilities the thought conjured up. Opening them again, he tightened his grip on her arm and inexorably drew her back up the steps to the terrace. "If we are missing at supper, your grandmama will have all her worst fears concerning me confirmed and will in all probability forbid me to speak to you!"

As she imagined the likelihood of his paying any attention to Lady Merion's strictures, a small, happy smile curved Dorothea's lips, and she allowed him to lead her back into the ballroom.

Almost immediately they came face to face with Edward Buchanan. "Miss Darent, you're flushed! Perhaps I might take you for a walk in the gardens? I'm sure Lord Hazelmere will excuse you." The accusatory look he cast Hazelmere nearly did for Dorothea.

Hazelmere, who knew very well the cause of the delicate flush still apparent on her alabaster skin, smiled in a devilish way that brought his reputation forcibly to Edward Buchanan's mind, and said, "On the contrary! Lord Hazelmere is about to escort Miss Darent to supper. If *you* will excuse *us?*"

Receiving a curt nod, Edward Buchanan found his quarry had somehow side-stepped him and escaped. The first uneasy glimmer that Miss Darent might fall prey to the wicked blandishments of tonnish society awoke in his unimaginative mind.

Out of earshot, Dorothea asked, "Am I really flushed?" She felt delightful; not uncomfortable at all.

She could not interpret the slow grin that spread across the Marquis's face. "Delightfully so," was all the answer she got.

After much stopping to talk to acquaintances on the way, they finally gained the supper-room. Fanshawe and Cecily had saved them seats at a corner table well provided with an array of delicacies. As Hazelmere helped Dorothea to her chair Fanshawe, after one glance at her, caught his friend's eye, his look clearly stating that he had every idea of what they had been up to. Hazelmere grinned back.

Relieved to see him no longer in the hips, Fanshawe turned back to assure an excited and insistent Cecily that he would take her to see the fountain court.

When they rose from the table Fanshawe said to Hazelmere, "Don't forget your promise to your mother! I've kept my side of it. I couldn't bear it if she was to quiz us all the way back to Cavendish Square."

"Ye gods! I'd forgotten." Hazelmere turned his most charming smile on Dorothea. "Miss Darent, my mother is here somewhere in this mêlée and has made me promise to introduce you. Will you allow me to take you to her?"

She raised her fine brows, but consented to be led on a search for the Marchioness. As she moved through the crowd on Hazelmere's arm she could not resist saying, "I'm tempted to ask why Lord Fanshawe is so anxious you keep your promise."

Laughing down at her, he replied, "I wouldn't if I were you. The answer would do nothing for your composure." The caress in his eyes made her feel decidedly odd.

He finally located his mother, seated on a chaise in a corner of one of the salons, busily chatting to an acquaintance. On seeing them approach, this lady tactfully withdrew and Hazelmere made the promised introduction.

Lady Hazelmere had been prepared by her friends' letters to find Dorothea Darent a particularly pretty girl. The stunning goddess her son introduced was considerably more attractive than she had anticipated. She smiled delightedly at this vision in ivory satin.

Motioning Dorothea to sit beside her, the Dowager made very large eyes at her son, signifying how impressed she was by his taste. Hazelmere, correctly interpreting the glance, returned it with a smile clearly saying, "Well, what did you expect?" Receiving in reply an unmistakable sign that she wished to be left alone with Miss Darent, he had little choice but to obey. Making his adieus to Dorothea, he bethought himself of another matter and departed to find Lady Merion.

Relieved of his distracting presence, Lady Hazelmere found that she was being regarded by an enormous pair of green eyes. With an ease born of long experience, she instituted a conversation on totally unexceptionable matters, carefully steering clear of any mention of her son. She quickly discovered that the child before her had poise and confidence, combined with a refreshing frankness. It was not difficult to understand her son's desire for the lovely Miss Darent. That he meant marriage she had no doubt, else he would never have consented to introduce her. As their conversation progressed she discovered that humour and a ready wit could be added to Miss Darent's charms and was well satisfied with his choice.

By the time Lord Alvanley came to claim Dorothea for the last dance of the evening Lady Hazelmere was wondering how much longer her son would wait. As Dorothea moved away on Alvanley's arm she wondered whether his conquest of the elegant young woman would be as smooth as he would certainly expect. In a flash of very unmaternal feeling she hoped that, for Dorothea's sake, it would not be *quite* that easy. Hazelmere was far too used to getting his own way—a set-down would make him much more human.

Chapter Eight

The next afternoon found the Marquis perusing various documents dealing with estate business which his mother had brought from Hazelmere. Over the years he had developed the habit of paying flying visits to his numerous estates while stationed in London for the Season, fitting these between his social engagements. This year, however, he had neglected business while pursuing Miss Darent. Never a lax landlord, he knew he could not put off visiting Hazelmere.

Glancing up at the clock on the mantel, he saw it lacked a quarter to three o'clock. The weather was fine, with a light breeze tossing the cherry blossoms from the trees in the Square. He rang for Mytton and gave orders for his curricle with the greys to be brought to the door immediately. He then went upstairs to throw a series of orders at Murgatroyd's head. Ten minutes later, immaculate as ever in top-boots and a coat of Bath superfine, he descended the steps of Hazelmere House. Climbing to the box-seat of his curricle, he nodded a dismissal to Jim Hitchin, adding, "Be ready to leave for Hazelmere when I return."

He tooled the curricle around to the other side of the

square and pulled up outside Merion House. Tossing the reins to an urchin, he strode up the steps to the door. He was admitted by Mellow. "Is her ladyship in, Mellow?"

"I regret to say, her ladyship is presently unavailable, my lord."

Hazelmere frowned. "In that case, perhaps you'll enquire whether Miss Darent can spare me a few minutes?"

"Certainly, my lord."

Mellow showed him into the drawing-room and left to find Miss Darent. Climbing the stairs, he wondered if he should risk awakening his employer. After weighing the matter, he rejected the idea. His lordship had his horses with him and would not like to keep them standing. Finding Miss Darent alone in the upstairs drawing-room, he conveyed his lordship's message.

Dorothea, their visit to the Richmond House orangery in mind, was unsure of the propriety of seeing Hazelmere alone. But Cecily had gone out driving with Lord Fanshawe, and Lady Merion had still not emerged from her bedchamber. So she descended to the drawing-room but cautiously left the door open when she entered.

Hazelmere, on whom such little subtleties were not lost, smiled warmly as he took her hand, kissed it and, as was fast becoming his habit, did not release it.

"Miss Darent, will you come for a drive in the Park with me?"

Ferdie had told her that Hazelmere, for the most chauvinistic of reasons, rarely took ladies driving in the Park. She was therefore perfectly conscious of the honour being done her. Deciding that she could not possibly forgo such an invitation, she replied with alacrity, "Why, yes, if you'll give me time to find my pelisse."

Releasing her hand, Hazelmere, long inured to feminine

ideas of time, felt constrained to add, "Ten minutes, no more!"

Dorothea laughed over her shoulder as she disappeared from the room. She surprised him by returning in less than ten minutes and, as they left the house, revealed something of her knowledge of him by exclaiming, "Good heavens! You have your greys!"

Retrieving the reins and suitably rewarding the attendant urchin, Hazelmere climbed to the driving seat. As he leant down to help her up to sit beside him he answered, "As you say, Miss Darent, my greys. And what do you know of my greys?"

This shaft fell wide, however, as she could reply with perfect composure, "Ferdie told me you rarely drive your greys in the Park."

Ferdie had told her rather more than this. Hazelmere's greys were considered to be the fastest and best matched pair in the country. His lordship, if Ferdie was to be believed, had been offered vast sums for them but, as he had bred and reared them on the Henry estates, he would not part with them for any price.

"Ah, Ferdie," mused Hazelmere, suddenly seeing that Ferdie's line in inside intelligence could become a two-way street.

Conversation was necessarily suspended as he gave all his attention to negotiating the crowded streets, with the high-couraged and restless greys taking exception to numerous sights and sounds along the way. Dorothea could only admire his skill in successfully gaining the gates of the Park. Once inside, the curricle tooled along at a decent pace and Hazelmere turned his attention to her.

Much to his relief, she wore no hat, so that her face, surrounded by dark curls, was completely visible. As he watched she turned her head to smile up at him, brows lifting in mute question.

Carefully considering it in the dispassionate light of morning, Dorothea had reluctantly dismissed their interlude in the orangery as inconclusive. She had instigated it in the hope that his reponse would give her some clue to his feelings. But, while the result had been deliciously exciting, it had taught her little. That Hazelmere was well qualified to introduce her to forbidden delights had never been in doubt. While she wished with all her heart that he would say something, anything, to explain himself to her, she was depressingly certain that he would not choose the Park, with his greys in hand, as the place to do so. But presumably he had brought her here to tell her something.

"Miss Darent, I find I must leave London for a few days. Estate business demands my attendance at Hazelmere."

"I see." Dorothea was not overly put out by this revelation. If she had thought about it she would have assumed that he must need to visit his estates fairly regularly. Then she remembered her coming-out ball. The sky seemed to darken. The face she turned to him was decidedly pensive as she wondered how to phrase her question.

Hazelmere, watching her thoughts pass across her face, solved her dilemma for her. "I'll be returning on Tuesday evening, so I'll see you next on Wednesday night."

As he watched the sunshine return to her face he felt he should need no further proof of her feelings for him. Her actions and responses in the orangery had been so very revealing. He was tempted to ask her then and there to marry him, but his real dislike of trying to converse with a lady while holding a highly dangerous pair of horses made him repress the impulse. There would be plenty of time later, in more appropriate surroundings. *God!* he thought, shaken. Imagine proposing in the middle of the Park!

They continued around the Park, stopping to exchange greetings with a number of acquaintances. Hazelmere, not wanting to keep his horses standing, kept these interludes to a minimum. As they completed their circuit he headed the greys for the gates. "The weather is turning, Miss Darent, so I hope you'll not mind if I return you to Cavendish Square forthwith?"

"Not at all," she replied, "I know how honoured I've been to be driven behind your greys."

Looking up, she found herself basking in that warm hazel gaze. "Quite right, my child," he murmured. "And do remember to behave yourself while I'm away."

Incensed by the proprietorial tone, she turned to utter some withering remark, but, quizzically regarded by those strangely glinting eyes, remembered just how often he had extricated her from difficult situations. She was saved from having to reply by their emergence into the traffic, his attention once more claimed by his horses. By the time they reached Cavendish Square she had convinced herself of the wisdom of ignoring his last remark.

Pulling up outside Merion House, Hazelmere jumped from the curricle and lifted her down. He escorted her up the steps and, as Mellow opened the door, raised her hand to his lips, saying with a smile, "*Au revoir*, Miss Darent. Until Wednesday."

Sunday and Monday saw the Darent sisters attend a number of smaller functions in the lead-up to their own coming-out ball. While Cecily flirted outrageously with her young suitors, most as innocent as herself, Dorothea wisely refrained from giving any of the callow youths worshipping at her feet the slightest encouragement. However, no amount of icy hauteur seemed to deter Edward Buchanan. Unfortunately even Lady Merion was of the opinion that time was the only cure for that particular pest.

So, to her deep irritation, Dorothea found herself too often for comfort in Mr Buchanan's company. His conversational style drove her to distraction, while his continual and gradually more pressing attempts at gallantry awoke a quite different response. Her sanity was saved by the attentions of Lords Peterborough, Alvanley, Desborough and company, who, much to her delight, seemed almost as accomplished as Hazelmere in the subtle art of deflating pretensions.

Lady Merion sat staring bemusedly at the list in her hand. Was this really the best of all possible arrangements? She had been engaged in the arduous task of deciding the seating at her dinner table for Wednesday night since first thing on this dismal Tuesday morning. The house was a shambles, with caterers and florists coming in to set up their trestles and stands ready for the presentation of their wares the next night. The servants were everywhere—cleaning and polishing every bit of brass, silver and copper in the house, lovingly shining every lustre of every chandelier. Tomorrow night was the highlight of the Season as far as they were concerned and not one of Lady Merion's glittering guests was going to find the least little thing wrong.

Glancing at the ormolu clock on her mantel, she saw that it was nearly time for luncheon. In a last effort to detect any flaw in her design, she returned her attention to her list. Finally satisfied, she laid it aside and went downstairs to the morning-room, where all their meals this week had been served while the dining-room and drawing-room were redecorated. With the aid of that expert in all things fashionable, Mr Ferdie Acheson-Smythe, she had decided that her main rooms would look well in a clear pale blue, touched with white and silver, so much more striking than the common white and gold. This colour scheme was repeated throughout the main areas of the house and continued into the ballroom. The flowers for the ballroom were to be blue and white hyacinths, white wood anemones and trailing white jasmine.

The pale blue, white and silver theme would provide the perfect backdrop for her granddaughters' ball-dresses. The culmination of a prodigious effort, they were considered by Celestine among the best pieces her genius had ever created. Dorothea's dress had been both difficult and immensely satisfying. Celestine herself had scoured the warehouses to find precisely the right weight of silk in a green that perfectly matched Dorothea's eyes. The dress was shocking in its simplicity. Cut so low as to be ineligible for a younger débutante, the neckline was essentially parallel with the tiny puff sleeves, kept off the shoulder, leaving the shoulders quite bare. The bodice was shockingly snug. From the raised waistline the skirts smoothly flared over the hips, then fell heavily to the floor.

Cecily's dress, though far less stunning, was still a perfection of simplicity. Of a clear and pristine aquamarine silk, the creation, with rounded neckline and raised waist, trimmed with seed-pearls, set off her youthful figure to best advantage.

In spite of the lowering skies, the sisters had ridden in the Park as usual that morning and had been occupied since with their mail. Joining their grandmother at the luncheon table, they continued to chatter in their artless way, telling her whom they had seen and who had sent greetings. Gazing at their happy faces, she felt a pang of dismay. Soon, too soon, these young things would be gone and her house would return to its previous existence. She was not looking forward to such a quiet future at all.

Lady Merion had decreed that there would be no riding on the day of their ball. Both young ladies were to remain in bed until ten o'clock, when they could join her in the morning-room for breakfast and open the coming-out presents sent by their numerous wellwishers. They could walk around the park in the square if they wished, but after luncheon were to rest until it was time to dress. She had a horror of Cecily becoming feverish from excitement or, worse, of Dorothea succumbing to a migraine.

On hearing this plan for her day, Dorothea declared that she was more likely to become comatose from boredom. However, grateful to her grandmama for all her efforts on their part, she agreed to abide by her strictures.

By the time the sisters appeared at the breakfast table it was covered with bouquets and boxes and trifles of every imaginable type. Trimmer, Betsy and Witchett were called in to assist, and both girls, disclaiming any interest in food, settled down to sort through the welter of presents.

Entering upon this scene, Lady Merion stopped, thunderstruck. ''Good lord! I don't think I've seen anything to equal it!'' She added two boxes to the piles, one in front of each of her granddaughters. ''There, my loves! I don't think any grandmama has had two granddaughters who've given her so much pleasure.''

Both girls impulsively rose and hugged and kissed her before opening her presents. To Cecily went a tiny pearl brooch made to adorn the neckline of her ballgown. Dorothea, opening the red leather case she found under the wrapping, gasped as her eyes fell on the single strand of perfect emeralds within. "Oh! Grandmama! They're beautiful!"

After these gifts were tried on and duly admired Lady Merion urged them to continue opening their presents while she joined in the game of exclaiming and laughing over who had sent what.

While the presents today showed a greater degree of extravagance than the more common tributes, both girls had received their share of bouquets and poems and such-like throughout the Season. However, while she frequently received bouquets from Lord Alvanley and the other members of Hazelmere's set, all of whom had, each in their own way, worshipped at her feet, from the Marquis himself Dorothea had not received so much as a primrose. She did not know that Hazelmere, expert in such matters and knowing the opposition's ways too well, had omitted to send her such tributes as a deliberate tactic. Consequently, when she came to a small package amid the jumble and, unwrapping it, found a box from Astley's she did not connect it with him.

It was not common to send débutantes jewellery. Intrigued, she pushed aside the surrounding wrappings and cleared an area so that she could examine this gift more closely. "I wonder who sent this," she murmured to herself.

Lady Merion heard her and came to her side. "How very odd! Open it, my dear, and let's see. There's sure to be a card inside."

However, on her opening the box no card was found. Inside lay the most exquisitely delicate brooch, composed of emeralds and rubies in gold, in the shape of a blackberry. A slow smile appeared on Dorothea's face. What audacity!

Lady Merion, seeing the smile, was at a loss. It was

Cecily who, looking up from her own concerns, saw the brooch in her sister's fingers and immediately made the connection. "Oh! Is that from Lord Hazelmere?" Raising her brown eyes to Dorothea's blushing countenance, Cecily giggled.

Lady Merion grasped the straw. But what on earth did blackberries have to do with Hazelmere? However, knowing that gentleman, she guessed the gift was far from innocent. She baldly stated, "Dorothea, I forbid you to wear that tonight!"

"Oh, no! Don't do that, Grandmama! See, this tag from Mr Astley says he has taken the liberty of designing the brooch so it can be used as a pendant off the emerald string. How very thoughtful."

Examining the brooch and then the string of emeralds, Dorothea discovered the secret of joining them and regarded the composite piece critically. It was perfectly balanced and looked both expensive and utterly unique.

"Dorothea, I don't know what that brooch signifies, and I'm not sure I want to know," declared Lady Merion in her most authoritarian tones. "But, whatever Hazelmere means by it, you can't seriously intend to wear it tonight. Just think how conspicuous it will be! How on earth would you face him while wearing it?"

"Why, with my customary composure, I should hope," returned her wilful granddaughter. "I really couldn't refuse the challenge, Grandmama. You know I couldn't."

Reflecting that she knew nothing of the sort, Lady Merion was visited by a strong suspicion that Hazelmere was leading Dorothea into deep waters. But, in the circumstances, there was little she could, in reality, do.

The only deviation from Lady Merion's rigid schedule was caused by Edward Buchanan. Without warning, he appeared on the doorstep and refused point-blank to accept Mellow's frigid denial of the ladies of the house. By dint of mentioning Herbert Darent, he prevailed on Mellow to admit him to the morning-room while that worthy conveyed a message to his mistress.

Lady Merion came downstairs, huffily indignant, and sailed into the morning-room. Five minutes later, looking slightly stunned, she emerged and went looking for her elder granddaughter.

Ten minutes later Dorothea, paler than usual, descended the stairs. She paused for a moment, eyeing the morning-room door with revulsion. Then, drawing a deep breath, she entered.

It was worse than she had imagined. Lady Merion had mentioned the bouquet of daisies—*daisies!*—already wilting. What she had not found words to describe was the incredible smug conceit of the man holding them.

"Ah! Miss Darent!" Abruptly words seemed to fail Mr Buchanan. Then, unfortunately, his tongue regained its major habit and he spoke. "I suspect, my dear, that you know very well why I'm here." His archness made Dorothea feel decidedly unwell. Luckily he was standing on the other side of a small round table and she had every intention of keeping it between them.

He seemed to find nothing remarkable in her silence and continued with unabated cheerfulness. "Yes, my dear! All right and tight, I'm here to beg the honour of your hand! I doubt you expected a declaration quite so soon, before your coming-out even. Not many young ladies can claim to be settled so successfully before being presented, what?"

She could stand it no longer. "Mr Buchanan. I thank you for your offer but I'm afraid I cannot consent to marry you."

"Oh, no difficulty there, my dear. Edward Buchanan knows how these things are done. Lord Herbert has already given his consent. All we need now is for you to say the word and we can announce it tonight at your ball."

Hazelmere, rather more perceptive than Mr Buchanan, could have told him that that was precisely the wrong thing to say to a lady as independent as Dorothea Darent. Colours flying, she made no effort to conceal the loathing she felt. "Mr Buchanan. You appear to be labouring under a misapprehension. Herbert Darent may be my guardian but he has no power to coerce me into marriage. I will not accept your proposal. I have no wish to be married to you. I trust I make myself plain? And now, if you'll excuse me, we're very busy. Mellow will show you out."

She swept out of the door, head high, pausing to instruct Mellow to see to their unwelcome visitor before continuing, thankfully and triumphantly, upstairs.

Later that evening, just before her dinner guests were due to arrive, Lady Merion stood in her hallway and watched her granddaughters descending the stairs. Her bosom swelled with pride and a well-earned sense of satisfaction. They were superb!

Cecily, leading, was a vision of childlike innocence, a twinkle in her big brown eyes belying any attempt at gravity. But Dorothea! Breathtakingly lovely, she came elegantly down the stairs, her innate poise allowing her to carry the stunning gown to maximum effect. She was a sight that would stop any male heart. Especially Hazelmere's! thought her ladyship with a touch of vengeance as her eyes alighted on the blackberry pendant. Dorothea had been right to wear it, she grudgingly admitted, for the pendant set off the whole to perfection, lying glinting green and red against her granddaughter's alabaster skin.

Within minutes Mellow announced Ferdie, who had promised to come early to lend them his support. Entering the drawing-room, he stopped stock-still and simply stared.

"Oh, I say!" was all the elegant Mr Acheson-Smythe could manage. At this evidence of appreciation all three ladies went into whoops of laughter, and a far less formal atmosphere greeted the remaining guests, who began to arrive promptly thereafter.

The drawing-room was soon abuzz with conversation. Lady Jersey and Princess Esterhazy complimented both girls with obvious sincerity. As Dorothea moved away to talk to Miss Bressington, Sally Jersey turned to Lady Merion. "M'dear, I just can't *wait* to see Hazelmere's face when he comes through the door and sets eyes on that vision."

"Sally, don't say things like that! I'm dreading that either he or Dorothea or both will forget where they are and do something quite scandalous tonight!"

"I hardly think, for once, anyone would blame him if he did!"

At exactly that moment Mellow announced the Marquis of Hazelmere and the Dowager Marchioness. While no one was ill-bred enough to stare, Hazelmere was well aware that all eyes, save one set of emerald green, were trained on him. He resisted the temptation to look for Dorothea and instead, with his usual urbane air, led his mother to pay their respects to Lady Merion.

Lady Hazelmere, not under any such compulsion, sought out Dorothea and in an undertone designed for him alone, said, "My dear, you are lost! That girl is the most stunning sight I have ever seen!"

Hazelmere, hazel eyes laughing, replied, "Thank you, Mama. I rather supposed that to be the case, seeing how closely all these tabbies are watching me."

Lady Hazelmere chuckled and turned to compliment Lady Merion on her charges. Relinquishing his mother to the group of old friends around their hostess, Hazelmere skilfully drifted into the crowd.

The Hazelmere party was closely followed by the Eglemonts. Under cover of the bustle this created, with most attention being distracted by the sight of Lord Fanshawe greeting Cecily Darent, Hazelmere approached Dorothea where she stood talking to his younger sister, Lady Alison Gisborne. This vivacious blonde, having no doubt who her brother's inamorata was, had introduced herself to Dorothea. Seeing him, she smiled broadly and announced, "Hello, Marc! Yes, I'm just going to see Mama, who I know is dying to say something to me!" She laughed up at him and departed.

"How well my younger sister understands me," he murmured, raising Dorothea's hand to his lips as usual. He was thankful for the few minutes he had had to grow accustomed to the vision she presented.

Risking a glance up at him, Dorothea found his hazel eyes glinting, and as he smiled at her she felt that the rest of the room could disappear for all she cared. Smiling back, she said, "I must thank you for your gift, Lord Hazelmere."

"Ah, yes. I hoped it would act as a token of pleasant memories," he replied, raising a long finger to touch the pendant and only just resisting the temptation to caress the skin on which it lay.

She had expected some outrageous remark. "Yes, I always found Moreton Park woods particularly restful." Her serenity was so complete that, if he hadn't known better, he could have thought she had forgotten her first meeting with him entirely.

Laughingly acknowledging the adept return, he took her breath away by murmuring provocatively, "You have grown so very expert at fencing with me, my dear, that I fear I'll have to resort to…more direct methods."

The emerald eyes flew to his, but just what she would have said in response they never knew, for at that moment Marjorie Darent approached them.

While the rest of the company had the good manners not to interrupt the conversation between Miss Darent and Lord Hazelmere, Lady Darent felt no such restriction. Seeing Dorothea being monopolised by a man she considered one step removed from a rake, she saw her duty clearly. Recently arrived, she had not yet spoken to Dorothea and, being short-sighted, it was not until she was within a few feet that the full effect of Dorothea's gown struck her.

Favouring the Marquis with what she believed was a gracious smile, she spoke to Dorothea immediately. "My dear! Don't you think a shawl would be more becoming over that gown?"

Hazelmere felt Dorothea stiffen and almost imperceptibly they drew closer together. "I think not, Cousin," replied Dorothea, holding her temper with a superhuman effort. "I'm hardly cold. And besides," she continued hurriedly, seeing that her cousin had missed the very large hint and was about to explain herself more fully, "I would hardly embarrass Grandmama by adopting so provincial a style of dress."

Lady Darent stiffened.

Only just preventing himself from applauding, Hazelmere intervened. "Miss Darent, I believe my mother is trying to attract our attention. If Lady Darent will excuse us?'' With a nod to that outraged lady, he firmly removed Dorothea from her orbit.

As they moved away he glanced down at the beauty by his side. "Good girl! If you hadn't said that I'm afraid I had something much worse in mind. Remind me that, despite the other...skills I've yet to teach you, I don't need to teach you how to insult someone."

A gurgle of laughter, quickly suppressed, greeted this sally, and Dorothea turned her sparkling eyes to his face. The Marquis's mother, towards whom they were headed, viewed this exchange with a peculiar smile. She had never thought to see her son so obviously in love.

The conversation continued to hum and the heat in the drawing-room rose, until Mellow, resplendent in new long-tailed coat, announced dinner. Hazelmere, as the most senior of the peers present, would normally have led in Lady Merion, but Herbert Darent found that he was to perform this office, leaving the Marquis to attend Miss Darent. Cecily was squired by Lord Fanshawe, and the others obligingly took care of themselves.

The dinner was a resounding success and not a single incident occurred to mar Lady Merion's pleasure. Conversation flowed on all sides, even Marjorie finding in the half-deaf admiral by her side someone with whom she shared some common ground. As all had expected, Hazelmere and Dorothea seemed oblivious to all others, as were Cecily and Fanshawe opposite. Due to Lady Merion's strategic planning, no one was the least put out by this, except Lord and Lady Darent. Luckily those disapproving figures were too far removed to exert any dampening influence on the sparkling scene in the middle of the table.

With the removal of the last course, the ladies rose and departed for the drawing-room, leaving the gentlemen to their port. At a dinner preceding a ball the ritual separation was usually kept to a minimum. But Lady Merion was taking no chances. She had enlisted the aid of the Earl of Eglemont to ensure that Herbert did not prose on in his accustomed way and drive everyone else to distraction.

For this service Lord Eglemont was an inspired choice. He knew that none of the younger gentlemen present would have the least inclination to remain kicking his heels over the port. And who could blame them? In his view, a dinner and ball was the time for some fun, and even he would rather be back in the drawing-room, watching what devilment Marc and Tony, and even Lord Harcourt and Ferdie, could concoct, than listening to that pompous windbag Herbert Darent.

Herbert, therefore, found the discussion he instituted on the latest ideas of rotation farming taken out of his hands and wound up by Lord Eglemont, who then further usurped his role and led the gentlemen back to the drawing-room.

Lady Merion heaved a sigh of relief when she saw them return. The room was pleasantly a-hum with conversation generated by the groups of young and old scattered through it. Lords Hazelmere and Fanshawe, re-entering the room to find the Misses Darent chatting avidly with groups of friends, wisely made no attempt to disengage them, but made themselves as inconspicuous as possible.

Hazelmere strolled over to his mother. "Ah, Mama! I'd meant to ask earlier. Do you know if my esteemed elder sisters will be gracing the ball tonight?"

Lady Hazelmere's strait-laced elder daughters were every bit as great a burden to her as they were to her son. "I fervently hope not, my dear!" She turned and, leaning across Sally Jersey, addressed Lady Merion. "Hermione, you didn't invite Maria and Susan, did you?"

To both mother and son's dismay, Lady Merion nodded. "Yes. And both accepted."

Lady Hazelmere turned back to her son, pulling a face. He bent to whisper in her ear. "In that case, it would be wise if you dropped a word of warning in my loving sisters' ears, regarding the wisdom of giving myself and Miss Darent a suitably wide berth tonight."

Lady Hazelmere looked at him in surprise. He smiled down at her in his usual maddening way before moving off into the room. She spent some minutes trying to solve the riddle, finally deciding that he must mean to do something that would incense her elder daughters. What it could be she had no idea but, as she turned to Sally Jersey sitting beside her, she found she was not alone in suspecting her son of being up to something.

"Anthea, what on earth is that boy of yours up to? He and Tony Fanshawe are behaving very coolly."

"I've really no idea, Sally. You should know mothers are always the last to be told anything. But I must say," she went on, "I do think you're right. They're certainly planning something."

As the time for the ball approached Lady Merion moved her dinner guests up to the ballroom. The florists and decorators had excelled themselves, but the exclamations and congratulations of the ladies were soon drowned by the arrival of the ball guests. The chatter and talk as acquaintances met swept like a wave across the room as all the ton rolled up to Lady Merion's ball.

Dorothea and Cecily were stationed at the head of the stairs with their grandmother to receive the guests. For the next half-hour they were completely absorbed in greeting and being presented to the ton at large. As the surge of arrivals started to ease and then reduced to a trickle the ballroom was close to overflowing, and all the glittering throng of the élite of London society were present. The room looked magnificent, and Lady Merion felt she had achieved the very pinnacle of success. Catching Mellow's eye, she gave the signal to start the ball. As he moved majestically down the room the guests parted to clear an area for the first waltz.

Traditionally the first section of the first waltz was danced only by the young lady in whose honour the ball was held. Tonight Dorothea would go first down the room, followed by Cecily, before the rest of the guests joined in. If strictest protocol was followed Dorothea would be partnered by Herbert and Cecily by Lord Wigmore, Lady Merion's cousin. However, when approached by her ladyship, Lord Wigmore had readily relinquished this task, chuckling when he heard who was to take his place. Herbert was simply informed that, as he did not waltz, a suitable replacement had been found. He was put out but did not have the gumption to cause a fuss. His grandmother wisely refrained from telling him who was to lead his ward out.

She had also, under orders, not told her granddaughters who their partners were for this all-important first dance. This had placed no strain on her inventiveness, as neither girl had thought to ask, both imagining that Herbert and Lord Wigmore were inescapable fixtures. So, with inward trepidation, Lady Merion, standing between the two girls at the top of the shallow steps leading down to her ballroom and, seeing the musicians preparing to strike the first chords, said, "Off you go, my loves! Your partners are arranged and will meet you at the bottom of the steps. And my very best wishes for a most wonderful ball for you both!"

The sisters moved down the stairs, Dorothea slightly in advance, carrying herself with that self-confident air that drew all eyes. Inwardly she was dreading this dance. She knew Herbert could not waltz to save himself. The next few minutes could be hideously embarrassing. Then her already huge and glittering eyes widened even further as, stepping on to the ballroom floor, she saw the Marquis of Hazelmere coming towards her, magnificent and smiling as ever.

He bowed to her and she automatically curtsied gracefully. He raised her and she went into his arms with her usual total abandon, her face radiant and her eyes sparkling with laughter. As they turned with the dance she cast a quick glance across to find Cecily had been met by Fanshawe. She sighed with relief, and said in heartfelt accents, "Oh! You have no idea how thankful I am that it's you!"

Hazelmere smiled as they slowly went down the room. "Neither your grandmother nor I felt horrible Herbert was a suitable partner for you, nor that the not nearly so horrible but staid Lord Wigmore was quite right for Cecily."

Alive to the silence around them, Dorothea, laughter in the big green eyes she did not dare take from his face, asked, "Are we making a scandalous spectacle of ourselves?"

Hazelmere, still smiling, murmured, "I rather suspect we are. But I doubt if it's for the reason you suspect."

She looked her question.

For a moment the hazel eyes glinted. He elected to answer only half of the query. "While my dancing the first waltz with you, and Tony with Cecily, is not precisely correct, it's nevertheless acceptable in the circumstances of your having no near male relatives other than Herbert, who everyone knows can't dance."

"So they may disapprove but they can't condemn?"

"Exactly so."

They had reached the end of the ballroom and Hazelmere expertly executed a difficult turn, sending them back through the other couples now on the floor.

"Incidentally," he continued, "this is also the one occasion when I can with impunity waltz twice with you. This dance is special and not listed on the programme and therefore doesn't count. So, my dear Miss Darent, may I have the double pleasure of the supper waltz and of escorting you to supper?"

Thinking that that would ensure a most enjoyable evening, she laughingly agreed. As the last notes drifted down the room they glided to a halt and he led her back to Lady Merion's side. Reluctantly relinquishing her, he kissed her hand and, with a peculiar smile that made her unruly heart somersault, disappeared into the gathering crowd of well-wishers.

Lady Hazelmere's reaction to that first waltz was much the same as that of many in the watching crowd. When Hazelmere took Dorothea into his arms the entire company held its breath, usually the prelude to an outburst of censorious whispering. However, all the censorious minds simultaneously realised that there was nothing particularly scandalous after all. A minute's reflection convinced the leading ladies that Lady Merion had pulled off a major coup. The gentlemen, almost to a man, found the incident highly entertaining.

What particularly tickled Lady Hazelmere's quirkish sense of humour was the outrage engendered in a large number of the more staid female breasts by the way her son and the lovely Dorothea danced. The ton had thought they were accustomed to the sight of Miss Darent in Lord Hazelmere's arms. But they had only seen them dancing in a crowd of other couples, not alone on a deserted ballroom floor. Tonight the first shock had come when Dorothea went so readily into his arms. But the way they moved together had really set the cat among the pigeons! So graceful, so completely attuned to each other that the intimacy which obviously existed between them was displayed for all to see. That performance had bordered on the indecent. Even more wonderful, thought the knowing Lady Hazelmere, was that not one word could be said of the matter. Not one single movement, not one flicker of an eyelash, had been in any way improper. The most censorious of the tabbies would not dare breathe a word for fear of being, quite justly, accused of having a mind of somewhat questionable taste. It was highly unlikely that her wicked son had not known how it would be. Equally certain that the lovely Dorothea was quite innocent in the matter. Well, no, perhaps not innocent, amended her ladyship, but Dorothea could certainly not have known how revealing that dance would be. No gently nurtured female could possibly have gone through with it.

At least I now know why Marc wanted me to warn off Maria and Susan, she thought. And, thinking just how scandalised her elder daughters were bound to be, she laughed and went to carry out his commission.

For both Darent sisters their coming-out ball was the most enjoyable night of the Season. They were fêted and saluted at every turn. Dorothea danced with every one of Hazelmere's close friends, with whom she now enjoyed an easy acquaintance. She also danced with Herbert, but in a quadrille, which he performed adequately if not gracefully. It was more than halfway through the evening before she found herself once more in the Marquis's arms, going down the floor in the supper waltz.

Guessing that she must have been making constant conversation, he did not press her to talk, merely murmuring, "Tired, my lovely Dorothea?"

For a moment his use of her name did not register. Then she looked up and found all inclination to question his right to use it evaporating. Meeting his eyes, she felt that deliciously warm feeling spread over her. So she assented to the question with a smile, her long lashes dropping to veil her large green eyes from his gaze in a manner he recognised only too well.

Smiling, he wondered if he dared tell her how she looked when she did that, or what the action commonly conveyed, but decided that after such an explanation she would in all likelihood not speak to him for a week.

Suppertime was hilarious. As Dorothea and Cecily were the twin foci of attention, they could not sit together. Instead, Dorothea and Hazelmere were surrounded by a reckless throng of his close friends. While he sat beside her, interpolating remarks only when the conversation threatened to get too deep for her ears, they entertained her with numerous anecdotes, many reflecting on Hazelmere himself. They knew he was perfectly capable of putting a stop to it any time he wished, so when he made no move to dampen their spirits their hilarity knew few bounds. In this way the half-hour devoted to supper whizzed past until Dorothea was claimed by Lord Desborough for the first of the last three dances of the evening.

At the end of the measure she was hailed by a small group of her grandmother's acquaintances, older ladies whom she had not yet had time to talk to. Laughingly dismissing Desborough, she went to spend a few minutes in their company. Eventually excusing herself, Dorothea passed slowly through the crowd, stopping to chat here and there, dispensing just the right degree of notice at each halt. Turning from one such encounter, she was addressed by Miss Buntton, a blonde ice-maiden two years her junior. "My dear Miss Darent," said Miss Buntton in her normal frigid accents. "Your gown is really so superb! Truly esoteric! But I fear my mama would never permit me to wear such a gown. She always says it does no good to stand out in a crowd."

Dorothea, long inured to Miss Buntton's waspish jealousies, thought she really made it too easy. "I'm sure, my dear Miss Buntton, that you run no risk of displeasing your mama." With a smile of gentle malice, she was about to move on when another, older woman, whose name she could not recall, standing on the other side of the blonde beauty, intervened.

"Miss Darent! I've been hoping to meet you. I'm Lady Susan Wilmot, Hazelmere's sister."

Dorothea touched the hand graciously held out to her and murmured something suitable. But Lady Susan was already speaking. "Yes, my dear. As I was just telling Miss Buntton, I was so pleased to see Hazelmere doing his duty by you tonight with that first waltz. He's so lax in certain responsibilities, but, given that Lady Merion must have asked him, as a favour, to replace Herbert, I was pleasantly surprised to see him behave so acceptably. Perhaps it's a sign that he's contemplating settling down. Of course, the lady he marries must have all the qualities—as she'll have to rule at Hazelmere. And naturally she can only come from the finest of family. Wealth, of course, is necessary; Hazelmere after all is one of the wealthiest himself." Her ladyship smiled, gimlet-eyes, on Dorothea. "I dare say I'm not giving away any secrets in saying that all the family have high hopes of our dear Miss Buntton here."

"Oh?" Unable to escape the net of her ladyship's eloquence and feeling oddly depressed, Dorothea could not resist a glance at our Miss Buntton. Good lord! The girl was actually simpering!

At that moment a hand touched her arm. "Dorothea! Here you are! Come and meet my brother-in-law. I've promised to introduce you." Lady Alison Gisborne's eyes met her older sister's across the little group. Lady Susan coloured.

Missing the byplay, Dorothea, with relief, nodded to Lady Susan and Miss Buntton and gratefully departed to meet Andrew Gisborne.

As the closing strains of the last waltz drifted across the ballroom, and tired couples turned to find their parties, Dorothea found herself at the side of the ballroom on Lord Alvanley's arm. His lordship was scanning the room, obviously looking for someone. "Ah, there he is!" Looking down at Dorothea, he explained, "Marc asked me to return you to him after the dance."

As they slowly made their way across the wide room, pausing to bid goodbye to departing guests, Dorothea saw Lady Alison pause by her brother, dragging on his arm to get his attention. For a moment Hazelmere listened as she spoke, clearly relating some message. Then she swiftly drew his head down to plant an affectionate kiss on his cheek and, with a cheerful wave, hurried to join her husband by the stairs.

By this time they had come up to the Marquis, who was conversing with an opulent beauty introduced earlier to Dorothea as Helen, Lady Walford. The four remained chatting for a few minutes as the company in the ballroom thinned. Then Lord Alvanley suavely offered Lady Walford his arm and, after taking their leave of Dorothea, they left.

Hazelmere, seeing the appreciative grin on her face, said, "Yes, Alvanley and I are very good friends." Her smile deepened. After a pause he continued, "My dear Dorothea, are you planning to ride in the Park tomorrow?"

This succeeded in capturing her attention from a group of guests nodding their goodbyes. "Why, yes, I think so," she replied.

"In that case, Ferdie and I, and probably Tony as well, will call for you at ten. Don't be late!" He kissed her hand and, recognising the portent of the flash in her green eyes, drew it through his arm; before she had time to tell him what she thought of his organisation of her morning, he strolled with her up the steps to her grandmother.

Lady Merion was exhausted. The evening had been an unqualified success, although in her opinion it would have proved less enervating if Dorothea and Hazelmere had been less accomplished dancers. However, she was not going to cavil at such a minor point and was in total charity with the world. Seeing them come up out of the deserted ballroom, she beamed. "My dears! Such a success it's been!"

"And all due to you, Grandmama!" replied Dorothea, impulsively hugging the old lady.

"Now be off with you, child!" said her ladyship gruffly. "Cecily has already retired. I'm sure Lord Hazelmere will excuse you."

Hazelmere lifted her hand from his sleeve and, elegantly dropping a kiss on her wrist, said, "Goodnight, Dorothea. I'll see you tomorrow morning."

With another glance of green fire she was gone.

Lady Merion watched this exchange and, once her granddaughter was out of earshot, said, "You do play close to the wind."

"Only with your granddaughter," came the outrageous reply. As she gasped he continued, "Am I correct in thinking the horrible Herbert that gorgeous creature's guardian?"

Knowing she was being distracted from her main grievance, she was forced to reply, "Yes, unfortunately."

"No matter." He shrugged, turning to take his leave.

But she had no intention of letting him escape so easily. Fixing him with a look that forcibly reminded him of his mother, she asked, "When are you going to ask for her hand?"

"In my own good time," he returned, unperturbed by this direct inquisition.

"So you intend to offer for her?"

At that he smiled. "Do you doubt it?"

"After that first waltz, no one present could doubt it!" she retorted acerbically.

"Which is precisely as I intended." With a smile of unruffled calm he bowed elegantly before descending the stairs.

Lady Merion watched his retreating back. For some reason she felt that, in spite of his cool handling of the affair, which she could not but applaud for the eminent good sense it showed, his success so far had been unnaturally easy. In her experience, headstrong young women like Dorothea were unlikely to appreciate his calm management of the affair. No, my lord, she thought, there's trouble ahead somewhere.

Chapter Nine

The riding party the next morning was a relaxed affair. From Cavendish Square came the Darent sisters, Hazelmere, Fanshawe, Ferdie and Mr Dermont. At the gates of the Park they were joined by Lord Harcourt and Miss Bressington. There were few others about at that hour, despite the clemency of the weather. Before long the three couples had parted, to amble down the glades and rides, totally absorbed with each other, while Ferdie and Mr Dermont were deep in discussion over the latest type of suiting.

As was often the case when she was alone in Hazelmere's company, Dorothea's composure was more apparent than real. She was having increasing difficulty maintaining the cool unconcern she felt was her only defence against those all-seeing hazel eyes. His presence physically disturbed her to the point where her mind no longer functioned with its customary clarity. Amid others, at balls and parties, where convention laid its restraining hand on his actions, she could retain sufficient command of her wits to deflect his subtle attacks. But when they were alone, with nothing to prevent him from leading her thoughts along avenues she knew to be as dangerous as they were exciting, she no longer felt confident of keeping him from guessing how deeply he affected her. In fact, she was no longer sure that she was hiding anything from him at all. She had no idea what he had made of her behaviour in the Duchess of Richmond's orangery. On the other hand, his imperious manners had abated not one whit. And he had yet to speak, even obliquely, of love.

As they rode side by side deep within the Park, far out of sight of the rest of their party, she was conscious of steadily increasing confusion. It was fraying her temper, particularly when the reprehensible creature beside her seemed not to know the meaning of uncertainty. His attitude was always one of complete assurance. She had a peculiar feeling of being inexorably caught up in something she did not comprehend, some trap baited with an irresistible lure, impossible to escape. And he was at the centre of it, drawing her ever closer.

Hazelmere took the opportunity to tell her he would again be away until some time in the next week. His brief trip to Hazelmere had revealed more examples of his neglect than his conscience would countenance. Having done all he could to impress upon the ton how definite his intentions towards her were, and what her response to his proposal was likely to be, he was determined to rectify the problems on his estates without delay. Other than the lady riding beside him, there was little to keep him in London; the débutante balls were not generally high on his list of enjoyable functions.

While she accepted the news of his projected absence prosaically enough, Dorothea was surprised by his final comments. "In my absence, if you should need help in any way, you can trust Ferdie or Tony, or Alvanley, Peterborough or any of the others of our set, for that matter.

We always help each other and they would unhesitatingly stand in my stead were there any need.''

She turned her wide-eyed gaze upon him, but was unable to see anything in his manner, other than a rueful twinkle in his eyes, to give her a clue as to what exactly he meant.

The twinkle was occasioned by the realisation that he had told her rather more than he had intended. He was slipping again. If she paused to consider she might wonder why his powerful friends should extend their protection to Miss Darent. That they would definitely do so to the future Marchioness of Hazelmere was a thought that might occur. He was sure she had no idea how publicly accepted their relationship had become and suspected that the realisation would be greeted, at least initially, with dismay, if not anger. It formed no part of his plans to force her hand thus early in the Season.

He then spent the best part of a pleasurable hour trying just how far into the realms of the improper he could lead her. He found it was rather further than his own rapidly diminishing control made safe. So, with a skill born of extensive practice, he adroitly disengaged, leaving her confused but with no idea of where they had been headed.

They were the last to rejoin the group, and the look on Hazelmere's face reminded Ferdie that he had a bone to pick with his lordship, and Tony too, come to think of it! In otherwise perfect harmony, the group made its way out of the Park and back to Cavendish Square, where Julia Bressington was to spend the day.

A select masquerade ball was to be held the following Thursday at the Bressingtons'. The Season's débutantes had been clamouring for a masquerade. Such events, commonplace some years previously, had fallen into disrepute because of the licentiousness they provoked and the difficulty in policing acceptable standards of conduct. However, wilting under the continued entreaties, a group of mothers had put their heads together and devised a compromise. While the ball was to be a masquerade, there were strict rules. Entry was by invitation only and everyone had to wear plain black dominoes over evening dress. Masks would be provided at the door, so the hostesses would know each face before any were permitted to enter.

Dorothea was disappointed when she realised that Hazelmere would not be back in time for the masquerade ball. She considered not going herself but, as chaperons were not permitted in the ballroom and Lady Merion was therefore taking a well-earned rest, Cecily did not like to go alone. To add to this, Lady Merion made various obscure comments about not wearing her heart on her sleeve or pining away just because a certain nobleman was absent from town. Not being obtuse, Dorothea took the point, and with good grace accompanied Cecily to the ball.

Entering the hall of Bressington House, they handed in their invitations and, approved by the hostesses, joined the queue leading to a table where the Misses Bressington were distributing masks. The sight of Dorothea affected Julia Bressington strangely. She tittered and then, looking highly conspiratorial, surreptitiously handed over a note.

Dorothea, waiting in line, opened the missive. It contained only one sentence: "Meet me on the terrace at midnight." She felt sure there was only one person who would dare send her such a peremptory command. So Hazelmere was coming to the ball after all. Presumably he would be late and so would have less time to find her in the crush.

Her mask was tied tightly across her face by a giggling

Julia, holding the hood of her domino in place and completely covering her hair. Despite this disguise, no sooner had she and Cecily stepped over the threshold than each was claimed by suspiciously tall, domino-clad figures.

Feeling a familiar arm about her waist and looking up into a pair of laughing hazel eyes, Dorothea instantly relaxed, laughing back.

"You're already here!"

"Already? How did you know I was coming at all?" he asked, thoroughly surprised.

"But you left me that note." As she said the words a dreadful premonition seized her.

"What note? No. Wait." He drew her into a window embrasure. "Show me," he commanded, holding out his hand.

Dorothea had put the note in the inside pocket of her domino. She drew it out and handed it to him.

Hazelmere read the single line of script, the lines about his mouth hardening. The idea of Dorothea attending the masquerade to fall victim to some gentleman as experienced as himself had been sufficient to drive him to conclude his business a day early. But what the hell was this note about?

Seeing Dorothea pale under her mask, he slipped his arm about her waist. Tucking the note into his pocket, he led her towards the centre of the room. "Remind me, my love, to show you my signature some time. Then, if I ever send you a letter, you'll know it's from me."

Deciding she was not going to be distracted by the ineligible epithet, which she knew had been included expressly for the purpose, she asked directly, "But who is it from, if not you?"

Hazelmere considered telling her some fanciful tale, anything to make her forget the incident, but one glance at her determined face warned him that that particular ruse was unlikely to succeed. He eventually answered, "I know no more than you, my dear."

A waltz started up and Dorothea found herself circling the floor in his arms. By the time the dance concluded he had succeeded in convincing her to put aside her thoughts on the mysterious note and give her undivided attention to him. She learned that the principal attraction of a masquerade ball was that a lady could spend the entire evening in the arms of one gentleman without causing a furore. For his part, Hazelmere had no intention of letting her go. Luckily, as most of the couples in the ballroom were similarly invariant and Dorothea found nothing amiss with this arrangement, his possessiveness passed unnoticed.

After their second dance he drew her into a shadowed alcove. There, with Dorothea standing, unconsciously, within the comforting circle of his arm, they swapped their news.

"And Lord Peterborough has been *so* attentive," sighed Dorothea, eyes dancing.

"Oh?" said Hazelmere, a frown in his eyes.

"Mmm," she murmured in confirmation, adding innocently, "He told me to tell you so."

The laugh this elicited made her tingle. His hazel eyes were wreaking havoc with her composure. "I must remember to thank Gerry next time I see him. In the meantime, sweet torment, come and dance."

For the rest of the evening Hazelmere devoted himself to making her forget the existence of the note. He tried every trick he knew to bemuse and amuse her, hoping to divert her thoughts sufficiently to enable him to leave her, unsuspecting, with Fanshawe while he kept her midnight appointment. But while she certainly paid attention to all he said, blushing delightfully at his more provocative suggestions, she clearly possessed a distressingly calm and collected mind. He suspected that she guessed the reason for his behaviour and, short of kissing her in the middle of the ballroom, he could think of nothing that might succeed in distracting her. As midnight approached he gave up the attempt.

The rules for the ball called for a general unmasking at midnight. As the clock over the door approached five minutes to the hour Hazelmere, knowing that Dorothea, too, was keeping track of the time, drew her over to the windows leading on to the terrace.

"Are you sure you want to go through with this?" he asked.

"But of course!" She assumed that his evident wish to spare her the midnight meeting stemmed from the belief she would be overcome by some missish sentiment. She felt slightly aggrieved that he didn't know her better.

"Before I permit you to go out on that terrace I want you to promise you'll do precisely as I say."

It was on the tip of her tongue to point out that it was her note and therefore her adventure, not his. And she certainly did not need his permission to go out on the terrace! But there was no time to argue, and the gleam of amusement in his eyes suggested that he had guessed her thoughts anyway. Mastering her annoyance, she agreed. "Very well. I promise. What must I do?"

"Open the door and go out, but don't shut it behind you. I'll stay behind in the shadows. Walk on to the terrace but, whatever you do, don't go more than halfway to the balustrade. And only go a few yards either side of the door. Understand?"

She nodded. Satisfied, Hazelmere held the heavy curtain aside for her to slip past, and followed her into the darkened alcove between the curtain and the window. He opened this and Dorothea moved out on to the moonlit terrace.

Directly in front of her was a flight of stone steps leading down to a gravel path, with the lawns and shrubbery in deepest shadow beyond. Mindful of her instructions, she moved to her left, keeping close to the house. She had only gone a few paces when a voice came to her from somewhere near the steps.

"Miss Darent! This way!"

At exactly that moment someone inside the ballroom flung back the curtain over the next window along and opened it, but then, as the call for the unmasking was heard, closed it again.

The sound of running footsteps retreating along the gravel path came clearly to both Dorothea and Hazelmere, still in the shadows. Stepping up to her, he whispered, "Stay here." He went past her and lightly down the steps.

The last echoes of the footsteps were dying in the distance. The rhododendron bushes that bordered the terrace were dense and taller than Hazelmere himself. A most convenient setting for an abduction, he thought grimly. He was too wise to go searching in the darkened garden, leaving Dorothea unattended on the terrace, even though it seemed as though the mysterious leaver of notes had departed. Removing his mask and pushing back the hood of his domino, he returned to the terrace.

"There's no sign of anyone now," he said. "A pity, but no harm done."

"But who could it be, to play such a silly joke?" she asked, tugging at the knots Julia Bressington had made in her mask strings.

"Here, let me." He reached over her and undid the mask, removed it and pushed the hood back from her hair.

Then, taking her face in both hands and tilting it up, he kissed her. After a moment his hands left her face to slip beneath her domino and gather her, unresisting, into his arms.

As the kiss deepened, Dorothea, again, lost all sense of time. He did no more than reinforce the lessons he had taught her in the orangery; there was no time for more. His experienced mouth claimed hers, gently persuading, while, under her domino, his hands drifted caressingly over her breasts, her waist and her hips. Then, reluctantly, he released her. Before she could recover he drew her hand through his arm and moved back to the door, saying in his usual manner, "We'd best return to the ballroom before our absence becomes too difficult to explain."

Back in the ballroom before she could gather her wits, Dorothea had no chance to say anything. They were quickly surrounded by friends, all laughing and talking at once. But during what was left of the ball she was conscious of the hazel eyes resting on her often, their expression doing nothing for her peace of mind.

Later, as they left the ballroom together, Hazelmere remembered the note. "Incidentally, my love, should you get any further notes inciting you to do anything the least bit improper and which purport to come from me, you might remember I'm much more likely to make such suggestions in person."

It was impossible to reply to that in any acceptable way. Dorothea wisely left it uncontested.

Leaving Bressington House a short time later, Lords Hazelmere and Fanshawe insisted on handing the Darent sisters into their carriage. Belatedly realising that she had allowed Hazelmere to monopolise her for the entire evening, Dorothea threw him a glance that she hoped conveyed her disapproval of his managing ways. She could hardly claim success, as he laughed and murmured in her ear that if she continued to cast such provocative looks at him he would be unable to resist the temptation to kiss her again. In the shadowy carriage drive he suited the action to the words, before helping a thoroughly flustered Dorothea into her grandmother's coach.

Hazelmere was more perturbed by the mysterious note and the incident on the terrace than he had let Dorothea guess. Walking back to Cavendish Square in company with Fanshawe, he considered the possible explanations.

Young heiresses had been abducted and held for ransom—that was one possible reason. However, most of the previous targets had been very wealthy. Dorothea, although commonly held to be well dowered, was not immensely rich. So, if it was an abduction attempt, the far more likely intention would be to have a touch at the Hazelmere coffers. It had never occurred to him that by making his interest in her so public he would make her a target for such attacks.

He considered the figure by his side. All was not well with his friend and, presuming from his silence on the matter that the cause was the younger Miss Darent, he did not like to add any extra burden to a brow already overwrought.

The romance between Fanshawe and Cecily was not proceeding as his lordship had hoped. He had discovered his love had a definite mind of her own and having once taken an idea into her head could hold to it buckle and thong in the face of all reason. She had objected to what she termed his proprietorial attitude at the masquerade, leaving him feeling decidedly rejected. While she had relented later, allowing him to escort her to their carriage, she had remained coldly aloof.

The two friends continued on their way, sunk in abstracted silence. They parted at the corner of Cavendish Square to retire to their respective chambers, troubled, for quite different reasons, over what the future held.

Chapter Ten

The Friday, Saturday and Sunday following the masquerade saw Hazelmere dancing attendance on Dorothea in a way that, had anyone still been watching, would have made them wonder at the power of love. Lady Merion was moved to make a number of rude comments to him when no one else was by, regarding the inadvisability of over-indulgence. Hazelmere listened politely and let the shafts fly by. He was thankful that his mother had returned to Hazelmere on Friday morning, archly refusing her dutiful son's offer of escort, saying she knew how many other things he had on his mind.

Keeping a watchful eye on Dorothea at the balls and parties in the evenings presented no great problem. He could with confidence leave her in the company of a great many friends, both his and her own. But from the time she returned from riding in the Park to the time she left Merion House for whichever of the evening's entertainments she was to attend, her day was a mystery to him.

On Friday he solved this by inviting her to drive with him in the Park in the afternoon. He almost committed the blunder of asking her to come out with him again on Saturday but, catching a glimpse of her face, realised that she was already becoming suspicious. She was quite capable of linking his sudden attentiveness with the incident at the masquerade. He returned to Hazelmere House and spent the rest of the afternoon trying to devise a means of keeping watch over her without being overly conspicuous.

The only other person he would have consulted was Fanshawe, but he was still having troubles of his own. He had to have better information on Dorothea's movements, but for some while the means of acquiring such intelligence did not present itself. It was only when a footman quietly entered to light the fire that the penny dropped.

Summoning his butler, he asked, "Mytton, is there any connection between my household and that of Merion House?"

Mytton, not sure what had occasioned this odd query, saw no reason to equivocate. "Young Charles, the footman, m'lord, is walking out with Miss Darent's new maid."

"Is he, indeed?" mused Hazelmere softly. He glanced up at his terribly correct and equally shrewd henchman. "Mytton, you may tell Charles that I wish him to find out for me, if he can, what Miss Darent's plans are for the morrow. He may take whatever time he needs. But I must have the information before tomorrow. Do you think he could accomplish such a task?"

"Young Charles, if I may say so, m'lord, is a most capable young man," responded Mytton gravely.

"Very good," replied Hazelmere, repressing a grin.

On returning home in the early hours of Saturday morning, he found that Charles had been every bit as capable as Mytton believed. Armed with Dorothea's plans for the next two days, he was able to confine his appearances to her usual morning rides in the Park, to a ball on Saturday night and to the party she attended on Sunday evening. At the party, he found himself again under suspicion.

"Just what are you about now?" Dorothea enquired as they glided around the room in the only waltz of the evening.

"I'd rather thought it was the waltz," returned Hazelmere, all innocence. "I'm generally held to be reasonably good at it."

Dorothea regarded him much as she would an errant child. "And I suppose it has always been your habit to attend such eminently boring parties as this?"

"Ah, but you forget, my love! My heart is at your feet. Didn't you know?"

While the words were what she longed to hear, the tone left Dorothea in no doubt of how she should treat them. She laughed. "Oh, no! You cannot distract me so easily. You'll have to think up a far more plausible excuse for your presence here, of all places."

"Is my being here so distasteful to you?" he asked, feigning seriousness.

Seeing the lurking twinkle at the back of the hazel eyes, she had no compunction in answering, "Why, no! I believe I would welcome even Lord Peterborough in such company as this!"

He laughed. "Very neat, my dear. But why, if this party is so boring, are you gracing it with your lovely presence?"

"I've no idea why Grandmama insisted on coming," she admitted. "Even she is not enjoying it, because Herbert and Marjorie are here. Thank heavens they leave for Darent Hall tomorrow. And Cecily! She's been going around as if the sky has fallen." Fixing him with a direct look, she continued, "Incidentally, if you have any interest in that matter, you could tell Lord Fanshawe to stop encouraging her to think herself up to all the rigs, because she's not. He has, and now she's annoyed because he won't let her do precisely as she wants. If he'll only tell her quite plainly he won't have it, she'll stop. She always responds to firm handling."

"Unlike her elder sister?" murmured Hazelmere provocatively.

"Precisely!" answered Dorothea.

Hazelmere had the opportunity to deliver her message to Fanshawe the next day. Thanks to Charles's continuing efforts on his behalf, he learned that Dorothea and Cecily were to attend a select picnic at the home of Lady Oswey, escorted by that pink of the ton, Ferdie Acheson-Smythe. Feeling he could safely leave Dorothea's welfare in Ferdie's capable hands for the day, he collected Fanshawe and they departed to watch a prize-fight on Clapham Common. As the sisters were going to the theatre that evening in company with Lord and Lady Eglemont, Hazelmere felt no need to attend this function either. It was the early hours of the next morning when their lordships, thoroughly pleased with their day away from the rigours of the Season and somewhat the worse for wear, returned to Cavendish Square and their beds.

Ferdie and Dorothea departed Merion House on the Monday morning, expecting to pass a pleasant day at the Osweys' house by the Thames at Twickenham. Cecily was querulous and moody, labouring under the twin goads of feeling, on the one hand, that she had treated Lord Fanshawe unfairly and, on the other, of not wishing him to order her life for her.

Observing her elder sister, she wondered why Dorothea, much more independently minded than herself, acquiesced so readily to the Marquis's suggestions. Noting the absent-minded smile that hovered on her lips as she gazed unseeingly out of the carriage window, she concluded that her sister was obviously in love with Hazelmere. She, in contrast, had clearly mistaken her heart. For surely if she was in love with Fanshawe she would be perfectly happy to allow his judgement to prevail? But he had been horridly strict and old-fashioned about her impromptu acquaintance with some of the more dashing blades present at the masquerade. The sneaking suspicion that he had been right in telling her that acquaintance with those particular gentlemen would not be to her advantage did not improve her humour. In an altogether dismal mood, she alighted from the chaise at Oswey Hall.

However, the glorious sunshine, blue skies and gentle breeze—perfect conditions for a picnic by the stream in the bluebell wood—raised even Cecily's spirits. Soon she was one of a group of chattering damsels busily comparing stories of encounters with the more eligible bachelors of the ton. Rather too old for such girlish pastimes, Dorothea settled by one of the Oswey cousins, come up to town from her home in west Hampshire to spend the Season with her relatives. Reticent and shy, Miss Delamere was grateful to the beautiful Miss Darent, who seemed happy to talk with her of country pastimes. Dorothea, who had not thought of the Grange for weeks, was quite content to make conversation on the topics that in years past had been her primary concern.

No chaperons were present other than the indolent Lady Margaret Oswey. Settled on a pile of cushions in the clearing where the picnic was held, she had no wish to bestir herself. Consequently only those gentlemen who could be trusted to keep the line even while out of her sight had

been invited. Ferdie was one of this select group. Lords
Hazelmere, Fanshawe and friends were, of course, absent.

After the repast Ferdie escorted two of the younger
misses to see the fairy dell, so named because of the mixture of bluebells, crocuses and tulips which grew there.
The dell was in the woods they had passed on their way
to the stream, and was reached by a path which branched
from the main one some little way back towards the
house. Having exclaimed to their hearts' content over the
colourful carpet lining the dell, the two young things reluctantly allowed him to lead them back towards the rest
of the company. Emerging on to the main track, one
young lady on each of his arms, they were approached by
a footman in search of Miss Darent.

"She's with her ladyship by the stream, I think," said
Ferdie. Perceiving the letter on the tray the footman was
holding, he asked, "Is that for Miss Darent?"

Assured it was and had just been delivered by a groom,
Ferdie, in benign mood, said, "Oh, I'll take it to her if
you like. Very good friend of Miss Darent."

As the footman had seen Ferdie arrive with the Darent
sisters, he saw no reason not to leave the missive in his
hands.

Ferdie needed both arms to escort the young ladies back
to the stream, so he deposited the letter in the inner pocket
of his coat. On reaching the clearing, he relinquished his
young charges but found that Dorothea had gone for a
ramble with Miss Delamere. Ferdie spent the rest of the
afternoon in a *tête-à-tête* with Cecily. As she had reached
the stage of needing someone's shoulder to cry on, he did
not have an easy time of it. However, by the end of a
lengthy discussion in which featured all the real and imag-
inary shortcomings of an unnamed peer with whom he
was well acquainted, he felt he had made some headway

in getting her to think of things from his lordship's point of view, rather than only her own.

Although he had enjoyed his day, Ferdie heaved a sigh of relief as the Merion carriage drew away from Oswey Hall late in the afternoon. After his difficult time with Cecily he completely forgot the letter for Dorothea.

The next day this missive resurfaced. Dorothea and Cecily had sent a message that they would not be riding that morning. Ferdie assumed Cecily had had a difficult time the evening before. As Lord Eglemont was convinced she would shortly be his daughter-in-law, Ferdie's imagination did not have to work overtime to understand that their visit to the theatre might have proved an ordeal.

He was consequently breakfasting in languid style when his valet, Higgins, appeared at his elbow. "I found this in your coat pocket, sir."

As it was common for him to forget letters and notes and leave them in his clothing, Ferdie thought nothing of this and opened the unaddressed letter. Reading the lines within, he frowned. He turned the single sheet over and then back and read it once more. Propping it against the salt cellar, he stared at the letter as he finished his coffee. Then he refolded it and called his valet. "Higgins, in which of my coats did you find this?"

"In the blue superfine you wore at Lady Oswey's picnic yesterday, sir."

"Ah. Thought that might be it."

Ferdie dressed rapidly and set out for Hazelmere House, fervently hoping that his cousin had not already departed for a morning about town. Luck favoured him. The Marquis was descending the steps of Hazelmere House in company with Fanshawe as he entered Cavendish Square. Out of breath, he waved at them. Staggering at seeing the impeccable Mr Acheson-Smythe in anything resembling a hurry, they halted and waited for him.

"Ferdie!" exclaimed Hazelmere. "What the devil's got into you?"

"Never seen you move so fast in my life!" said Fanshawe.

"Need a word with you, Marc. Now!" Ferdie gasped.

Hazelmere saw that his cousin was looking unaccustomedly serious. "Let's go back into the house."

They re-entered Hazelmere House and headed for the library. Hazelmere sat behind the desk. Fanshawe perched on a corner of it and both looked expectantly at Ferdie, who had dropped into a chair facing them. Still struggling to catch his breath, he drew out the letter and threw it on the desk in front of his cousin. "Read that."

Hazelmere, suddenly equally serious, complied. Then he looked at Ferdie, his face impassive. "Where did you get this?"

"Was supposed to be delivered to Dorothea at Lady Oswey's picnic. Met the footman on the way and offered to take it to her. Put it in my pocket and forgot it. Higgins found it this morning and, not knowing what it was, I opened it. Thought you'd like to see it."

"So Dorothea never got it?"

Ferdie shook his head.

Fanshawe was totally in the dark. "Will someone please tell me what is going on?" he pleaded.

Without comment Hazelmere handed him the letter. The message it contained read:

My dear Miss Darent,

I cannot imagine that the company at Lady Oswey's picnic is quite as scintillating as that to which you have become accustomed. So, why not meet me

at the white wicket gate at the end of the path
through the woods? I'll have my greys and we can
go for a drive around the lanes with no one the wiser.
Don't keep me waiting; you know I hate to keep my
horses standing. I'll expect you at two.

Hazelmere.

Like Ferdie, Fanshawe had no difficuly recognising Hazelmere's writing and signature and knew the letter in his
hand was a hoax. Eyeing his friend with an unusually
grim look, he asked simply, "Who?"

"I wish I knew," replied Hazelmere. "It's the second."

"What?" The exclamation burst from Fanshawe and
Ferdie in unison.

Laying the letter Ferdie had brought in front of him,
Hazelmere opened a drawer and took out the note Dorothea had received at the Bressingtons' masquerade. Once
they were side by side, it was clear that the same hand
had written both. Fanshawe and Ferdie came around the
desk to study them over his shoulders.

"When was the first one sent?" asked Fanshawe.

"The masquerade. That attempt would have succeeded
to admiration except I returned to London a day earlier
than expected. It was handed to Dorothea in the hall at
Bressington House. She was surprised to find me already
there. She'd believed the note. Hardly surprising, as it's
exactly the sort of thing I might be expected to do."

"You should have told me. We might have baited a
trap!" exclaimed Fanshawe.

"We did spring the trap," Hazelmere answered with a
fleeting grin. "Dorothea went out on to the terrace at midnight and I was in the shadows behind her. A voice, which
neither of us recognised, called her towards the steps
down on to the path. But then some others in the ballroom

opened another door on to the terrace and whoever it was took fright. I wasn't about to give chase and leave Dorothea alone on the terrace."

"And you saw nobody?" asked Ferdie. Hazelmere shook his head, going back to studying the second letter.

"Very likely she'd have gone to that gate if Ferdie'd remembered to give her the note," said Fanshawe.

"No. She won't be caught by that ruse again," said Hazelmere. "But what puzzles me most is who the writer of these missives could be."

"Got to be someone acquainted with you," put in Ferdie.

"Yes," agreed Hazelmere. "That's what is particularly worrisome. I'd thought it was one of those abduction plots at first."

"Shouldn't have thought the Darent girls were sufficiently rich to attract that sort of attention," said Fanshawe.

"They aren't. I am," replied the Marquis.

"Oh. Hadn't thought of that."

All three men continued to study the letters, hoping that some clue to their writer's identity could be wrung from them. Fanshawe broke the silence to ask Ferdie, "Why do you say whoever it is must know Marc?"

"Writing's not his, but the style is. Just the sort of thing he would say," replied the knowledgeable Ferdie.

"Can't know you all that well. You never drive young ladies around, let alone behind your greys," his lordship pointed out.

"With one notable exception," corrected Hazelmere. "To whit, Miss Darent."

"Oh," said Fanshawe, finally convinced.

"Precisely," continued Hazelmere. "It's someone who at least knows me well enough to write a letter in a style that could pass for mine. Someone who also knows I have driven Miss Darent behind the greys, who knows I'm very particular about keeping my horses standing and who knew I was out of town and not expected to attend the Bressington masquerade.''

"Therefore," concluded Ferdie, "one of us. Of the ton, I mean. At least as an accomplice."

"That would appear the inescapable conclusion," agreed Hazelmere. He continued to stare at the letters.

"What're we going to do?" asked Fanshawe.

"Can't call in Bow Street," said Ferdie, decisively. "Very heavy-footed. Create all sorts of rumpus. Lady Merion wouldn't like it; Dorothea wouldn't like it."

"*I* wouldn't like it either," put in Hazelmere.

"Quite so," agreed Ferdie, glad to have this point settled.

"As far as I can see, the only thing we can do is keep a very careful watch over Dorothea," said Hazelmere. "She won't be taken in with any messages, but, as we don't know who's behind this, we'll have to ensure no one who could possibly be involved is given any chance to approach her alone."

"Just us three?" Fanshawe enquired.

Hazelmere considered the question, the hazel gaze abstracted. "For the moment," he eventually replied. "We can call in reinforcements if necessary."

"What are they doing now?" asked Fanshawe.

"Resting," replied Ferdie. Seeing their surprise, he explained. "Went to the theatre last night with your parents, dear boy. Result—Cecily's exhausted."

"Ah," said Hazelmere with an understanding grin. Fanshawe frowned.

"Going riding with them this afternoon," continued

Ferdie, "then the Diplomatic Ball at Carlton House this evening. That's easy—we'll all be there."

"Well, Ferdie, m'lad," said Fanshawe as he rose to leave, "you'll just have to keep us informed of where Miss Darent means to be and then make sure at least one of us is there. Shouldn't be too hard. They can't be gallivanting all over town still, can they?"

Ferdie reflected that their lordships, normally engrossed in their own pursuits, had very little idea of just how crowded a young lady's calendar could be. He sincerely hoped they would not have to keep up their surveillance for long.

Moments later, as he descended the steps in their company, arriving on the pavement ahead of them, he gave voice to an idea that had been rolling around in his head for some time. "Actually, as far as I can see, the easiest way to solve all these problems is for you two to hurry up and marry the chits! Then Marc could spend his entire day with Dorothea, if necessary, and Cecily wouldn't be moping around, and I could go back to living a quiet life again."

Seeing that their receipt of this advice was not favourable, he hurriedly waved at them. "No? I'm off! See you tonight at the ball."

The Diplomatic Ball at Carlton House was so named because all the diplomatic corps and delegations stationed in London attended. Sponsored by the Prince Regent, attendance by all those invited was virtually obligatory. These included all the year's débutantes, the majority of the peers present in London and the élite of society. It amused the Prince to think that for one night in the Season they all danced attendance on him. While the cream of the ton considered this function supremely boring, the ne-

cessity of being present when the Prince arrived ensured
that all summoned came early.

Knowing his Prince, Hazelmere realised that, while it
was hardly likely that Dorothea would be kidnapped from
the ball, both she and Cecily could face a threat from a
different source. After discussing the possibilities, he and
Fanshawe called at Merion House when they knew the
sisters were riding with Ferdie. They found Lady Merion
at home and, having outlined the perceived problem, it
was agreed that both of them would accompany the Merion party to Carlton House, using the large Hazelmere
town carriage.

Ferdie was taken aback at finding them in attendance
when he called at Merion House that evening. A quick
word from Hazelmere brought comprehension to his eyes.
"Good heavens! Never thought of that!"

"Never thought of what, Ferdie?" asked Dorothea. She
had witnessed the exchange and, her curiosity aroused,
had come to see if she could surprise from him some
explanation for the appearance of their lordships.

Ferdie could never think quickly in such situations. He
could find no glib words to answer her. Dorothea knew
that if she waited long enough he was bound to say something helpful. She had reckoned without Hazelmere, who
calmly stepped in with a blatant lie. "Ferdie, I believe
Lady Merion has been trying to catch your eye these
minutes past."

"What? Oh, yes! Got to see your grandmama." With
this explanatory aside to Dorothea, he crossed the room
to her ladyship's side with the alacrity of a rabbit escaping
a snare.

Dorothea looked at Hazelmere in disgust. "Spoil-
sport," she said.

"It's hardly fair to try to trip Ferdie up. He's definitely

not in your class. You can attempt to get the story out of me if you like.''

''As you obviously have no intention of telling me, it would be wasted effort, I fear,'' she replied, adding, ''In such matters, I am, after all, definitely not in your class.''

''True,'' returned Hazelmere, taking the wind out of her sails. The emerald glance he received in reply spoke volumes.

With Ferdie come, there was nothing more to delay their departure and soon they were settled in the carriage and on their way. The Hazelmere town coach was a luxurious affair and easily sat the six of them, despite the voluminous ballgowns peculiar to this affair. To some extent, the Diplomatic Ball had temporarily replaced the more formal presentations of previous years. Due to the problems besetting the royal family, these had been suspended. But the tradition of all-white, waisted, full-skirted ballgowns for the débutantes, worn with white ostrich plumes in their hair, had transferred to the Prince Regent's Diplomatic Ball.

The all-white ensemble made Cecily look ethereal. Dorothea, with her dark hair and green eyes contrasting with the white, looked divine. As usual, Celestine had taken full advantage of Dorothea's age and figure and the bodice was cut low, while the waistline had been subtly altered to emphasise her tiny waist and the swell of her hips. On entering the Merion House drawing-room, Hazelmere, setting eyes on her, knew he was justified in anticipating trouble at Carlton House.

It took no more than ten minutes to drive the short distance to the Prince Regent's London residence, but, owing to the crowds, it was nearly an hour before they reached the head of the stairs and heard their names announced as they entered the ballroom. As His Highness

was convinced that he had a particular susceptibility to
colds and chills, the rooms were already overheated. Dorothea was glad she had not brought a shawl. Hazelmere,
glancing down at her as she walked by his side, uncharacteristically wished she had.

With Fanshawe escorting Cecily and Lady Merion on
Ferdie's arm, they strolled down the ballroom, stopping
to chat to acquaintances and friends. They had agreed that
the safest place for the Misses Darent to make their curtsy
to the Prince Regent was where the élite of the ton usually
congregated. Lady Jersey and the other patronesses of Almack's would be there, as would most of their lordships'
close acquaintances. In such august company, the chances
of His Highness issuing one of his unwelcome commands
was considerably reduced.

They had reached this position and were busy greeting
their friends when a general stir running through the
crowd announced the entrance of the Prince Regent. As
the now portly Prince, accompanied by two of his confi-
dants, strolled down the ballroom the assembled ranks of
gentlemen bowed and the ladies sank into the deepest of
curtsies. This movement passed like a wave down the long
room, arrested every now and again as His Highness
paused to exchange a word with one of the favoured or,
more frequently, to ogle a beautiful woman. Viewing this
behaviour as her Prince approached, Dorothea thought it
hardly appropriate for one of his years and position. In
this, the majority of those around her agreed.

As the wave of curtsying ladies reached her, and the
débutante to her left sank down, Dorothea did likewise,
bowing her head as she had been taught. She was supposed to maintain this pose until His Highness had passed.
While she waited, frozen into immobility, she realised that
his feet, the only part of him within her range of vision,

gaudily clad in bright red ballroom pumps with huge gold buckles, had stopped a short distance away. Risking an upward glance through her lashes, she discovered the Prince's protuberant pale blue eyes fixed on her. He smiled archly and came to take her hand and raise her to her feet.

As the others around her abandoned their obsequious stances she was aware of Hazelmere close behind her in the crush, a little way to her right, his hand now resting lightly at her waist. Mrs Drummond-Burrell moved slightly on her left. This movement, almost imperceptible though it was, distracted the Prince, who then became aware of those around her. She watched as the distinctly lecherous look faded, and then disappeared altogether, as His Highness's gaze met Hazelmere's over her right shoulder.

The Prince inwardly cursed. He had been informed that the most attractive débutante this year was Miss Darent, but that to suggest she might like to entertain him in private would be unwise, as she was considered by the ton to be virtually affianced to the Marquis of Hazelmere. While there were some among the peers he could ignore, Hazelmere was not one of them. But, seeing the luscious dark-haired beauty curtsying to him, he had entirely forgotten the warning until recalled to his surroundings by the censorious eyes of Mrs Drummond-Burrell and then Hazelmere's cool gaze. So, instead of what he had been going to say, he smiled in quite a different way, almost charmingly, and said, "You are really very beautiful, my dear." With a nod, he released her hand and, still smiling, moved on.

Dorothea sensed the almost palpable relief around her. As the Prince continued along the ballroom and the ranks of his subjects broke up she turned to Hazelmere and, not knowing how to phrase the question, raised her enquiring eyes to his.

"Yes, that was it," he assented, smiling as he drew her hand through his arm. "You did very well, my love."

Ignoring provocation she knew to be deliberate, she asked, "Why didn't you tell me he could be so...well, like that?"

"Because one can never tell if he will be."

"Is that why I was with you and not with Grand-mama?"

"His Highness is occasionally misguided enough to make...suggestions, which in your case would be totally inappropriate."

"I see. And he would not do so while you were about but might well have done if I had been with Grandmama only?"

Hazelmere, who would have much preferred she had not realised that, merely nodded. He knew it would not be long before she deduced the reason that his presence had protected her from the Prince's importunities. After one glance at her pensive face he headed for the area of the huge ballroom given over to dancing.

At Carlton House the social rules that applied every-where else did not hold sway. The principal ladies of the ton deplored the licence permitted under the Prince Regent's influence. Previously Hazelmere had found these lax standards very useful. Now he was concerned that Dorothea was not unknowingly led into difficulties through her innocence of just what was possible at Carlton House.

Reaching the dance-floor and hearing the musicians strike up, without a word he drew her into his arms and into the waltz. There were no dance cards at Carlton House and the waltz was the only dance permitted. She had not spoken again. Hazelmere, wishing that Carlton House had a deserted orangery, felt how stiff and distant she was as they glided down the floor. But as they progressed, in spite of herself, she relaxed into his familiar arms. He saw that they had attracted the attention of a number of gentlemen not normally present at any of the ton gatherings and determined to return her to Lady Merion immediately the dance ended. Looking down at her calm face, he realised with a jolt that he had no idea what she was thinking. She was normally so completely frank with him that it had not occurred to him that she could withdraw so entirely. Uncertain what to do for once in his life, he remained silent.

As the dance ended he raised her hand to his lips, bringing a familiar green spark to her enormous eyes. Smiling down at her, he drew her hand through his arm and led her to find Lady Merion. Relinquishing her to her grandmother with real regret, he was relieved to see Alvanley claim her for the next dance. To be overly attentive would only exacerbate her mood, so he resigned himself to not dancing with her again and drifted off in search of his friends.

Dorothea was in a state of utter confusion, which having to make a pretence of polite conversation did nothing to help. As the weeks of the Season had passed she had come to accept that she and Hazelmere would, in time, perhaps later in the Season, come to an understanding—a mutually agreed understanding. But now it appeared she was to have no say in the matter at all! Everyone already knew she would marry Hazelmere. Even the Prince Regent knew!

The sensation of being an entirely helpless puppet with Hazelmere pulling the strings fuelled her anger. While she had been falling desperately in love with him, worrying over whether or not he loved her, he had somehow convinced the world that she was his. How *dared* he take her so much for granted?

She fumed inwardly, her temper simmering, denied the natural outlet of confronting him in person. She spent three waltzes entirely consumed with plotting what she would say to him on the morrow. He would be made to realise that she was no milk-and-water miss to be manipulated to suit his convenience!

Dancing with one after another of his friends, all of whom, she now realised, treated her as they would a friend's wife, did nothing to improve her temper. None of her partners guessed her true state; her composure was complete, her serenity convincing. It was, therefore, with an air of dangerous resklessness that she viewed the debonair Frenchman bowing before her and begging the pleasure of the next waltz. She had just been returned to her grandmama by Lord Desborough, who had moved away into the still considerable crowd.

With Lady Merion's consent she allowed the Comte de Vanée to lead her on to the floor. He had, so he informed her, only recently arrived from Paris. As he expertly guided her through the other dancers the Comte kept up a flow of general conversation, to which Dorothea paid little heed. Until she heard him mention Hazelmere's name.

Without hesitation she broke into his discourse. "I'm so sorry, Comte, I'm afraid I didn't catch what you just said."

"Ah, *mademoiselle,* I was only saying it is so like the Marquis to secure the most beautiful women as his mistresses—the lovely Lady Walford, for instance, whom you can see over there, talking with his lordship."

Dorothea glanced where he indicated and glimpsed Hazelmere deep in conversation with Lady Walford, his dark head bent close to her fair one, listening intently. Even to her inexperienced eye, the pose argued a degree of familiarity. Feeling her heart literally descend to her slippers, she required every ounce of her well-practised poise to meet the Comte's eyes with her habitual calm. But that young man had felt her stiffen when she had seen Hazelmere and Lady Walford and was more than satisfied with his success. Too wise to belabour the point, he continued in his light-hearted recitation of ton affairs.

Unknown to the Comte, his words plunged Dorothea even deeper into misery than he could have hoped. If she was confused before, she was now utterly wretched. The sole vision in her tormented mind was of Hazelmere in intimate converse with Lady Walford. All the rest seemed to sink beneath a miasma of pain.

On the previous Sunday, before her departure for Darent Hall, Marjorie Darent had sought a private interview with Dorothea, in order, as she saw it, to do her duty. "As Herbert is your guardian and I am his wife," she had carefully begun, "I feel it is my duty to tell you it's common knowledge that Lord Hazelmere is trifling with your affections. I've been told he has acted in exactly this manner with many other susceptible young ladies. I regret to say, your resistance to his charm is most likely the attraction that draws him to your side. Neither Herbert nor I would wish to criticise your grandmama, but we are deeply pained to see you in the toils of such a man."

Dorothea had listened with a patience born of her certainty that none of it was true. Marjorie had no idea how Hazelmere behaved towards her. And there was no chance that Lady Merion would blindly permit his attentions were these other than honourable.

Marjorie had gone on to enumerate his lordship's many

failings—gambling, racing, addiction to boxing and other low forms of sport, finally coming to the point of her visit. "It is my distressing duty to speak plainly to you, my dear. Lady Merion likely feels such subjects should not sully the ears of innocent maids, but, in the circumstances, it is right you should know. Forewarned, after all, is forearmed!"

Dorothea's lively imagination had run riot at this juncture. She was agog to learn what secret life Marjorie had invented for his lordship. The explanation, when it had come, was so mundane that she had almost giggled.

"My dear, the man is a rake! A very highly born rake, I'll agree. But a rake none the less! Why, the stories I've heard of his mistresses, many of them as well born as you or I, and all of them the most ravishing creatures. As you are yourself, my dear."

The insinuation that Marjorie had managed to infuse into this last statement had nearly overset Dorothea. The idea of Hazelmere offering her a *carte blanche* was so ridiculous that she had had to take a deep breath to stop herself from laughing aloud and ruining her pose of polite attention. As it was, Marjorie had taken the indrawn breath to signify shock at his lordship's perfidy.

Her cousin had concluded by stating that neither Herbert nor she would countenance any further communication with the Marquis. Dorothea had managed to keep her temper by reminding herself it was her grandmother, not Marjorie, who had charge of her in London.

After Marjorie had left Dorothea had put her warnings entirely from her mind as the ludicrous imaginings she had been sure they were. But now that it seemed as if one, at least, of her cousin's facts was not wrong she was forced to question whether she really knew Hazelmere at all.

She had assumed there had been many women in his past—he could hardly have attained his undoubted experience of her sex without practice. But she had imagined these women were of the *demi-monde* and, furthermore, definitely in his past and not cluttering up his present life. Lady Walford, however, belonged to the ton, and she was obviously part of Hazelmere's present.

Dorothea heard not a single word of the rest of the Comte's conversation. Just before the dance ended she noticed Cecily dancing with Fanshawe. From her sparkling eyes, Dorothea concluded that they had made up their differences. Fanshawe, catching a glimpse of her through the throng, looked surprised, but they were immediately separated by the movement of the dance, so Dorothea failed to see what had excited his attention. At the end of the dance the Comte punctiliously delivered her to her grandmother and immediately took his leave of them, disappearing into the crowds. His departure was rapid because he, too, had seen Fanshawe's surprised look and, unlike Dorothea, knew the cause.

As the Comte could have predicted, it was not many minutes before Hazelmere materialised at her elbow. Immediately noticing her drawn face, he forebore to ask what the matter was, instead suggesting to Lady Merion that they could with impunity leave the ball, as the Prince had retired. Her ladyship, disliking the tone of the entertainment, readily agreed. As Fanshawe and Cecily reappeared at that moment, it only remained to find Ferdie before they could leave. This was easily accomplished, and the party departed Carlton House.

Seated opposite Dorothea in the carriage, Hazelmere desperately sought for a clue to what had so agitated her. Tony had told him that she had danced with one of the French diplomatic staff, a man of questionable standing.

But it seemed unlikely that anything he could have said would have so overset her. He sensed that under her outward calm she was close to tears, but he had no idea why. Knowing he would get no chance to ask her directly, and so could not comfort her, only added to his frustration.

The carriage drew up outside Merion House and the ladies were escorted within. Ferdie left on foot and, sending the carriage on, Hazelmere and Fanshawe walked across the square. For more than half the distance Fanshawe kept up a rapturous monologue on the delights of love. He had made good use of Dorothea's advice, borrowing some of Hazelmere's arrogance to lend it weight, and it had been most successful.

Realising that Hazelmere was not responding and catching sight of his friend's serious face, Fanshawe exclaimed, "Don't tell me you two have fallen out?"

Hazelmere grinned at the tone. "To be perfectly truthful, I don't know whether we have or not."

"Great heavens! You're worse than us!"

"Unfortunately true."

"Well," continued Fanshawe, "why don't you just use Dorothea's advice on herself?"

"I have been reliably informed that firm handling will not work with the elder Miss Darent," replied Hazelmere with the ghost of a smile.

"Which means very likely it will," rejoined Fanshawe, still in exuberant vein.

"As a matter of fact, you speak more truly than you know," returned Hazelmere as they parted on the steps of Hazelmere House.

Not as observant as Hazelmere, neither Lady Merion nor Cecily noticed the strained look in Dorothea's eyes. Her ladyship retired to bed with a headache, and Cecily was so bubbling over with her own happiness that for once her sister's pallor escaped her sharp eyes. To Dorothea's relief, she was able to retire to her bed without having to answer any difficult questions.

She lay staring at the window for what felt like hours. Her heart would not accept what her mind knew to be fact. While Hazelmere had been dancing attendance on her, making her lose her heart with his easy address and gentle caresses and those *wicked* hazel eyes, he had been simultaneously enjoying a far more illicit relationship with the beautiful Lady Walford. And what was more, she thought, wallowing in misery, that meant he was not in love with her at all.

It had taken her a long time to sort it out, but now, at last, she had it clear: Hazelmere had to marry, so he had decided she would do. Not the icily uncomfortable Miss Buntton, but a naïve country miss, not at home in the ton, someone who would be a sweet, conformable, entirely acceptable and totally manipulable wife, providing him with heirs and presiding over his household while he continued as he always had, enjoying the more exotic delights provided by the likes of Lady Walford. And, most likely, her apparent indifference was the lure that had drawn his eye. She was a challenge and a convenient conquest, all rolled into one.

For the first time since she had come to London she thought longingly of the Grange, where life had been so much simpler. No having to deal with imperious peers with beautiful mistresses who made one fall in love with them for entirely selfish reasons. It was close to dawn before she finally drifted into troubled sleep.

On entering his house, Hazelmere went into the library and, pouring himself a large brandy, settled down to stare into the dying fire.

When he had decided to wait until later in the Season before asking for Dorothea's hand he had not envisaged the current tangle of their affairs. He still had no clue what had gone wrong tonight and had no right to ask for an explanation. And, while previously she might have given him one, tonight she had realised how public he had made their relationship. She had not been pleased. God only knew what she would say if she learned that an announcement of their marriage was considered imminent! He grinned as he imagined her fury. Still, he could not regret his manipulation. After his behaviour in Moreton Park woods and at that blasted inn she would never have believed he was meek and malleable. If he had let her have her head in the matter of choosing her own husband she would undoubtedly have landed herself with some boring slowtop, too dimwitted to exercise any control over her. And she certainly needed someone to control her, to watch over her, to care for and cherish her—he shuddered to think what trouble she would have landed herself in had he not been there, time and again, to rescue her. Half the time she had not even recognised danger when she saw it. Such as in him.

That still surprised him. She certainly recognised the danger in Peterborough and Walsingham. But never, from that first moment in Moreton Park woods when he'd held her and kissed her as she'd never been kissed before, had she shown the slightest consciousness of danger in his company. Another one of her odd quirks, but one for which he was profoundly thankful.

He suspected that her dislike of his authoritarian ways stemmed from her habit of getting her own way in most things and of being able to manipulate people like Cecily,

Lady Merion and Ferdie into doing much as she wished. Her refusal to attempt to wring from him the explanation for his presence at Merion House earlier in the evening suggested that she recognised the futility in cajoling or trying to manipulate him. Which was just as well. He had no intention of ever allowing her to do so. Still, he thought, a smile hovering at the corners of his mouth, he had no objection to her trying.

With a sigh he doggedly drew his mind back to his present problems. She had withdrawn from him and while, in normal circumstances, he would not have doubted his ability to bring her around, there were too many unexplained incidents occurring for him to feel easy. He glanced towards his desk, where the two mysterious notes lay in a drawer. There was someone else playing this hand and as yet he did not know who it was.

There was only one possible course of action. His steward on his Leicestershire estate was begging for his attendance. In travelling there, he would pass through Northamptonshire, not far from Darent Hall. Rapidly reviewing his engagements, he remembered a luncheon on the morrow. Very well, he would leave later in the day for Leicestershire and call in on horrible Herbert on the way back. Then, he supposed, he really should tell his mother, which meant an evening spent at Hazelmere. Seven days in all. He would be back in London by Tuesday next.

He did not like to leave her, but as he had no idea if any further attempt on her would be made, it would be wiser to solve the potential problem by marrying her as soon as possible. Abducting the Marchioness of Hazelmere would be a far more difficult task than abducting Miss Darent. In fact, he would make sure it was entirely impossible. He tossed off the last of the brandy and went to bed.

Comfortably settled between his silken sheets, he listened to Murgatroyd's footsteps die away down the hall. Their interlude in the Richmond House orangery had left no room for doubt of her feelings for him. And in her subsequent actions she had, albeit unwittingly, confirmed his hopes. She loved him. Beneath his frustration, that knowledge ran like a heady pulse, a constant source of joy and wonder. And from it had been born the patience to see the game through, to let her have her Season of independence before he claimed her. Aside from any other consideration, he had enjoyed her spirited resistance, her attempts, becoming less and less successful with time, to conceal her response to him. He sighed. For good or ill, her time had run out. Tuesday next would see the end of the game. And the start of so much more.

He stretched, conscious of the tenseness lying just beneath the surface. He should never have kissed her. Now every time he saw her he was shaken by an urgent desire to do it again. And every time he gave way to the impulse he was increasingly aware of an even more urgent desire to take her to bed. The warmth of her hair, her smooth skin, the sweetness of her lips and, more than anything else, those tantalising green eyes had all become so strongly evocative that, for the first time in his considerable experience, his desire was no longer subject to his control. Aside from anything else, marrying her soon would end the torture. He slid himself into a more comfortable position and, thinking of emerald eyes, lost touch with reality.

Chapter Eleven

Next morning Lady Merion remained in bed, unwell after the stuffy atmosphere of Carlton House. Dorothea, unrefreshed by her troubled sleep, went to enquire after her health. Her ladyship immediately noticed the dark rings under her granddaughter's large eyes and insisted she remain in bed for the rest of the morning. Sure that if she rode in the Park this morning she would meet Hazelmere, and feeling that normal conversation with him was as yet beyond her, Dorothea agreed.

Cecily was undisturbed by the change in plans, as she had arranged to go driving with Fanshawe that afternoon. She wrote to Ferdie to cancel their morning engagement and, at Dorothea's suggestion, asked him to escort her sister for a ride that afternoon.

When the afternoon came Ferdie and Dorothea duly set off for the Park. Ferdie, not generally observant, noticed that Dorothea was not her normal self. Thinking to distract her, he rattled on about the Carlton House ball and the Prince Regent's set, and anything else that came into his head. Understanding his benign impulse, Dorothea tried to put on a happier face and to ignore the fact that he,

too, seemed to consider her virtually betrothed to Hazelmere.

They had entered the Park and were ambling along the
grass verge of the carriageway when, glancing ahead, she
suddenly stopped. Breathlessly she cut into Ferdie's description of Lady Hanover's new wig. "Ferdie, I want to
gallop over to those trees. I think there are freesias growing there."

Precipitately she set the bay mare cantering towards a
stand of oak to their left. Ferdie, taken by surprise, turned
his own horse to follow. As he did so his gaze alighted
on an approaching carriage. It was Hazelmere's curricle,
the Marquis driving his greys with Helen Walford beside
him. The brief glimpse of his cousin's face before his
horse moved off was quite sufficient to tell Ferdie that
Hazelmere had seen Dorothea's sudden departure. The ap-
palling fact that Dorothea had knowingly cut his cousin
in the middle of the Park dawned on a horrified Ferdie.

"What on *earth* do you think you're doing?" he demanded as he came up with her by the trees. "That was
Hazelmere!"

"Yes, I know, Ferdie," replied Dorothea, contrite as
she realised that he was really distressed.

"Well, I'll be hanged if I know what you're up to,"
he continued, "but I can tell you that cutting people like
Hazelmere in the middle of the Park is not the thing at
all!"

"Yes, Ferdie. I'd like to go home now, please."

"I should dashed well think so!" he exclaimed, knowing that Hazelmere would shortly be following them.

On the way back to Cavendish Square Ferdie tried to
impress upon Dorothea the magnitude of her sin. Not
knowing what had caused her to behave in such an extraordinary way, he felt that if he could induce her to

behave with something like contrition when she shortly faced his cousin she might stand a better chance of surviving the ordeal. Ferdie knew, as few others did, that, while Hazelmere appeared to have the easiest of tempers, this was a fiction. The Marquis of Hazelmere had a very definite temper; he just did not lose it often.

Ferdie did not know that Dorothea was already acquainted with Hazelmere's temper. Seeing him driving his greys with the lovely Lady Walford by his side, she simply could not bear to stay and politely exchange pleasantries with them. Although she knew she had behaved badly and Hazelmere had every right to be angry, she, too, was decidedly aggrieved and was almost looking forward to an interview with his lordship. Luckily Ferdie had no idea of her thoughts—that anyone could look forward to an interview with Hazelmere in a rage was far too bizarre a concept for him to have understood.

Reaching Merion House, Ferdie escorted her indoors, past the interested Mellow and into the drawing-room. There he got a glimmer of the underlying story. Dorothea, pacing about the room like a caged tigress, seemed to the distracted Ferdie to be more incensed than contrite.

"How *dare* he approach me while driving that woman?" she finally burst out.

Ferdie stared. "What's wrong with driving Helen Walford?" he asked, fearing that her reason must be slipping.

"But surely you know? She's his mistress!"

"What?" Ferdie positively goggled. "No! You've got that wrong! Very sure she's not Marc's mistress."

Remembering his connection with Hazelmere, Dorothea paid no attention to him, convinced that he would take his cousin's side in any argument.

An imperious knock fell on the street door. Ferdie,

glancing out of the window, saw Hazelmere's curricle standing outside.

Seeing Dorothea pointedly move away from the carriageway, Hazelmere was thunderstruck. What the *devil* was she about, behaving like that to him? Too well attuned to his whereabouts to allow his entirely understandable rage to be evident, it was nevertheless some minutes before he could trust his voice to ask Helen Walford, "My dear Helen, do you mind if I return you to your friends? I'm departing for Leicestershire shortly and I believe I've some unfinished business to attend to."

Lady Walford was well acquainted with Hazelmere's temper, as she had often, in her childhood, been the cause of it. Looking into the hazel eyes, normally warm and amused, and finding them as cold and cloudy as agate, she merely smiled her agreement. She hoped Miss Darent had more backbone than the normal run of débutantes, for she was undoubtedly in for a most uncomfortable interview. The fact that Hazelmere was head over heels in love with her would not, as might be supposed, help her at all. Like all the Henrys, he possessed an unexpected puritanical streak which would lead him to demand of his wife-to-be a far higher standard of conduct than he might tolerate in less favoured ladies. Consequently she feared that his Dorothea was in for a particularly torrid time.

Having set Lady Walford down amid her friends, Hazelmere drove immediately to Merion House. Arriving there, without a word he threw the reins of his curricle to a bright-faced urchin and strode up the steps to the door.

Admitted to the house by an intrigued Mellow, he merely asked, in a deceptively gentle voice, "Where is Miss Darent, Mellow?"

"In the drawing-room, my lord."

"Thank you. You need not announce me."

He strolled across the hall and opened the drawing-room door. Setting eyes on Ferdie, he smiled in a way that made Ferdie decide to do whatever he wished. Holding the door open, Hazelmere said, "I believe you were leaving, Ferdie."

There was no doubt about the command, but Ferdie, recognising the hardness in the hazel eyes, was having second thoughts about the wisdom of leaving these two together. But as he glanced at Dorothea his decision was unexpectedly taken out of his hands. "Goodbye, Ferdie," she said.

So Ferdie went. He discarded the idea of telling his cousin that Dorothea seemed to think Helen Walford was his mistress. In his opinion, if anyone was going to talk to Hazelmere about his mistresses it had better be Dorothea herself. Hearing the drawing-room door shut with a click behind him, he decided it might be wise to inform Lady Merion of the reason for, and the likely outcome of, the interview being presently conducted in her drawing-room.

Returning to the hall some five minutes later, having explained the situation as fully as he could to Lady Merion upstairs, he found the drawing-room door still shut. Viewing this with misgiving, he departed for his lodgings.

After shutting the door behind Ferdie, Hazelmere moved into the room. "Very wise of you, my dear. There's no need for Ferdie to get caught up in this."

He paused to strip off his driving gloves and cast them on a side-table. One glance at Dorothea, standing beside one of the wing chairs by the fireplace, her hand clutching its back, informed him that she was every bit as angry as he was. He had no idea why, but the knowledge served to make him rein in his temper sufficiently to ask, in a relatively calm voice, "Do you think you could possibly explain to me why you cut me in the Park?"

Despite the calmness, the undertones succeeded in igniting her smouldering temper. "How *dare* you approach me while driving that woman?"

Looking into her furious green eyes, Hazelmere felt, like Ferdie before him, that he had lost the thread of the conversation. "Helen?" he asked, mystified.

"Your mistress!" she replied scathingly.

"My what?" The words came like a whiplash, and Dorothea winced. Even angrier than before, Hazelmere moved to within a few feet of her, everything about him radiating barely leashed fury. Eyes narrowed, he asked, his voice deceptively soft, "Who told you Helen Walford was my mistress?"

"I don't think that need concern you—"

"You mistake," he broke in. "It concerns me because Helen Walford has never been, is not and never will be my mistress. So who, my credulous Miss Darent, told you she was?"

Looking into the stormy hazel eyes, Dorothea knew she was hearing the truth. "The Comte de Vanée," she finally replied.

"A man of little importance," he said dismissively. "It may interest you to know that I have known Helen Walford since she was three. However," he continued, moving forward so that he was standing directly beside her, forcing her to turn from the chair that up until then had been between them, "that aside, you have still not explained why, regardless of what you might have thought, you presumed to censure me in such a public manner."

Although his voice was low and even, Dorothea could not miss the suppressed anger. She knew she had been in the wrong, but his next words banished any notion of apologising.

"I've told you provincial manners will not do in London," he continued. But there he stopped, for she rounded on him with such naked rage in her eyes that he was taken aback.

"How *dare* you speak to me of manners? Explain yours, if you can! I know you've been dancing attendance on me purely to see if you could make me fall in love with you, just because I didn't succumb to your legendary charm. Oh, Cousin Marjorie explained it all, so—"

That was as far as she got. Hazelmere paled as her words struck him. But as he caught the gist of her argument the already frayed rein he had kept on his passions snapped. In one swift, practised movement he swept her into his arms and his lips came down on hers in a kiss almost brutal in its intensity. Panicked, she struggled, but, as before, his fingers entwined in her hair, holding her head still, while the arm around her tightened, locking her in his embrace. And then, in the space of time between one heartbeat and the next, the tenor of the kiss changed to one of unbelievable sweetness. Her interest caught, her lips parted in response to his subtle command and she found herself floating in a sea of sensation. Dazed, she felt desire flooding through her, growing stronger with every second, rapidly building to a force she, in her inexperience, had no hope of restraining. She realised that she was responding in the most shameless way to his ardent kisses. She no longer cared. The only thought in her disjointed mind was the hope that he wouldn't stop.

His lips left hers to brush kisses on her upturned face, on her forehead, her eyelids, her chin and her delectable white throat. Recapturing her reddened lips, he gently explored the sweet softness within. She moaned, the sound an audible caress, her arms slipping around his neck, her fingers twisting in his dark hair as she held him to her. Inwardly smiling, he allowed the kiss to deepen, fanning the racing flames of her desire until they coalesced into a conflagration that threatened to consume them both. Then, reaching to the depths of a passionate nature that in every way matched his own, he demanded, and received, a surrender so complete and unequivocal that he knew beyond doubt she would be his, body and soul, whenever he so desired. Entirely satisfied, he drew her closer, moulding her body to his, allowing her to feel the extent of his desire for her.

Dorothea was nearly mindless. Some tiny part of her consciousness was detached enough to be shocked and horrified, dismayed as his experienced hands roamed over her, his practised caresses sending ripples of desire from the top of her head to her toes. The rest of her was in no mood to listen. She supposed he would have to stop some time—but oh, she would enjoy this while it lasted! Still, surely not even Hazelmere would seduce her in her grandmother's drawing-room? Would he?

The tremor that ran through her jolted him to his senses. He would have to leave her, and soon, if he was to leave her at all. And, as they were in Merion House and not one of his establishments, leave her he must. If he looked into her eyes he would not be able to go. And at the moment he was in no mood to talk to her. He needed time away from her to sort out what had happened—right now he wasn't sure of anything other than his physical need for her. And that required no words to describe. He knew they had passed the point of easy withdrawal; there was no gentle way to stop now. So, abruptly bringing the kiss to an end, he released her and, disentangling her hands from his hair, put her from him almost roughly, before, turning brusquely, he walked straight to the door, picking up his gloves on the way, and, opening the door, left the room.

In the hall he encountered Mellow. As his face had assumed its normal mien and his hair was cut in a style that disguised Dorothea's rumpling, Mellow assumed that there had been no major fireworks. He hurried to open the door for his lordship.

Leaving the house, Hazelmere headed across the square to his own mansion. While an observer unfamiliar with him would have detected nothing amiss, he was experiencing a degree of mental turmoil that effectively prevented him from thinking clearly. Anger, frustration, hurt pride and a peculiar sense of elation were only some of the emotions running riot in his mind. He would have to leave, get out of London, before his fevered brain would cool sufficiently to accurately assess just where they now stood. Entering Hazelmere House and seeing Mytton come forward from behind the green baize door, he paused at the foot of the stairs. "I've decided to leave for Leicestershire immediately. I expect to return on Tuesday next. Send Murgatroyd up to me and tell Jim to put the bays to and have the curricle at the front door in ten minutes."

"Yes, m'lord," replied Mytton, who, acquainted with the Marquis since that gentleman's childhood, returned immediately to the servants' hall to inform the household of his lordship's orders, adding that their master was in the devil's own temper. Without further discussion they all sped to their tasks, Murgatroyd almost running up the stairs.

Standing before the mirror to remove the diamond pin in his cravat, Hazelmere suddenly turned to his valet, hurriedly packing. "Murgatroyd, see if you can catch Jim before he leaves the house. Tell him I've left the curricle outside Merion House. If he's already left for the mews you'd better send one of the footmen after him and come back to me.''

After one stunned moment Murgatroyd was out of the door and down the stairs as fast as dignity would allow. Hazelmere ruefully surveyed his own reflection. If his servants had not already realised the cause of his present mood, the fact that he had walked away and left his greys outside Merion House would doubtless clarify the issue.

Murgatroyd reached the servants' hall just as Jim, attired in the Hazelmere livery, was preparing to leave. Hearing his message, the entire population of the servants' hall simply stared. Then all those with any legitimate claim to be in the front of the house headed for the street door. Opening it and looking across the square to Merion House, Mytton, Jim, Murgatroyd and Charles gazed in silent awe at the curricle.

''My gawd! I'd never've believed it if I hadn't seen it for myself,'' said Jim.

With much shaking of heads, they all resumed their activities, Jim crossing the square to retrieve the precious greys and Murgatroyd hurrying upstairs to inform his lordship that the carriage was being prepared.

In the end, Jim had to walk the bays for five minutes before his master appeared. On his way downstairs Hazelmere recalled the one player in the game who did not know where he was going but should. He went into the library. His eye alighted on a pile of correspondence, delivered that afternoon. He flicked through the envelopes, leaving most unopened. His attention was caught by a plain envelope of poor quality, addressed in a strong hand to ''Mr M. Henry'. Opening it, he scanned the enclosed pages. When his eyes lifted he remained standing, gazing at nothing, his long fingers beating a thoughtful tattoo on the desk-top. Then, with a frown, he crammed the letter into his coat pocket and sat to compose a suitably informative note to Ferdie. This was not easy. He still could not concentrate properly, particularly when reviewing that interview at Merion House. Finally he wrote a simple set of statements, informing Ferdie that he had to leave for Leicestershire on estate business and would be back in London on Tuesday next, that Tony knew this, that he and Tony had informed their close friends of the attempts on Dorothea over lunch that day and they would assist in keeping an eye on her. He ended with a simple request to Ferdie to look after Dorothea for him.

Signing this epistle, he bethought himself of one last item. Raising his pen, he added a postscript. He would much prefer if Ferdie could manage not to tell Dorothea of their fears for her safety. Smiling ruefully, he fixed his seal to the letter and rang for a footman. He did not have much confidence in Ferdie's ability to distract Dorothea once she became suspicious, as she undoubtedly would long before he returned. Handing the letter over with instructions that it be delivered to Mr Acheson-Smythe's lodgings immediately, he strode out of his house to the waiting curricle.

Released from that passionate embrace, Dorothea stood by the chair, too stunned to move. Hearing the front door shut, she put her fingers to her bruised lips. Her eyes slowly refocused. Then, drawing a shuddering breath, she went to the door, opened it and, without even noticing Mellow, went up the stairs to her chamber.

Lady Merion, hearing her footsteps, came out of the morning-room. Five minutes after Ferdie had left her she had come downstairs. There was, she had felt, a limit to how long she could leave Dorothea alone with Hazelmere. All had been silent in the drawing-room. Taking a deep breath and waving Mellow away, she had opened the door. Seeing Dorothea locked in Hazelmere's arms, she had immediately closed it again. With a decidedly pensive expression, she had informed Mellow that she would sit in the morning-room and if anyone should call he was to show them in there. Now, glimpsing the retreating figure at the top of the stairs, she sighed. With a resigned air she rang for tea.

Despite her ignorance of the details of the recently conducted interview, she thought Dorothea would need at least half an hour to cry herself out. Far too wise to try to talk sense to a young lady in the first flush of tears, she calmly reviewed what she knew of the afternoon's events. None of it made a great deal of sense. She would have to extract sufficient details before she could begin to understand what it was about; she was too old to leap to conclusions.

Finishing her tea, she went purposefully upstairs.

Reaching her bedchamber, Dorothea shut the door, threw herself on her bed and gave way to her tears. For the first time in years she wept unrestrainedly, a mixture of relief, bewilderment and pent-up emotions pouring from her, disappointment and a barely recognised frustration lending their bitter flavour to her woe. For ten minutes the storm continued unabated. Finally, through exhaustion, the whirling kaleidoscope that was her mind slowed down and the racking sobs died. She was propped up against her pillows, dabbing ineffectually at her brimming eyes with a sodden handkerchief, when her grandmother knocked and entered.

Seeing her normally calm and collected granddaughter

in the shadows of the bed, her large eyes enormous and swimming in unshed tears, Hermione walked over and plumped herself down on the end of the bed. Dorothea gulped and whispered, "Oh, Grandmama, what am I to do?"

Recognising her cue, Lady Merion responded briskly. "The first thing you'll do, my dear, is to wash your face and get yourself a fresh handkerchief. Go on, now. You'll feel a great deal better." As Dorothea rose she continued, "And after that I think we'll have a long talk. It's time you explained to me just what you and Hazelmere have been about."

At that, Dorothea's green eyes returned to her grandmother's face, but she made no comment. While she washed and dried her face, and then ransacked her dressing-table for a clean handkerchief, the capacity for rational thought returned. Her grandmother undoubtedly deserved an explanation. But there were so many questions still unanswered. Pensive, she returned to her seat on the bed.

Lady Merion opened the conversation with a simple request to be told all about it.

Dorothea grimaced, then drew a deep breath and plunged in. "Last night, at the ball, the Prince...well, it was obvious he believed...knew, that...there is...a...connection between myself and Lord Hazelmere. I realise, now, that most people know that some sort of...understanding exists between us."

"After that first waltz at your come-out, I should think they would!" snorted Lady Merion.

"Waltz?" echoed Dorothea in confusion. "What do you mean?"

Lady Merion sighed. "I didn't think you knew." She eyed her granddaughter shrewdly, then said, "Over the past weeks your feelings for Marc Henry have been be-

coming daily more visible. Oh, I don't mean you wear
your heart on your sleeve! Far from it. But no one, seeing
the two of you together, could doubt your interest in him.
And, given his attentiveness since the start of the Season,
his intentions have been quite clear. Why, after your ball,
he told me he would offer for you. In his own good time,
he said. Just like him, of course.''

Dorothea listened to her grandmother's explanation,
comprehension dawning. It occurred to her that she could
do a great deal worse than to appeal to her experienced
grandparent for further clarification. ''Actually,'' she said,
''I wondered whether he was…well, merely looking for
a suitable bride. He must marry. I gather his family have
been badgering him for years to do so.'' Resolutely she
drew a deep breath and brought forth her most secret fear.
''When he met me in Moreton Park woods I think he got
the idea from something I said that I had no expectations
of marrying. And when I didn't behave like all the others
I thought maybe he felt I would do.'' She paused, gathering strength to continue. ''I wondered if he thought that,
as I didn't have any great hopes of marriage, I'd be happy
to enter into…I suppose the correct phrase is 'a marriage
of convenience', which would leave him free to continue
with his mistresses as before.''

Lady Merion's face went blank. Then she threw back
her head and laughed. When she could command her
voice she said, ''Well! I'm glad Hazelmere's carefully
orchestrated wooing has got the result it deserved.''

Bemused, Dorothea looked at her expectantly, but her
grandmother waved aside the unspoken question. ''My
dear Dorothea, I came into the drawing-room this afternoon while you and Hazelmere were…somewhat engaged. In my experience, a man contemplating a *mariage
de convenance* does not set out to seduce his prospective

bride before proposing.'' A grin of unholy amusement still lit her ladyship's sharp face. ''After the way Hazelmere's been behaving over you, my dear, I should think you must be the last person in the ton to realise he's in love with you.''

''Oh.'' Hope and a sneaking suspicion that it was all too good to be true warred in Dorothea's breast. Hope won, but the suspicion was not entirely vanquished.

Lady Merion broke in on her thoughts. ''Ferdie mentioned some misunderstanding over Helen Walford.''

''The Comte de Vanée told me she was Hazelmere's mistress. He denied it.''

Lady Merion almost groaned aloud. She closed her eyes. Finally opening them, she asked, her tone resigned, ''You asked him, I suppose?''

''Well, he wanted to know why I cut him in the Park,'' said Dorothea, rapidly regaining her normal equilibrium. ''He said he'd known her since she was a child.''

''So he has. Helen Walford's father is a distant connection of Lady Hazelmere and, as a child, Helen often spent her summers at Hazelmere. In age she is some years younger than Ferdie. She was something of a tomboy, and she often plagued Marc and Tony, who treated her much as they treated Alison. As I recall, they were always hauling her out of some scrape or other, and with no very good grace, I can tell you!

''Helen unfortunately made a most unsuitable marriage. Arthur Walford was a rake and a gamester. He killed himself, much to the relief of everyone. No one knows the full story, but Hazelmere was involved. Helen once asked him how her husband died. He told her she didn't need to know but should content herself with the fact.''

''That certainly sounds very like him,'' said Dorothea,

sniffing. Clearly Hazelmere's habit of managing things was a long-standing and deeply ingrained characteristic.

"Anyway, Hazelmere has always treated Helen exactly as he does Alison. I assume he was astonished that you thought she was his mistress?"

Recalling his face at the time, Dorothea nodded. "But why did the Comte de Vanée tell me she was?"

"My dear, I'm afraid you'll have to get used to the malicious tongues of certain people you meet. There are more than a few who'd like to cause trouble for Hazelmere and will seek to use you to do it." Her ladyship paused, eyeing her granddaughter's elegant profile. "Incidentally, I would not, if I were you, ever bring up the subject of Hazelmere's mistresses. I grant you, he has had a few. Well," she amended, realising the inadequacy of this description, "more than a few. A positive parade, in fact, and all of them the most gorgeous of creatures! But, my dear, Hazelmere's mistresses are very definitely *not* your concern, and if he follows in his father's footsteps they'll be confined to his past. It's highly unlikely, given how much in love with you he is, that you'll find yourself having to turn a blind eye to such liaisons in the future, unlike so many other ladies."

Dorothea inclined her head in acknowledgement of this excellent advice.

Lady Merion, watching her, saw tiredness creep over the pale face. She leaned forward and patted Dorothea's hand reassuringly. "My dear, you're worn out. I'll have a tray sent up, and you really should have an early night. We'll have to consider how best to go on but I think we should leave further discussion until tomorrow."

Dorothea, feeling strangely wrung out and curiously elated at the same time, nodded her acquiescence and kissed her grandmother's cheek before Lady Merion, suddenly feeling her age, left the room.

When Trimmer brought her dinner tray to her, Dorothea, contrary to her expectations, was feeling quite hungry. Nibbling the delicate chicken, she pondered her state. None of what had happened should have been a shock. But the fact remained that things had changed. Somehow, hand in hand with the Marquis of Hazelmere, she had stepped from the safe shores of fashionable dalliance into a realm where forces stronger than any she had ever known seemed set to steal her very soul. Thinking of how she had felt in his arms that afternoon, she shivered. He would never let her forget how much she wanted him. He had certainly won that bet. Some part of her rational mind suggested, faintly, that she should be incensed over his subtle machinations which would so easily have overridden any objections from her. But the truth was... The truth was that she had no objections. None at all.

Absent-mindedly she picked up the bowl of Witchett's special tisane. Sipping it, she relaxed in her chair, the warmth of the fire welcome as night fell. Thinking back, she could not recall a single incident where he had seriously professed any devotion. That had been one of the factors that had drawn her to him. Beside all the others and their protestations of undying love, his calm authority had been a welcome relief. Instead, if she had been able to think clearly where he was concerned, she would have seen the true meaning behind that peculiar warmth which shone in his hazel eyes, the care he had continually shown her, even, as she had discovered the morning after, to the extent of hiring a bodyguard to watch the stairs during the night at that inn. It was not hard to believe her grandmother's view. But oh! What she would give to hear it, clear and unambiguous, from his lips.

She stared into the fire as if in the flames she would find his face. She had no firm idea of what was to follow and, as she yawned again, realised she was too tired to accurately assess the possibilities. They would have to wait until morning.

Trimmer entered and unobtrusively removed the tray. She helped Dorothea change, then silently withdrew.

Lying in the depths of the feather mattress, Dorothea heaved a deep sigh and snuggled down in the bed. Under the subtle influence of Witchett's tisane, she dropped into a deep and dreamless sleep.

Dorothea awoke early the next morning, refreshed but strangely lethargic. She stayed in her room, staring out of her window at the cherry trees in the Park, now in full leaf. At nine o'clock she emerged from her bedchamber and descended to the morning-room. Cecily, she was informed, was spending the morning with the Bensons in Mount Street and had cancelled their morning ride with Ferdie. Relieved of two worries, Dorothea gave silent thanks to be spared the traumas of satisfying her sister's curiosity. Having drunk a cup of coffee and nibbled a piece of toast, she decided it was still too early to go up to her grandmother. On impulse, she called for Trimmer and went for a walk in the square.

The sun was shining, and a light breeze blew wispy clouds across the sky. Revelling in the fresh air, she walked through to the other side of the park, paused to glance briefly at the silent mansion opposite, then briskly returned to Merion House. By now Lady Merion would have left her bed. Ascending the stairs, she was surprised to see Ferdie on his way down.

Having received his cousin's note, Ferdie had decided that if Dorothea was not to be told of the danger then it was high time someone informed her ladyship of the threats to her granddaughter. He had also been able to set Lady Merion's mind at rest regarding the inevitable gossip arising from the incident in the Park. At the party he had attended the previous night he had found this had incurred little attention, and what comment there was had described it as just a lovers' quarrel.

As luck would have it, Lady Jersey had witnessed the encounter. She had immediately afterwards attended a select tea party at Mrs Drummond-Burrell's and, of course, had bubbled over with the news of Miss Darent's odd behaviour and the Marquis's likely response.

While there had been more than a few disapproving comments, the tone had been set by Mrs Drummond-Burrell herself. A friend of Hazelmere's, she had been impressed by Dorothea and heartily approved the Marquis's choice. In response to a disparaging remark that Miss Darent had properly cooked her goose, as Hazelmere would never stand for such behaviour, that most steely of Almack's patronesses had coolly observed, "Dear Sarah, I really don't think you fully appreciate Miss Darent. How often have any of us seen Hazelmere so much as thrown off balance?" The ensuing silence had assured her that she had captured the attention of the room. "I cannot help thinking," she had continued, "that any young lady who can shake that gentleman's calm deserves our congratulations. If she can make the Marquis realise that he cannot control absolutely everything, I for one will applaud her." Thus Dorothea's actions had come to be regarded as a successful attempt to defy his lordship, with the likely result being no more than a tiff.

Pausing to exchange greetings with Dorothea, Ferdie said, "I'll call for you at three."

"Oh, Ferdie, I don't know that I can."

"Not a matter of can or can't, you must," answered that knowledgeable gentleman. Realising that she did not understand, he suggested, "Go see your grandmama. She'll explain."

And with a nod and a wave he descended to the hall and, accepting his hat from Mellow, quit the house. Dorothea surrendered her pelisse to Trimmer and entered her ladyship's sanctum.

Lady Merion had already had much to think about that morning. The news that Dorothea had been the subject of two abduction attempts had shocked the old lady. But, considering the steps already taken to protect her, she could not think of anything more that could be done. She had rejected Ferdie's suggestion that Dorothea be warned, informing him that his cousin was already the cause of enough turmoil in Dorothea's life, without adding this to the account. Hazelmere's absence was not comforting. On the other hand, it would give Dorothea time to adjust to his idea of her future.

She had been pleasantly surprised and not a little relieved to hear of the lack of speculation over the scene in the Park. She particularly appreciated Ferdie's offer to ride with Dorothea in the Park that afternoon. "Won't do for her to hide away, you know," that young gentleman had sapiently remarked.

When Dorothea entered the room Lady Merion smiled and waved her to the comfortable chaise. "You're looking a great deal better, my dear."

"I feel a great deal better, Grandmama," replied Dorothea, dutifully kissing her cheek and then gracefully sitting beside her.

Noting her calm and confident manner, Hermione nodded. "I think it's time we had some plain speaking." Having made this promising beginning, she paused to marshal her arguments. "To begin with, I expect you'll admit Hazelmere has seriously engaged your affections?"

Smiling at the careful phrasing, Dorothea responded easily, "I've been in love with Lord Hazelmere for some time."

"As I said, he's already told me he intends offering for you. In his own good time," continued her ladyship. "But what I want to know is, how will you reply?"

A gurgle of laughter escaped Dorothea. "Oh, Grandmama. Do you really think I'll have any choice?"

Lady Merion snorted. "To be perfectly honest, my dear, I doubt it. Hazelmere is well aware of your feelings. And, from what I saw in the drawing-room yesterday, your *verbal* agreement is merely a formality." She watched her calm and cool granddaughter blush rosily. "Mind you," she went on, "it's a nuisance, having a husband who knows too much, but you can't have everything. Still, I don't think it's a bad bargain—his father was just the same, and Anthea Henry was the happiest married woman in town."

To Dorothea, it seemed safest to accept this assurance in silence.

Deciding that there was nothing more she could do to aid Hazelmere, Lady Merion continued briskly, "Very well. Now we must decide how you should go on. You must not give the gossips any reason to suppose that anything other than the mildest of disagreements has occurred between you."

Dorothea's brows rose in a thoroughly haughty manner.

"Quite!" nodded Lady Merion. "But you'll be guided by me and Ferdie in this matter. Ferdie is so useful at times like these; he always knows how things will appear and what one must on no account do. You must continue to appear at all your engagements as usual, and you must appear entirely your normal self." Looking at her grand-daughter, she remarked acidly, "That doesn't seem to be causing you any great difficulty at the moment."

Turning huge green eyes upon her grandmother, Dorothea smiled in a serenely confident way, which, under the circumstances, Lady Merion found oddly disconcerting. "Grandmama, I promise I'll behave at all times in a befitting manner. But you really cannot expect me to be the same as I was before the Diplomatic Ball."

Lady Merion, not entirely sure of its portent, accepted the qualified assurance. "One last thing. Ferdie told me Hazelmere has gone out of town until Tuesday, to one of his estates. Not," she continued in response to the question in Dorothea's eyes, "because of your quarrel. He'd already told his friends he meant to depart by yesterday evening."

Digesting this news, Dorothea decided that, all in all, a few days to polish her newly discovered public persona without distraction would not go amiss. Besides, she was beginning to feel that there were a few tricks left to be played in the game between herself and the arrogant Marquis. When he next appeared, she intended to be well prepared.

Chapter Twelve

Ferdie and Dorothea arrived at the Park and joined the groups of ladies and gentlemen milling about, exchanging greetings and the latest *on-dits*. More than a few eyes were directed Dorothea's way. Chatting in a relaxed and animated fashion with Lord Peterborough, riding beside her on his bay, she had herself well in hand. To all who were interested, she appeared entirely at ease.

Mrs Drummond-Burrell, sitting haughtily in her barouche, waved to them to attend her. As they drew up she complimented Dorothea on her looks and then embarked on a conversation with all three. At no time did she refer to the most noble Marquis of Hazelmere, nor the incident in the Park. Looking into the cool blue eyes, Dorothea smiled warmly, acknowledging the message.

Released from her side, they next fell victim to Lady Jersey. In stark contrast, she tried by every means possible to extract some comment from Dorothea on Hazelmere and what had happened after they had left the Park. Dorothea's practice in verbal fencing with his lordship left her well equipped to deal with opponents like Sally Jersey. She successfully turned aside all that lady's probing questions. As she accomplished this with an amused tolerance, very reminiscent of Hazelmere himself, Lady Jersey was more entertained than enraged by her refusal to be outwitted. Finally escaping her clutches, they rode on.

"Phew!" exclaimed Ferdie as soon as they were out of earshot. "Never seen Silence so hell-bent on getting an answer!"

While they encountered a number of ladies similarly intent on learning the details of Dorothea's last meeting with the Marquis, Lady Jersey's inquisition was by far the most comprehensive, and Dorothea easily handled these less inveterate busybodies.

On returning to Merion House, having parted from Lord Peterborough at the Park gates, Ferdie confessed to being thoroughly satisfied with Dorothea's performance. Overhearing this remark, addressed to her grandmother, Dorothea's eyes twinkled. "Why, thank you, Ferdie," she said meekly.

Not sure how to take this and finding her confidence slightly alarming, Ferdie assured them that he would call at eight to escort them to the evening's rout, and made his escape.

During the following days Dorothea found Hazelmere's friends keeping a protective watch over her and was amused by their endeavours to conceal this. Intrigued, she quizzed Ferdie for the reason and finally, in desperation, he retreated behind his absent cousin. "Best ask Hazelmere if you want to know about it." Correctly understanding this to mean that his lordship had left instructions that she was not to be told, she refrained from pushing Ferdie further. Finding that the words "Hazelmere said so' acted as a talisman, Ferdie used the phrase increasingly. He fervently hoped his cousin would not be out of London longer than anticipated.

As she had all of Hazelmere's closest friends dancing

attendance on her, Dorothea used the opportunity to lead them into describing their many interests and amusements. In so doing, they often gave her information on Hazelmere, and she slowly built up a more complete picture of his complex personality. For their part, his lordship's friends found the task of guarding her a pleasure. More than one found himself mesmerised by those large green eyes. Her natural assurance was much more apparent in Hazelmere's absence and, added to that, she now gave the impression of being fashionably distant, as if waiting for something or someone. However, not one of them found anything in her manner to suggest that she was other than completely content with Hazelmere's suit. So, roundly cursing his lordship's infernal luck, even the volatile Peterborough succumbed to her subtle invitation to be friends, and then the entire crew were her devoted slaves.

Fanshawe, viewing proceedings from the distance of his pursuit of Cecily, now close to success, could think of only one reason for Dorothea's serene manner. But, having heard from Ferdie of their last meeting, and knowing from Cecily's silence that Hazelmere had not proposed and forgotten to mention it, he was left wondering. From their friends' behaviour, he guessed Dorothea had succeeded in the not inconsiderable feat of adding them to her circle of doting admirers. Hazelmere would get something of a shock when he found to what use she had put his watchdogs. Luckily he was more likely to be amused at their susceptibilities than annoyed at her success. Life was going to be interesting when the Marquis returned to town.

For Dorothea, the time passed in a dull whirl she would readily have traded for the sight of his lordship's hazel eyes, preferably smiling at her. She was not entirely looking forward to her next private meeting with him, foreseeing a certain awkwardness in explaining why she had behaved as she had. But she would rather have faced it sooner than later. Unfortunately she could do nothing but wait and, with so many people endeavouring to please her, she felt it would be churlish to complain, even though her enthusiasm for fashionable pursuits had waned.

The only truly dreadful moment occurred at the Melchetts' ball on Saturday night. She might have guessed, had she thought of him at all, that Edward Buchanan would, like a distempered ghost, return to haunt her. He had heard of the encounter in the Park and had listened with interest to the speculation on the outcome. To his mind, Miss Darent's options were rapidly diminishing.

He accosted her as she stood by the side of the dance-floor in company with Lord Desborough. Unfortunately the musicians had had a slight accident, and in the unexpected interval the guests were strolling about, conversing in small groups. Desborough had not previously met Edward Buchanan and so accepted at face value his claim to acquaintance with Dorothea. Knowing she would be mortified by Mr Buchanan's gallantries, Dorothea asked Desborough to fetch her a glass of lemonade, hoping in the interval to dispose of her unwelcome suitor. Her plans backfired, and instead she found herself in a small ante-room with Edward Buchanan again pressing his suit.

"I have, after all, got your guardian's blessing. And now there are these rumours about your behaviour with Hazelmere. What I say, my dear, is that none of your fancy beaux will have you now." He cocked an eyebrow at her and his ponderous voice gained in weight. "Too top-lofty, that lot. You've queered your pitch there, right enough. You'd do well to lower your sights, my girl. Hazelmere and his set are out of your reach now. You should consider my proposal, indeed you should!''

Rigid with anger, Dorothea struggled to control her voice. ''Mr Buchanan! I will tell you for the last time: I do not wish, in any circumstances, to marry you! I trust that is plain enough. I will not change my mind. It was unwise in the extreme for Herbert to have encouraged your suit. I'm sorry, but I must return to the ballroom.''

She moved to sweep past him where he stood, his back to the door. As she did so Desborough, who had been looking all over for her, appeared there. Sheer relief showed on Dorothea's face. At the same moment Edward Buchanan grabbed her by the shoulders and attempted to kiss her. She struggled frantically, averting her face.

Almost instantly Buchanan was bodily plucked from her and thrown roughly against the wall. In considerable surprise he slid down to sit on the floor, his legs splayed out in front of him and an idiotic look on his face. Desborough, adjusting the set of his coat before offering his arm to Dorothea, turned at the last moment to say, ''Be thankful it was me and not Peterborough, Walsingham, or, God forbid, Hazelmere. Any of those three and you would be nursing rather more bruises and, very likely, a few broken bones as well. I suggest, Mr Buchanan, that you trouble Miss Darent no longer.'' And, with that, he ushered a deeply grateful Dorothea back into the ballroom.

The upshot was that Hazelmere's friends never, ever, left her unattended again, whether in the ballroom, the Park, or any other gathering of the fashionable.

Hazelmere's entire attention was devoted to controlling the frisky bays as he threaded through the crowded streets of the capital. Once they had passed the village of Hamp-

stead and started over Finchley Common he dropped his
hands and the bays shot forward. With the horses driven
well up to their bits, the curricle rocketed past coaches
travelling at conventional speeds. Jim Hitchin, hanging on
grimly behind, kept his lips firmly shut and prayed that
his master's customary skill did not desert him. As the
evening wore on and the shadows started to spread, throwing inky patches across the road, concealing pot-holes and
ruts, Jim expected their pace to ease. But no change in
speed was detectable as they left Barnet behind and raced
onwards up the Great North Road towards the George at
Harpenden, where they spent the night on such trips as
these.

Jim kept silent, more from fear of distracting the Marquis than from reticence. But, when Hazelmere overtook
the north-bound accommodation coach just before St Al-
bans on a tight curve with less than inches to spare, Jim,
in considerable fright, swore roundly.

"What was that, Jim?" came Hazelmere's voice.

"Why, nothing, m'lord," replied Jim. Unable to help
himself, he added, "Just if you was to be wishful to break
both our necks I could think of few faster ways to do it."

Silence. Then Jim heard his master laugh softly. "I'm
sorry, Jim, I know I should not have done that." And the
curricle slowed until they were bowling along at a safer
pace.

Yes, and you're still up in the boughs, thought Jim. Just
as long as you keep this coach on the road, we'll survive.

It was late afternoon on Thursday when they reached
Lauleigh, Hazelmere's Leicestershire estate between Mel-
ton Mowbray and Oakham. His steward, a dour man
named Walton, had not erred in demanding his attendance. There was an enormous amount of work to be done

and they made a start on it that evening, going over the accounts and planning the activities of the next two days.

Walton, hearing from Jim of the likely change in his lordship's affairs, made sure that anything requiring his authorisation was dealt with. He was under no illusion that he would be able to summon his master north again that Season. Accustomed, like most of the Marquis's servitors, to keeping a weather eye out for his temper, in this case Walton guessed it was unlikely to be directed at him, and his flat tones droned in Hazelmere's ears incessantly over Friday and Saturday.

Hazelmere called a halt on Saturday afternoon and retired to his study, informing Jim that they would leave early the next morning. The events of the past two days, entirely divorced from those of the Season, had succeeded in restoring his calm. By forcing his mind to deal with such mundane affairs, he had managed to shut out the turmoil of emotions he had experienced on leaving Dorothea until now, when he felt infinitely more capable of dealing with them.

While it was warm in the south of the country, in Leicestershire the winds blew cool in the evening and the fire was alight. Pouring himself a drink, he dropped into the comfortable armchair before the hearth, stretching his long legs to the blaze. Cupping the glass in both hands, he gazed into the leaping flames.

Conjuring up the image of a pair of emerald eyes, he wondered what she was doing. Ah, yes. The Melchett ball. Away from the endless round of London during the Season, he was even more conscious of how much he wanted her by his side. That meeting in the drawing-room at Merion House had had about it an air of inevitability. He'd been so angry with her when he'd walked in the door— admittedly more from hurt pride than righteous indigna-

tion. And she'd been so surprisingly angry with him!
Thankfully, she had promptly told him why. He grinned.
All the dictates of how a young lady should behave had
been overturned in the space of a few minutes. He could
imagine no other female—apart from his mother, perhaps—who would dare let on that she even knew of his
mistresses, much less question him on the subject.

As his relationship with Helen Walford was so well
known among the ton, it had never occurred to him that
a different version could be presented to Dorothea. Very
clever of the Comte. He vaguely recalled some difficulty
with Monsieur de Vanée over one of the barques of frailty
who had at one time resided under his protection. What
had been her name? Madeline? Miriam? Mentally he
shrugged. The Comte's lies had undoubtedly been the
cause of Dorothea's distress that night, coming on top of
the incident with the Prince. Hardly surprising that she
had baulked at meeting Helen and him in the Park.

But why, *why* had she flung that drivel about her being
no more than a challenge at him? Even if Marjorie Darent
had impressed it on her, surely she didn't believe it? He
sipped the fine French brandy and felt it slide warmly
down his throat. No—she hadn't believed Marjorie's tales.
The Darents had left London on Monday, so any conversation between Dorothea and Marjorie must have occurred
earlier. But Dorothea had behaved normally at that hor-
rendous party on Sunday night. And at the Diplomatic
Ball she'd been entirely unconcerned until the Prince's
performance had opened her eyes too far. Even then, she
had not been distraught, only, as he had expected, angry
with him. It had only been later, after the Comte's inter-
ference, that she had been shattered and almost in tears.
Well, his actions in her grandmother's drawing-room

should have settled that. She couldn't possibly have missed the implication of that kiss.

It had not occurred to him until that day that by loving her he had put into her hands the power to hurt him. Since he was naturally strong and self-reliant, there were few close to him whose opinions mattered enough to affect him—his mother and Alison, Tony and Ferdie and, to a lesser extent, Helen. That was about it. And Dorothea mattered far more than all of them combined. But if such vulnerability was what one had to put up with, then put up with it he would. She had only lashed out at him because she was hurt by his imagined perfidy. He would simply ensure that such misunderstandings did not occur in the future.

So where did that leave them now? Much where they had been before, except that presumably she now knew he loved her. Assuming that events progressed as he intended, there was no reason that they could not be wed in a month or so. Then his frustrations and her uncertainties would be things of the past.

He brought his gaze back from the ceiling whence it had strayed and fixed it once more on the dancing flames. He was happily engaged in salacious imaginings in which Dorothea figured prominently when his housekeeper entered to inform him that dinner was served.

He reached Darent Hall, close to Corby and not far off his direct route, just before ten o'clock. He threw the reins to Jim, who had run to the horses' heads, with a command to keep them moving.

Admitted to the hall, he spoke to the butler. "I am the Marquis of Hazelmere. I wonder if Lord Darent could spare me a few moments?"

Recognising the quality of this visitor, the butler

showed him into the library and went to inform his master. Herbert was engaged in consuming a leisurely breakfast when Millchin announced that the most noble Marquis of Hazelmere required a few words with him. Herbert's mouth dropped open. After a moment he recovered himself enough to reply, "Very well, Millchin, I'll come at once, of course. Where have you put him?"

Millchin told him and withdrew. Herbert continued to stare at the door. He had little doubt what Hazelmere wanted, but Marjorie had insisted that he was not in earnest and, even if he was, that he could not be considered suitable. In this instance, adherence to his wife's wishes was entirely impossible. Herbert was already uncomfortable before he entered his library to face Hazelmere, who somehow seemed more at home in the beautiful, heavily panelled room than its owner.

The interview was brief and to the point, conducted as it was by Hazelmere rather than Herbert. Having listened to the Marquis's request, Herbert felt forced to reveal that he had already given Edward Buchanan permission to address Dorothea.

At mention of Mr Buchanan, Hazelmere's look became uncomfortably intent. "Do you mean to tell me you gave Buchanan permission to address your ward without checking his background?" The precise diction made Herbert even more nervous.

"I gather he owns an estate in Dorset," he flustered. "And, of course, he knows Sir Hugo Clere."

"And learned from Sir Hugo that Miss Darent had inherited the Grange, no doubt. For your information, Edward Buchanan owns a tumbledown farmhouse in Dorset. He's penniless. The reason he's in London is that, after his most recent attempt to run away with a local heiress,

Dorset is too hot for him. I'm surprised, my lord, that you take such little care over your duties as guardian.''

Herbert, brick-red with embarrassment, remained silent.

''I assume that, as you are acquainted with my family and my standing in society and as my wealth needs no detailing, you have no objection to giving *me* your permission to address Miss Darent?''

The scathing tones made Herbert wince. ''Naturally, should you wish to address Dorothea, of course you have my permission,'' he said, squirming, then unwisely added, ''But what if she's already accepted Buchanan?''

''My dear sir, your ward is a great deal more discerning than you are.'' Now that he had obtained Herbert's approval, the only other information Hazelmere required was the name of the family solicitors who would handle the marriage settlements.

Herbert was strangely diffident on this question. ''I believe Dorothea uses Whitney and Sons, in Chancery Lane.''

It took the Marquis a moment to assimilate this. Then he asked, eyes narrowed, ''So Miss Darent's solicitors are her own, not yours?''

''My aunt's crazy idea,'' said Herbert defensively. ''She had the oddest notions. She decided it was best that both girls controlled their own fortunes.''

''So,'' pursued Hazelmere, drawing on his gloves, ''when the Misses Darent marry, control of their fortunes remains in their hands?''

''Well, yes,'' said Herbert, glancing directly at him. ''But that wouldn't worry you, surely? Her estate is nothing compared to yours.''

''Oh, quite,'' agreed Hazelmere. ''I was merely wondering whether you gave that information to Buchanan. Did you?''

Herbert looked blank. "No. He didn't ask."

"I thought not," said Hazelmere, a highly cynical smile curving his lips. Disclaiming any desire to dally with his relations-to-be, he re-entered the hall, to find that he was not destined to escape an encounter with Marjorie Darent. Her ladyship was looking even more severe than usual and directed a look of such magnitude at her husband that Hazelmere almost felt sorry for him.

"Lord Hazelmere—" she began.

But Hazelmere was determined that the conversational reins would remain in his hands. "Lady Marjorie," he countered. "I'm sure you'll forgive my not staying. I've concluded the business I had with your husband and it's most urgent I return to Hazelmere at once. My mother, you realise."

"Lady Hazelmere is ill?" asked Marjorie, struggling to keep abreast of this flow of information.

Hazelmere, unwilling to expose his mother to letters of condolence on her relapse, simply looked grave. "I'm afraid I'm not at liberty to discuss the matter. I'm sure you understand."

He bowed elegantly over her hand, nodded to Herbert and escaped.

He reached Hazelmere on Monday afternoon. His mother was resting, so, seeing the glint in his steward's eye, he gave his attention to the host of minor matters Liddiard had waiting for him. He delayed his appearance in the drawing-room until just before dinner. If they were free of servants his mother would lose no time in asking him why he was home, and he would rather face the inquisition after dinner than before.

As it transpired, he entered the drawing-room immediately in front of Penton, his butler. Lady Hazelmere, recognising the strategy, pulled a face at him as he bent to kiss her cheek. He merely gave the smile he knew infuriated her, telling her as it did that he was perfectly aware of what she wanted to say to him but had no wish to hear it—at least, not yet. Her ladyship reflected that her son was growing to resemble his father more and more.

Over dinner he kept up a steady flow of inconsequential anecdotes, detailing the fashionable happenings since she had left London. Lady Hazelmere, knowing he would say nothing to the point in front of the servants, listened with what interest she could muster. Finally, after the covers were removed and the servants withdrew, she drew a deep breath. "And *now* are you going to tell me why you're here?"

"Yes, Mama," he replied meekly. "Only I do think we might be more comfortable in your parlour."

Functioning in a similar way to Lady Merion's upstairs drawing-room, her ladyship's parlour was a cheerful apartment on the first floor of the large country house. The curtains were already drawn, shutting out the twilight, and a small fire was burning merrily in the grate. Lady Hazelmere sat in her favourite wing chair by the hearth, while her son, after pulling it further from the flames, elegantly disposed his long limbs in its partner opposite.

He then smiled at his impatient parent. Her ladyship, inured by the years to such tactics, asked bluntly, "Why have you come to see me?"

"As you correctly suppose, to tell you I'm about to offer for Dorothea Darent."

"Very punctilious, I must say."

"You know that I always am. In such matters as these, at least."

Aware that this was true, she ignored the comment. "When is the wedding to be?"

"As I haven't asked her, I cannot say. If I have my way, as soon as possible."

"I must say, I've wondered at your unusual patience."

He shrugged. "It seemed a good idea at the time. She'd only just arrived in town, and if she'd refused it would have caused considerable awkwardness for a number of people."

"Yes, I can appreciate that. But why the change of heart?"

He looked hard at her. "Hasn't Lady Merion written to you this week?"

"Well, yes," she admitted. "But I'd much rather hear it from you."

Hazelmere sighed and succinctly outlined the events preceding his departure from the capital. He also described the two attempts to abduct Dorothea, learning in the process that his mother already knew of these via a recently informed Lady Merion. When he finished, Lady Hazelmere looked at him, perplexed. "But if she's in danger, why are you gallivanting all over the country?"

"Because the others are looking after her and it seemed more sensible to marry her as soon as possible and remove her from any danger at all," he explained patiently. "As I had to go to Lauleigh, I looked in on Herbert Darent on the way back."

She eventually conceded. "Yes, I suppose you're right, as usual. I assume Herbert was only too thrilled?"

"As a matter of fact, no," he replied with a grin. "I think that indescribable wife of his has convinced him I'm no better than a rake and shouldn't be allowed to marry into the family."

Lady Hazelmere was speechless.

After a moment Hazelmere said, "I take it you approve?"

His mother dragged her mind from contemplation of Lady Darent's manifold shortcomings. "Of course! She's very suitable. In fact," she said, warming to her theme, "she's *eminently* suitable, as among her numerous qualities she can include the unique accomplishment of having attracted your interest!"

"Exactly so," he returned, amused. "And, as I've been at great pains to make our attachment abundantly clear to the ton, I really don't think the announcement will surprise."

"When I think of that waltz at the Merion House ball!" Anthea Henry closed her eyes, continuing faintly, "So very shocking of you, my dear!"

Hazelmere, not deceived, replied, "Coming it much too strong, Mama!"

She opened eyes brimming with laughter. "But it was! You had all the tabbies with their fur standing on end!"

Both mother and son allowed the conversation to lapse while they relived fond memories. Her ladyship finally stirred. "When will you speak to her?"

"As soon as I can arrange to see her. Wednesday probably. If she's agreeable we'll come here for a few days. It would be useful, I imagine, for her to see the house."

Lady Hazelmere sighed. Hermione's weekly letter had been perfectly candid. Clearly, despite minor misunderstandings, her arrogant son had, as usual, triumphed, and all would proceed as he decreed. Even the headstrong Dorothea had apparently been tamed. If things continued in this fashion Marc would soon grow to be utterly impossible. She had had such hopes of Dorothea. Still, at least she would now have a daughter-in-law. Even if nothing else, they could swap stories of her impossible son. And, knowing her son, she could look forward, with as much confidence as possible in such matters, to a grandchild within the year. The thought cheered her. So, resigned, all she said was, "Yes, that would be wise. We'll have to arrange to refurbish the apartments next to yours."

Chapter Thirteen

Hazelmere returned to London, driving a new pair of black horses, leaving the bays in the country to recuperate. The curricle flashed into the mews behind Hazelmere House late in the afternoon. Discussing the performance of the new pair with Jim, he strolled out of the stables as Ferdie rode into the mews, leading two horses.

Thoroughly worn out with his role as chief confidant and protector, Ferdie was delighted to see his cousin. Dismounting and handing over the reins to Jim, he reflected that the source of the horses the Darent sisters rode was one of the better kept secrets in this whole affair. He could imagine what Dorothea would say when she learned that her bay mare had all along belonged to Hazelmere. He hoped they would be married by then and she could discuss the subject with Hazelmere rather than him. He turned to his cousin. "Relieved to see you back!"

"Oh?" The black brows rose interrogatively.

"Not that anything's happened," he hastily assured him. "But Dorothea knows something's going on and it's getting more and more difficult to know what to say."

"Poor Ferdie! It sounds as if it's all been too much for you."

"Well, it has!" returned Ferdie, incensed. "Here she's gone and turned all your friends into her most devoted slaves—oh, yes! Didn't expect that, did you?" He had the satisfaction of seeing the hazel eyes widen. Nodding decisively, he continued, "Rather think it's been her holding the reins in your absence, not us!"

Hazelmere, eyes dancing, sighed. "I see I was mistaken in thinking it safe to leave you all in charge of Miss Darent. I might have guessed it would turn out the other way. Why on earth you have allowed her to assume the whip hand, I know not. Obviously I'll have to intervene and save you all."

"All very well for you. It's you she loves, not us! Never seen a lady so capable of making us all jump to her tune. Better take her in hand straight away!"

Hazelmere laughed at this blatant encouragement. "Believe me, Ferdie, I intend to—with all possible speed. But not tonight, I think. It's Alvanley's dinner for me. I can't remember if there's anything else on."

"No, nothing of note. I'm to escort Dorothea and Cecily to a quiet little party at Lady Rothwell's. Just the younger crew, so I'm looking forward to an uneventful evening. Mind, though! Tomorrow she's all yours!"

"Oh, quite definitely!" As they strolled back into Cavendish Square Hazelmere added, "In fact, you can assist in your own relief by informing Dorothea that I'll call on her tomorrow morning."

Regarding his cousin with misgiving, Ferdie answered, "Well, I'll tell her. But she'll probably insist on going riding or think up some important engagement on the spot."

"In that case," Hazelmere said, his voice silky smooth, his lips curving in anticipation, "you had better add, in your most persuasive tones, that she would do very much better to meet me next in private rather than public.''

Ferdie, doubting that he could deliver that statement with quite the force Hazelmere could, nodded reluctantly. "Yes, all right, I suppose that'll do it."

"You can take it from me that it will," responded Hazelmere gravely. Laughing at Ferdie's outraged countenance, he clapped his cousin on the shoulder and went into his own house, leaving Ferdie to wander on to his lodgings.

Some two hours later Fanshawe was attempting to tie his neckcloth in the latest fashion when the knocker on his door was plied with unusual insistence. With an oath he discarded his latest attempt and testily recommended his man, standing mute with an armload of fresh specimens, to see who on earth it was.

A minute later, just as he was once again engrossed, the door opened.

"Hartness, who on earth have you sent these to? They're too floppy to do anything with!"

Came an amused voice in reply, "A poor cobbler always blames his lathe."

He twisted around, ruining any chance he had of correctly tying his next attempt. "Oh, you're back, are you?"

"As you see," replied Hazelmere. "I'd said I would be, after all."

"Never know where you'll be or not. Where'd you get to—just Leicestershire?"

"Lauleigh, Darent Hall and Hazelmere," responded the Marquis.

Fanshawe took a moment to work this out. "Thought that might be it," he said sagaciously. "Have you seen Dorothea yet?"

"No. I thought that after my flying around the country I deserve Alvanley's dinner. And Ferdie tells me they're to attend a boring party tonight, so all should be safe until tomorrow."

"Tomorrow. Good! Where'd you say Darent Hall was?"

"Ah, lies the wind in that quarter?"

"You're not the only one who can suddenly decide for reasons unknown to get leg-shackled to a managing female!" responded his lordship tartly.

Laughing, Hazelmere said, "It's in Northamptonshire, not far from Corby. Easy to find if you ask. Here! For the lord's sake, let me tie that or Jeremy will be wondering what's become of us! Stand still!"

He rapidly tied his friend's cravat, his long fingers creasing the stiff material into the required folds. "Right, done. Now let's get going!"

Fanshawe, admiring the finished product, mused, "Not bad."

Finding his coat thrown at his head, he laughed and, putting it on, joined Hazelmere on the stairs.

Jeremy Alvanley had been in the habit of giving a dinner for his closest friends every year for six years. It had become an event in their calendar, a gentlemen-only gourmet affair with the best of the latest vintages to wash the delicacies down. All their set made every effort to attend, and the occasion usually proved highly entertaining. This year's dinner was no exception. The conversation flowed as freely as the wine. Much of this consisted of regaling Hazelmere with the problems they had faced in looking after Miss Darent. All of them knew of the scene in the Park, but none of them could begin to imagine what had happened afterwards. However, they were well acquainted with Hazelmere and had therefore been surprised at Dorothea's subsequent performance. Finding him in his normal benign mood, none of them was quite sure what to think. But, as he was obviously genuinely entertained by the stories of their difficulties, they took every opportunity to impress on him how arduous their labours had been.

Though they did not know it, their stories confirmed for Hazelmere what Ferdie and later Fanshawe had told him: clearly Dorothea had taken charge, realising that, to some extent, they were acting under his direction. That she had succeeded in captivating them was apparent. He was amused to hear that the only sure way they found to escape her subtle questioning had been to invoke his name. That this had succeeded told him that she had known precisely what she was about in her handling of this group of gentlemen whom he would have described as among the most hardened to feminine wiles.

During the evening Desborough paused by his chair to enlighten him regarding Edward Buchanan. The black brows drew together. Then he shrugged. "I might have expected him to make some such attempt. Thankfully, you were there." With a quick smile Desborough moved on.

After dinner it was their custom to adjourn to White's for the rest of the evening, or, more correctly, until the small hours of the next morning. By eleven o'clock they were deeply engrossed in play.

Ferdie, Dorothea and Cecily arrived at Lady Rothwell's punctually at eight, to find carriages waiting to convey them to a surprise party at Vauxhall. Neither Dorothea nor Ferdie was enthusiastic; Cecily was ecstatic. As it was virtually impossible to withdraw politely, Dorothea and the even more reluctant Ferdie were forced to accept the change with suitable grace.

At the pleasure gardens Lady Rothwell had hired a

booth facing the dancing area, gaily lit with festoons of coloured lanterns. The younger folk joined in the dancing, while Dorothea and Ferdie stayed in the booth, watching the passing scene. Lady Rothwell sat keeping a shrewd and motherly eye on all her young charges.

Dorothea had heard that Hazelmere was expected to have returned that day. Speculation on their next meeting was consuming more and more of her time. Glancing at her pensive face, Ferdie recalled his cousin's message. He could hardly deliver it in Lady Rothwell's hearing. "Would you like to view the Fairy Fountain, Miss Darent?"

Dorothea had no wish to view the Fairy Fountain but thought it odd that Ferdie should imagine she would. Then she caught the faintest inclination of his head, and, intrigued, agreed. Lady Rothwell made no demur to their projected stroll and Dorothea left the booth on Ferdie's arm. Once out of sight and sound of her ladyship, she lost no time. "What is it you wish to tell me, Ferdie?"

Thinking she had a bad habit of making it difficult to lead up to things by degrees, Ferdie answered baldly, "Met Hazelmere this afternoon. Gave me a message for you."

"Oh?" she replied, bridling.

Not liking the tone of that syllable and fast coming to the conclusion he should have told his high-handed cousin to deliver his own messages, Ferdie was forced to continue. "Said to tell you he would call on you tomorrow morning."

"I see. What a pity I shall miss him! I do believe I have to visit some friends tomorrow morning."

"Told him so." Ferdie nodded sagely. Under Dorothea's bemused gaze, he hurriedly explained, "Told him you would very likely be engaged."

"And?"

Liking his role less and less, Ferdie took a deep breath and continued manfully, "He said to say you would do better to meet him in private rather than in public."

The undisguised threat left Dorothea speechless. Seeing her kindling eyes, Ferdie decided it was time to return to safer and more populated surroundings than the secluded walk they had entered. "Take you back to her ladyship," he volunteered.

Seething, Dorothea allowed him to take her arm and they retraced their steps. She was incensed. More than that, she was *furious!* How *dared* he send such a command to her? However, as she strolled back to the booth by Ferdie's side common sense reasserted itself. If her last meeting with Hazelmere was any guide, she would be wise to avoid provoking him further. The thought of refusing his suggested interview only to meet him next in the middle of a ballroom was enough to convince her to accede to his request.

Shortly after Dorothea and Ferdie had left, Lady Rothwell was joined by Cecily, thoroughly enjoying herself, accompanied by Lord Rothwell. Noticing Cecily's high colour, her ladyship sent her son for some ices from the pavilion. Cecily sat down beside her and was in the middle of a delighted description of the sights when they were interrupted by a knock on the door.

At her ladyship's command, an individual in attire proclaiming the respectable gentleman's gentleman entered the booth.

"Lady Rothwell?"

"Yes?"

"I have an urgent message for Miss Cecily Darent." The man proffered a sealed letter.

At a nod from Lady Rothwell, Cecily took it, broke the seal and spread open the single sheet. Reading it, she paled. Reaching the end, she sat down weakly in the chair, allowing her ladyship to remove the letter from suddenly nerveless fingers.

"Good heavens!" exclaimed Lady Rothwell, quickly perusing the missive. "My dear, I'm so sorry!"

"I must go to him," said Cecily. "Where's my cloak?"

"Don't you think you should wait for Dorothea and Ferdie?"

"Oh, no! They might be half an hour or more! Surely there can be no impropriety? I must not delay. Oh, please, Lady Rothwell, please say I may go?"

Her ladyship was not proof against Cecily's huge pansy eyes. But it was with definite misgiving that she watched her disappear down the walk to the carriage gate in the company of Lord Fanshawe's man.

Ten minutes later Ferdie and Dorothea regained the booth. Lady Rothwell had sent her son away and was trying to rid herself of a strong suspicion that she had erred in allowing Cecily to leave. She looked up with relief.

"Oh, Ferdie! I'm so glad to see you. And you too, my dear. Cecily received a most disturbing message and has gone off with Lord Fanshawe's man."

Neither Ferdie nor Dorothea understood much of this, but, seeing the letter her ladyship was holding out, Ferdie took it.

To Miss Cecily Darent,

I am writing on behalf of Lord Fanshawe, who is currently in my surgery, having sustained serious wounds in a recent accident. His lordship is in a bad way and is asking for you. I am sending this note by the hand of his servant and I hope if he finds you you will allow this individual, who his lordship assures me is trustworthy, to escort you to his lordship's side. I need hardly add that time is of the essence.

Yours, et cetera,
James Harten, Surgeon.

"Oh, dear!" said Dorothea.

"Gammon!" said Ferdie.

"I beg your pardon?" asked Dorothea.

"This letter," he explained. "It's a hoax."

"But how do you know?" wailed Lady Rothwell.

"Because I know it's Alvanley's dinner tonight and then they always go on to White's. Every year, always the same. So wherever Tony is, Marc's with him. Bound to be. And Marc would never allow this. You may not know, but I do. Devilishly starchy on some things, Hazelmere."

Dorothea, knowing this to be the truth, gave voice to her thoughts. "But if it is a hoax, to what purpose?"

Ferdie realised they had all made a mistake in forgetting there were two Darent sisters. Dorothea and Lady Rothwell were obviously expecting him to answer. "Sorry to have to say this, but I'm afraid she's been abducted."

"I knew there was something wrong," wailed her ladyship. "Oh, dear! Whatever shall I tell Hermione?"

"Ferdie, what should we do?" asked Dorothea, wasting no time in histrionics.

Ferdie, whose brain could, under stress, perform quite creditably, paused for a moment. "Who else knew of this letter?"

"No one," answered Lady Rothwell. "William was out

getting ices at the time and I didn't like to show it to him.''

"Good. Dorothea and I will leave and return to Merion House. If any demand or message is sent, that's where it'll be. Lady Rothwell, you'll have to tell everyone Dorothea was feeling unwell and that Cecily and I took her home.''

Her ladyship, reviewing this plan, approved. "Yes, very well. And Dorothea, tell Hermione I'll keep silent about this. I feel responsible for letting Cecily go and I dread to think what your grandmother will think of me, my dear.''

Nodding, Dorothea murmured thanks and reassurances before she and Ferdie left for the carriages.

In spite of the coachman's best efforts, the journey to Cavendish Square took twenty tense minutes. Admitted to Merion House by a surprised Mellow, they found, as suspected, a recently delivered letter addressed to Dorothea. Lady Merion was attending a card party at Miss Berry's and would not be home for hours.

Ushering Dorothea into the drawing-room and shutting the door on Mellow, Ferdie nodded to the letter. "Best open it. Have to know what they want.''

Dorothea broke the cheap seal and read the contents of the single sheet, Ferdie looking over her shoulder.

My dear Miss Darent,

I have your sister in safe keeping and if you wish to see her again you will do exactly as I say. You should immediately set out in your carriage and travel to the Castle Inn at Tadworth, south of Banstead. Do not bring anyone with you or nothing will come of your visit and your sister's reputation will assuredly be lost. If you do not arrive before dawn I will be forced to conclude that you have informed the authorities and I will then have to flee the country, taking your sister with me. I am sure I can rely on your good sense. I remain,

> Your most obedient servant,
> Edward Buchanan, Esq.

"Good God! The bounder!" said Ferdie, disgust etching his fair face. "You can't possibly go to that place." After a pause he added, "But someone's going to have to."

Dorothea's mind was racing. In a way, it was partly her fault that Cecily had been abducted. If only she had been more careful of her younger sister and not so absorbed with her own affairs. It was Cecily for whom they had come to London to find a husband. Maybe she could have been firmer with Edward Buchanan, though it was difficult to see how. Weighing up the possible courses of action available to her, she answered Ferdie at random. "Yes, but who? And how?"

Ferdie had little doubt as to the who and how. "Best thing we can do is get hold of Hazelmere. Tony'll be with him and they'll know what to do. Sort of thing Marc's good at."

Dorothea's absent gaze abruptly fixed on Ferdie's face. She had no difficulty understanding his comments. But inwardly she groaned. The memory of how affairs stood between herself and the Marquis, never far from mind, reeled into focus. After the way they had parted the last thing she needed was this. To meet him next with a calm request to extricate her sister, essentially her responsibility, from the clutches of one of her own importunate suitors was a prospect she could not face. "No, Ferdie," she

said with calm decision. "There's no need for Hazelmere
or Fanshawe or anyone else to be involved."

Ferdie simply looked blank. Then stubborn. There ensued a totally unprofitable ten minutes of wrangling. Finally Dorothea suggested a compromise. "If you fetch
Grandmama, then she can decide what to do."

Relieved, Ferdie headed for Miss Berry's.

It was over an hour later that Mellow opened the door
to his mistress. On reaching the Misses Berry's trim little
house, Ferdie had sent in a message that Dorothea was ill
and consequently Lady Merion's presence was required
at Merion House. Instead of resulting in Lady Merion's
coming out, he had been summoned in. Lady Merion had
been engaged in a thrilling rubber and had desired to
know how desperately ill her granddaughter, last seen in
rude health, had become. Under the amused gaze of what
had seemed like half the ton, Ferdie had been forced to
assure her ladyship that Dorothea's state was not critical.
With a smile her ladyship had settled down to finish her
game.

But now, as she surrendered her fur wrap, Lady Merion
looked anything but complacent. A worried frown had
settled over the sharp blue eyes as she led the way into
the drawing-room. Ferdie followed and shut the door.

"Where's Dorothea?" asked Lady Merion.

Ferdie's face was blank as he scanned the room, almost
as if he expected to find Dorothea hiding in a corner. The
pale blue eyes stopped when they reached the white
square tucked into a corner of the mirror on the mantel-
piece.

Lady Merion, following his gaze, walked over and
twitched the envelope free. It was addressed to her. She
smoothed out the sheet. Then, one hand groping wildly,

she sank into a chair. Under her powder she paled, but her voice when she spoke was firm. "Drat the girl! She's gone off to get Cecily herself."

"What?"

"Precisely!" Lady Merion read the note again. "A lot of gibberish about being responsible for the mess." She snorted. "Says she can handle Buchanan."

A pause developed, Ferdie, for once, too incensed to break it. Eventually Lady Merion spoke again. "I'm not so sure she can handle that man. I think we should summon Hazelmere anyway. Dorothea seems set against it, but in the circumstances he should be told. It's time she realised that, as she's virtually affianced to him, she simply can't go careering off about the countryside like this, let alone keep it hidden from him." The sharp blue eyes turned on Ferdie. "So how do we get hold of him?"

Ferdie came to life. "Tonight it's easy. You write a note and we'll send it to him at White's. One night of the year you can be sure he's there."

Lady Merion nodded briskly and, going to the small escritoire, dashed off a note to Hazelmere.

Ferdie, engaged in some hard thinking, looked up as she sealed it. "Don't address it. I'll do that."

Lady Merion raised her brows but relinquished her seat without comment. Picking up the pen, Ferdie frowned, then inscribed the front of the note with his cousin's full title.

Summoning Mellow, Ferdie put the note into his hands and instructed him to ensure its immediate delivery to White's. No answer was expected. Together with Lady Merion, he settled down to wait.

As Ferdie had predicted, both Lords Hazelmere and Fanshawe were at their accustomed positions in the gaming-room. Hazelmere was holding the bank, and the rest of the table was comprised of their friends, all making every effort to break the bank. They had been playing for a little over an hour and had just got pleasantly settled in.

Hazelmere, dealing the next hand, was surprised to find an attendant at his elbow with a letter on a salver. Completing the deal, he picked up the letter and, glancing at the direction, used the silver-bladed knife to break the seal. He laid the missive on the table and returned his attention to his cards.

He had immediately recognised Ferdie's handwriting, but could not understand why his cousin should suddenly start to send letters to him under his full title. In fact, he could not understand why Ferdie would send him a letter at this time of night at all. Despite giving only half his mind to the game, he succeeded in concluding the first round and, while the other players were considering their next bids, he opened the letter.

The reason for Ferdie's departure from normal behaviour was instantly apparent. Rapidly scanning the lines, he managed to control his expression so that those watching could tell nothing from it. The letter ran,

My dear Hazelmere,

Cecily has been abducted by Edward Buchanan. In a note he has demanded Dorothea's attendance at some inn. After sending Ferdie to get me, Dorothea left for the inn. Ferdie suggests you may be able to help. We are at Merion House.

Yours, et cetera,
Hermione Merion.

Refolding the letter, Hazelmere stared pensively at the cards. Then, placing the letter in his coat pocket, he turned once more to the game. He rapidly brought this to a conclusion, refusing the opportunity to draw Markham further into the bidding. Pushing back his chair, he signalled to an attendant to remove the pile of rouleaus from in front of him. "I'm very much afraid, my friends, that you'll have to continue without me," he said smoothly.

"Trouble?" asked Peterborough.

"I trust not. Nevertheless, I'll have to return to Cavendish Square. Will you take the bank, Gerry?"

While Hazelmere and Peterborough concluded their transaction for transfer of the bank, Fanshawe frowned at the table. He had also recognised Ferdie's writing. Finally catching Hazelmere's eye, he raised his brows questioningly. Receiving an almost imperceptible nod in return, he also withdrew from the game. Minutes later the two friends descended the steps of White's. Once clear of the entrance, Fanshawe asked, "What is it? Not your mother?"

Hazelmere shook his head. "Wrong side of Cavendish Square." Without further comment he handed the letter over. They stopped under a street-lamp for Fanshawe to read it.

"Good lord! Cecily!"

"I'm afraid we protected Dorothea too well and so he changed his plans a trifle." Seeing Fanshawe still staring at the letter, Hazelmere removed this firmly from his grasp, saying, "I suspect we should hurry."

They covered the distance to Cavendish Square in less than ten minutes. Admitted to Merion House by the thoroughly intrigued Mellow, Hazelmere did not wait to be announced but led the way into the drawing-room.

Lady Merion started up out of her chair. "Thank God you're here!" Despite her wish to appear calm, the unexpected worry was a taxing burden. She was no longer young.

Hazelmere smiled reassuringly and, after bowing over her hand, settled her once more. Hearing the increasing commotion from the other side of the room as Fanshawe tried to piece together what had happened, he intervened. "I think we should start at the beginning."

His voice cut through the altercation with ease. Fanshawe and Ferdie looked at him, then his lordship abandoned his belligerent stance and Ferdie his defensive one. They seated themselves, Ferdie opposite Lady Merion and Fanshawe on a chair pulled over from the side of the room.

Hazelmere nodded his approval and perched on the arm of the chaise. "You start, Ferdie."

"Took Dorothea and Cecily to Lady Rothwell's, as I'd said. We all thought it was to be a quiet little party. Turned out to be a visit to Vauxhall."

"Couldn't you have stopped it?" interposed Fanshawe.

Ferdie looked at Hazelmere and replied, "Knew you wouldn't like it, but nothing to be done. Dorothea and Cecily wouldn't have understood. Couldn't simply refuse and come away."

Hazelmere nodded. "Yes, I see. What then?"

"At first all seemed fine. Nothing untoward. Young people only and no flash characters. Took Dorothea for a stroll." Nodding to Hazelmere, he explained, "Your message. When we got back to the booth Lady Rothwell told us Cecily had gone. A servant had come with a letter for her." Fishing in his coat pockets for the letter, Ferdie continued, "Fellow told Lady Rothwell he was your man, Tony. Here it is."

He handed the crumpled note to Fanshawe. As he read it his lordship's face grew unusually grim. Handing it on to Hazelmere, he looked at Ferdie. "And she went with him?"

"Lady Rothwell tried to stop her, but you know what Cecily is. After that we came straight back here."

"One moment! Did anyone other than Lady Rothwell know what happened?" asked Hazelmere.

"No, luckily," replied Fanshawe. "And she's promised to keep mum. Going to say Dorothea was unwell and Cecily and I escorted her home."

"She's a good friend," put in Lady Merion. "She won't say anything unhelpful."

"And then?" prompted Hazelmere.

"We found the letter from Buchanan waiting when we got here."

"Where's this letter?" asked Fanshawe.

Lady Merion and Ferdie tried to remember where they had put it. Then her ladyship realised it was on the escritoire. Hazelmere retrieved it and remained standing while he read the single sheet, Fanshawe looking over his shoulder.

"Is the writing the same as the others?" asked Fanshawe.

Hazelmere nodded. "Yes, all the same. So it was Edward Buchanan all the time." He folded the letter and returned to the chaise. "What happened next?"

"I suggested we send for you. Seemed the best idea. Dorothea didn't agree. Insisted there was no need. Couldn't see it, myself. Then she suggested I fetch Lady Merion. Meek and mild as anything! Thought that was a good idea, so I did. Didn't know she'd go haring off as soon as my back was turned! Didn't let on at all!" Ferdie's anger returned in full force.

Hazelmere smiled.

Lady Merion frowned. "Well? Aren't you going after her?"

The black brows rose, a touch arrogantly. "Of course. While I dare say Dorothea may manage Buchanan well enough, like you, I would feel a great deal happier if I knew exactly what was going on. However," he paused, hazel eyes fixed on an aspidistra in the corner, "it occurs to me that flying off in a rush might land us in a worse tangle."

"How so?" asked Fanshawe, seating himself again.

"At the moment Cecily is presumably at the Castle Inn at Tadworth, in the company of Edward Buchanan and associates. Dorothea must have left before midnight and it'll take her close to three hours to make the journey. It's now after twelve-thirty. We can probably make the distance in two hours, so we should reach the inn not far behind her." He paused for breath. "However, if we go flying down there we end with both Darent sisters mysteriously disappearing from London, and on the same night you and I, Tony, also mysteriously disappear. And what do we do when we catch up with them? Bring them back to London? But we wouldn't reach here until morning. The gossips would have a field-day."

As the truth of his words sank in, Lady Merion grimaced.

Ferdie's pale face went blank. "Oh."

"So what are we going to do?" asked Fanshawe.

Hazelmere grinned. "The problem is not insurmountable." Glancing at Lady Merion's worried face, he added with a smile, "It's a pity your inventive elder granddaughter isn't here to help, but I think I can contrive a suitable tale. Ring for Mellow, Ferdie."

Hazelmere asked for his groom to be summoned from Hazelmere House. While they waited he was silent, an odd smile touching the corners of his mouth. At one point he roused himself to ask whether Dorothea had gone alone.

Lady Merion answered. "Her note said she was taking their maid, Betsy, and of course Lang, her coachman, will be driving."

Hazelmere nodded as if satisfied and relapsed into silence.

Jim entered the room, cap in hand. Hazelmere studied him for a moment and then, smiling, began in a soft voice that Jim knew well. "Jim, I have a number of orders which it's vital you carry out to the letter and with all possible speed. The first thing you'll do is fig out the greys."

"What?" This exclamation broke from both Ferdie and Fanshawe simultaneously.

"No! Really, Marc! Can't have thought! The greys on bad roads at night!" blustered Ferdie.

Jim, watching his master, merely blinked. Fanshawe opened his mouth to protest, then caught his friend's eye and subsided.

"There's no point in having the fastest pair in the realm if one cannot use them when needed," remarked Hazelmere. Turning back to Jim, he continued, "After you've seen the greys put to, get a stable-boy to walk them in the square. Saddle the fastest horse in the stables—Lightning, I think. And then ride first to Eglemont." Turning to Fanshawe, he asked, "Your parents are at home, aren't they?"

"Yes," replied his lordship, mystified.

"Good. You, Jim, will demand to see Lord Eglemont, or, failing him, her ladyship. You'll tell them Lord Fanshawe will arrive before morning with Cecily Darent. He'll explain when he arrives. You're then to ride to Hazelmere and speak to the Dowager. You'll tell her that I'll arrive before morning with Miss Darent. Again, I'll explain when I arrive.'' Suddenly grinning, he added, ''It's probably just as well you won't know the whole story, so you can deny knowledge with a clear conscience.''

Jim, knowing the Marquis's mother well, grinned back. Hazelmere nodded a dismissal.

Fanshawe had worked out some of the plan in his friend's head and was grinning. Hazelmere refused to meet his eye, and instead turned back to Lady Merion and Ferdie. ''I'll only go through this once. We don't have time for repeat performances. Listen well and, if you see any points I've missed, say so. We have to ensure the story is watertight.''

Satisfied he had their attention, he started, ''Some time much earlier in the Season I unwisely described to Dorothea the beauties of seeing Hazelmere Water at sunrise. Dorothea told Cecily, and between them they made my life and yours, Tony, unbearable until we agreed to organise an excursion to see this wonder. With the aid of our respective parents, a plan was hatched. It's best to see this spectacle on a clear morning, and because none of us wished to spend a week or more in the country waiting for such an opportunity it was agreed that on the first clear moonlit night we would drive down in the carriage, view the Water at dawn, visit Hazelmere and Eglemont and return to town later.'' With a nod at Lady Merion he added, ''The party was to include your ladyship. Tonight is a clear moonlit night with the promise of a fine morning to follow. Perfect for our projected expedition. Did you say something, Tony?''

Fanshawe had put his head on his arms with an audible groan. Looking up, he said, ''All very well to save their reputations, but what about ours?''

Hazelmere grinned. "I don't expect this story to fool our friends. It's the rest of the ton I'm concerned about." He paused. "Console yourself with imagining how grateful Cecily is bound to be when you tell her of your sacrifice to preserve her reputation."

Lady Merion snorted. She wondered if Hazelmere expected Dorothea to be grateful. Then he was speaking again.

"To continue. It was arranged that Lady Merion and the Misses Darent would decide on the most appropriate night and then contact the two of us. At the Rothwells' party the girls realised tonight was the most suitable in weeks. So they excused themselves from the party on the pretext that Dorothea was ill and returned to Merion House. They sent a message to us at White's. Ferdie helped with that. And all the gaming-room saw me get the letter, and then we both left to return to Cavendish Square. So far, all's well. Then, after we arrived and agreed tonight was suitable, Ferdie went to fetch Lady Merion. What excuse did you give for summoning her ladyship, Ferdie?"

"That Dorothea was ill."

"So that fits too. However, when you arrived home, Lady Merion, it was you who felt truly unwell. Sufficiently unwell, at least, to baulk at a night drive down to Hazelmere. But rather than postpone the outing, and seeing that as of this afternoon Dorothea and I are betrothed..."

Hazelmere broke off, seeing the sensation this announcement had caused. "No," he continued in a weary tone, "I haven't asked her yet, but I do have horrible Herbert's blessing and she's not going to get the chance to refuse, so we will be by the time we return to London."

He paused but, when no one made any comment, continued, "Where was I? Oh, yes! In these circumstances, you suggested the maid Betsy could go in your stead. We left immediately. Dorothea and I went down in the curricle with Jim and Tony, and Cecily followed in the carriage with Betsy. We had decided that, as the Season is somewhat flat at the moment, we would all spend a few days in the country. So that is exactly what has happened and is going to happen.''

A pause ensued while they considered the tale. Lady Merion's mind was reeling as she considered the possible outcomes when Hazelmere calmly informed Dorothea that she was to marry him. She wished she could be there to see it. But it would do Marc Henry the world of good to meet some opposition for a change. She had little doubt he would succeed in overcoming it. So, an expectant smile curving her lips, she remained silent.

Then Hazelmere spoke again. "Now for the loose ends. You and I, Tony, are shortly to leave for Tadworth to remove the young ladies from Buchanan's hands and from there we'll proceed to Hazelmere and Eglemont. Lady Merion, you remain here and ensure we have no more rumours. Ferdie, you are the final player and you've probably got the most vital role.''

At these words Ferdie looked highly suspicious. Long acquaintance with his cousin made him wary of such pronouncements. "What am I to do?''

"First, I want you to place a notice of my betrothal to Dorothea in tomorrow's *Gazette*. There should be time. Then you must very subtly ensure the story of our romantic escapade is broadcast throughout the ton.''

"No!'' groaned Fanshawe, pain writ large on his countenance. "We'll never be able to show our faces at White's again!''

Hazelmere's smile broadened. "Even so. If everyone is

exclaiming over our idiotic behaviour they're unlikely to go looking for other explanations of tonight's doings." Turning back to Ferdie, he asked, "Have I missed anything vital?"

Ferdie was running the whole tale over in his mind. He brought his gaze back to his cousin's face, his eyes alight. "It's good. No gaps. I think I'll drop in on Ginger Gordon tomorrow. Haven't seen him in ages."

This was greeted by another moan from Fanshawe. Sir "Ginger" Gordon was an inveterate gossip, Sir Barnaby Ruscombe's chief rival. Even a few words in his ear could be counted on to go a very long way.

"Good! That's settled." Hazelmere glanced at the clock and rose. "Come on, Tony. We'd better go." Taking Lady Merion's hand, he smiled confidently down at her. "Don't fret. We'll bring them off without harm."

Turning to Ferdie, Hazelmere noted the smile of pleasant anticipation on his face. "Don't get too carried away, Ferdie. I do wish to live in London, you know."

Startled out of his reverie, Ferdie hastened to reassure his cousin that everything would be most subtly handled. As Fanshawe had finished taking his leave, Hazelmere merely threw him a sceptical glance as he moved to the door.

The friends strode rapidly across Cavendish Square. As they reached Hazelmere House Fanshawe said, "I'll go and get changed. Pick me up when you're ready?"

Hazelmere nodded and entered his house. Moments later his servants were flying to do his bidding, and inside ten minutes, attired more suitably for driving about the country at night, he mounted his curricle behind the restive greys and swept out of the square. Taking Fanshawe up at his lodgings, they made good time through the deserted city streets. Once clear of the suburbs, Hazelmere allowed the horses their heads and the curricle bounded forward.

Edward Buchanan's master plan began to hiccup from the start. The first phase was the abduction of Cecily Darent from Vauxhall Gardens. Having assumed that she was no different from the usual débutante, he was unprepared for the spirited resistance she put up when he grabbed her on one of the shadowy paths. Assisted by his valet, he had secured her hands and gagged her, but she had managed to kick him on the shin before they had bundled her into the carriage. Thus warned, he had kept her bound and gagged until he had been able to release her into the parlour, the only one in the Castle Inn, and lock the stout oak door on her.

The Castle Inn was a small hostelry. Not far from the major roads, it was sufficiently removed to make interruption by unexpected guests unlikely. The front door gave directly on to the taproom. Edward Buchanan stayed by the fire in the low-ceilinged room, sipping a mug of ale and smugly considering the future. It had finally dawned on him that the desirable Miss Darent, she of the Grange, Hampshire, as nice a little property as any he had seen, had ripened like a plum and was about to fall into the hand of the Marquis of Hazelmere. And his lordship didn't even need the money. It was grossly unfair. So he had set about rectifying the error of fate. But Miss Darent seemed possessed of an uncanny ability to side-step his snares. His attempts at the masquerade and the picnic had both come to naught. This time, however, he prided himself he had her measure. To save her young sister, she would, he was certain, deliver herself, and her tidy little fortune, into his hands. Her fight with Hazelmere and his lordship's absence from town had relieved his horizon of its only cloud. He smiled into the flames. Then, bored with his own company, he rose and stretched. Miss Cecily had been alone for nearly an hour. It should, therefore, be safe to venture in and discuss the beauties of the future with his prospective sister-in-law.

Opening the door of the parlour, he sauntered in. A vase of flowers flew at his head. He ducked just in time and the vase crashed against the door.

"Get out!" said Cecily in tones reminiscent of Lady Merion. "How *dare* you come in here?"

He had expected to find her weeping in distress and fear, totally submissive and entirely incapable of accurately throwing objects about the room. Instead she stood at the other end of the heavy deal table that squatted squarely in the middle of the chamber. On its surface, close to her hand, were ranged all the potential missiles the room had held. Eyeing these, he assumed an authoritative manner.

Waving his hand at her ammunition, he said in a confident tone, "My dear child! There's no cause for such actions, I assure you!"

"Gammon!" she said, picking up a small salt cellar. "I think you're mad."

A frown marred Edward Buchanan's contentment. "You shouldn't say such things of your future brother-in-law, m'dear."

It took Cecily all of a minute to work it out. "But Dorothea won't marry you."

"I assure you she will," returned Edward Buchanan with calm certainty. He pulled a chair up to the table and sat, a wary eye on the salt cellar. "And why not? Hazelmere won't have her now, not after she cut him in the Park. And none of her other beaux seems all that keen to come up to scratch. And after she comes down here to spend the night with me—well, just think of the scandal if she doesn't marry me after all.''

''Good lord! You really must be mad! I don't know what happened between Dorothea and Hazelmere in the Park, but I do know he's only gone out of town to his estates. He's expected back any day now. If he finds you've been trying to…to pressure Dorothea into marrying you, well…'' Words failed Cecily as she tried to imagine what Hazelmere really would do in such a situation.

But Edward Buchanan was not impressed. ''By the time his lordship finds out, it'll be too late. Your sister will be promised to me and Hazelmere will never stand for the scandal.''

''What scandal? If he killed you it would be simple to hush it up. Tony told me there's little Hazelmere couldn't do if he wished it.''

A niggling doubt awoke in Edward Buchanan's stolid brain. Memories of the tales of Hazelmere's prowess at Gentleman Jackson's boxing salon reverberated in his head. And Desborough's warning flitted through his consciousness. He shook such unhelpful thoughts aside. ''Nonsense!''

But Edward Buchanan was to find, as Tony Fanshawe already had, that Cecily's mind was of a peculiarly tenacious disposition. She continued to dwell longingly on the possible outcome once Hazelmere learned of his plans. No amount of persuasion could shake her faith that he would find out, and that sooner rather than later. As her description of the likely punishments in store for him passed from the general to the specific Edward Buchanan found himself totally unable to divert her attention. She was trying to recall what drawing and quartering entailed when she was interrupted by a knock on the door.

With enormous relief he rose. "That, I believe, will be your sister, m'dear."

Dorothea had spent the journey to Tadworth more in consideration of the possibilities of her next morning's encounter with Hazelmere than in worry over her imminent encounter with Edward Buchanan. She had no real fear of the bucolic Mr Buchanan and did not pause to question her ability to deal with him. She planned to march into the Castle Inn and, quite simply, walk out again with Cecily. If Edward Buchanan was so Gothic as to believe he could bend her to his will by such melodramatic tactics he would shortly learn his error. Her only worry was that her grandmother would bow to Ferdie's exhortations and inform Hazelmere. Hopefully, Lady Merion would hold firm. That way she could get Cecily and herself safely back to London and meet his lordship in the morning, having lost no further ground, bar the lack of a few hours' sleep.

Lang found the inn without difficulty. Entering, Dorothea saw at a glance that this was a respectable house. Reassured, she left Betsy and Lang seated in the taproom and knocked on the parlour door. When it opened she swept through, head held high, without so much as a glance at the man holding the door. She advanced towards her sister, stretching out her hands in greeting. "There you are, my love."

The sisters exchanged kisses and Dorothea pulled off her gloves. "Did you have a pleasant trip down?" she enquired.

Moving back to his chair after shutting the door, Edward Buchanan began to feel that all was not proceeding as it should.

Cecily took her cue from Dorothea. Ignoring their captor, they happily conversed in the most mundane manner, as if nothing at all untoward had occurred. Dorothea moved to the fire to warm her chilled hands.

Suddenly Edward Buchanan could stand it no longer. "Miss Darent!"

Dorothea turned to look at him, disdain in every line. "Mr Buchanan. I had hoped, sir, that you would by now have come to your senses and that I would not be forced into conversation with you."

The repressive tones stung. But Edward Buchanan had not come thus far to be easily turned aside. "My dear Miss Darent, I realise the events of the evening have come as a shock to you. But you must consider, m'dear. You're here. I'm here. You need to be married. I'm only too willing to oblige. If you think about it, I'm sure you'll see that Edward Buchanan's not such a bad bargain."

Eyes blazing, Dorothea replied scornfully, "You, sir, are unquestionably the most distasteful character it has been my misfortune to meet. I dare say you think you've been clever. Personally I doubt it! I cannot for the life of me understand your obsession with marrying me. However, other than as a source of irritation, it concerns me not in the least. By your presence you reveal yourself as anything but the gentleman you purport to be, and neither my sister nor I have the slightest wish to converse with you further!"

Edward Buchanan purpled alarmingly as the comprehensive condemnation poured over him. Rising abruptly, he knocked over his chair. "Ah, but I think you'll change your mind, m'dear. You wouldn't want it broadcast that I was alone with your lovely young sister for some hours tonight."

Both Dorothea and Cecily whirled to face him, contempt written clearly on their faces. But before either could speak Edward Buchanan went on, "Oh, yes. I think you'll change your mind. You've scuttled your chances with Hazelmere. Wouldn't do for your sister to let Fanshawe off the hook, too.''

Cecily was fairly hopping with rage. ''Thea, don't you listen to him! Oooh, just *wait* till Tony and Hazelmere hear of this!''

Dorothea laid a restraining hand on Cecily's arm as that spirited damsel was about to launch forth into further vituperative outpourings. Drawing herself to her full height, she spoke clearly, a distinctly martial light in her green eyes. ''Mr Buchanan. There will be no scandal. My sister and I will shortly be leaving this charming inn and returning to town in our carriage, accompanied by our maid.''

Edward Buchanan jeered, ''And what's to stop me passing on the tale of what happened here tonight?''

Dorothea's eyes opened wide. ''Why, Hazelmere, of course.'' She would have given anything not to have needed recourse to his lordship, but, as far as she could see, he was the best deterrent she had. Cecily's happiness was at stake now and she would do anything necessary to preserve her younger sister.

Her calm reference to the Marquis temporarily rattled Edward Buchanan. Then he recovered. ''Nice try, m'dear. But it won't do. Aside from the fact that all the ton knows you quarrelled with his arrogant lordship, I happen to know he's out of town. By the time he returns, the damage will be done.''

The gaze Dorothea bent on the hapless Mr Buchanan would have frozen greater men. ''My dear sir, if your information on the Marquis's movements is so reliable I presume you also know that he returned to London today. As for our relationship, I have no intention of edifying you with an explanation. Suffice to say that Lord Hazelmere has requested an interview with me tomorrow morning.'' She paused to let her words sink in. Then she turned to Cecily. "Come, my love. We should start back. I wouldn't like to be late for my meeting with Hazelmere.''

But Edward Buchanan was not yet defeated. "Easy to say, m'dear. But even if he is in town, who's to say he'll hear about it? No, I'm afraid I really can't let you leave.''

His stubborn belligerence ignited Dorothea's temper. "Oh, you silly man! I hope Hazelmere *doesn't* hear about it. The only reason I came down here is so that there's no reason for him to be involved. And if only you'd see sense you'd be assisting us to leave with all speed!''

"Hah! So he doesn't know!''

"He didn't know when I left, but I wouldn't wager a groat that he doesn't know by now.''

"There's still time to get married,'' mused Mr Buchanan. "I've a special licence and there's a clergyman of sorts in the village.''

Cecily's mouth dropped open. "You're quite mad,'' she informed Mr Buchanan.

"Mr Buchanan!'' said Dorothea in tones of long suffering. "Please listen to me! I will not marry you. Not now, not tonight, not ever.''

"Yes, you will!''

Dorothea opened her mouth to deny this charge but it remained open, her words evaporating, as a calm voice drawled from the doorway, "I'm shattered to disappoint you, Buchanan, but in this instance Miss Darent is quite correct.''

All eyes turned to see the Marquis of Hazelmere, standing in the doorway, shoulders negligently propped against the frame.

Chapter Fourteen

Dorothea would have given everything she possessed to know how long Hazelmere had been standing there. Across the room her eyes locked with his. Then, smiling faintly, he straightened and crossed to stand before her, taking her hand and kissing it, as was his habit. Dorothea struggled to master her surprise as the usual light-headedness swept over her. Under the warm hazel gaze she blushed. Hazelmere retained his clasp on her hand as he turned to view Edward Buchanan.

Fanshawe had been standing immediately behind Hazelmere and had entered the room in his wake, pointedly shutting the door after him. Cecily, with a suppressed squeal, had run to his side.

The arrival of their lordships left Edward Buchanan, at least temporarily, with nothing to say and nowhere to go. He was barely able to believe the evidence of his eyes, and all trace of intelligence had left his face, leaving it more bovine in appearance than ever. With the rug effectively pulled from under him, he stared in mute trepidation at Hazelmere, who stood, calmly regarding him, a considering light in the strange hazel eyes.

"Before we continue this singularly senseless conversation I should point out to you, Buchanan, that, on her marriage, Miss Darent's estate remains in her hands.''

Cool and precise, Hazelmere's words affected Edward Buchanan as if a bucket of iced water had been dashed in his face. For a matter of seconds sheer astonishment held him silent. Then, ''Why, that's...that's... I've been grossly deceived!'' he blustered. ''Lord Darent has misled me! And Sir Hugo!''

Cecily, Fanshawe and Dorothea received these interesting revelations in fascinated silence. Hazelmere said, ''Precisely. That being so, I think you'll need a holiday to recover from your...exertions, shall we say? A long holiday, I should think. On your estates in Dorset, perhaps? I have no wish to see your face again, in London or anywhere else. If I do, or if it comes to my ears you are again indulging in the practice of abduction or in any way inconveniencing anyone, I'll send your letters to the authorities with a full description of what took place. As all the notes are in your handwriting, and one is very conveniently signed, I'm sure they'll take a great interest in you.''

The steely words effectively reduced Edward Buchanan's grand plan to very small pieces. With his great chance fast disappearing downstream, he glanced wildly, first at Fanshawe and Cecily, and then at Hazelmere, Dorothea at his side, her hand still firmly held in his. ''But the scandal...'' His voice trailed away as he encountered Hazelmere's eyes.

''I'm afraid, Buchanan, you seem to be labouring under a misapprehension.'' The tones were icy enough to chill the blood in Edward Buchanan's veins. He suddenly recalled some of the other stories about Hazelmere. ''The Misses Darent are on their way to visit Fanshawe's and my families on our estates, escorted by their maid and coachman. Fanshawe and I were delayed in leaving town and so arranged to meet them here.'' There was a slight pause during which the hazel eyes calmly surveyed Mr Buchanan. ''Are you suggesting there is anything in that which is at all...improper?''

Edward Buchanan paled. Thoroughly unnerved, he hastened to reassure the Marquis, the words fairly tripping from his tongue. ''No, no! Of course not! Never meant to imply any such thing.'' One finger had gone to his neckcloth as if it was suddenly too tight. Retreat, disorderly or otherwise, seemed imperative. ''It's getting late. I must be away. Your servant, Misses Darent, my lords.'' With the sketchiest of bows he made for the door, slowing as he realised that Fanshawe still stood with his back to it. At a nod from Hazelmere, Fanshawe opened the door, allowing an agitated Edward Buchanan to escape.

Instantly the sounds of a hurried departure reached their ears. Then the main door of the inn slammed shut and all was quiet.

Inside the parlour the frozen tableau dissolved. Cecily openly threw herself into Fanshawe's arms. Dorothea saw it and wished she could be similarly uninhibited. As things were, she felt barely capable of preserving her composure.

''Oh, God! What a nincompoop!'' said Fanshawe. ''Why'd you let him escape so easily?''

''He's not worth the effort,'' replied Hazelmere absentmindedly, his eyes searching Dorothea's face. ''Besides, as he said, he'd been misled.''

Dorothea, trying to look unconscious of his meaning and failing dismally, tried to steer the conversation into lighter fields. ''Misled! I've been trying for weeks to get rid of him. If *only* I'd known!'' It suddenly dawned on her to wonder how Hazelmere had known. She felt strangely giddy.

Hazelmere saw her abstracted gaze. Noticing the assorted objects on the table, he seized on the distraction "Have you been using the abominable Mr Buchanan for target practice?"

Dorothea, following his gaze, was diverted. "No. That was Cecily. But she only threw a vase of flowers at him."

Looking to where she pointed, he saw the shards of the shattered vase. "Does she often throw things?" he asked faintly.

"Only when she's angry."

While he considered her answer Hazelmere picked up Dorothea's cloak and draped it over her shoulders. "More to the point, does she hit anything?"

"Oh, usually," Dorothea replied, strangely engrossed with the ties of the cloak. "She's been doing it since she was a child, so her aim is really quite good."

Glancing at Fanshawe, absorbed with Cecily, Hazelmere could not repress a grin of unholy amusement. "Do remind me, my love, to mention that to Tony some time. I should warn him of what he's about to take on."

Dorothea smiled nervously. Hazelmere reached around her to retrieve her gloves and handed them to her. Correctly interpreting his nod, she put them on. She looked up, to find his hazel eyes warmly smiling.

"I think we should leave this inn forthwith. Aside from getting you and Cecily safely away, it's by far too crowded for my liking."

She smiled back, ignoring the little thrill of anticipation the words and tone drew forth, perfectly content to do whatever he wished, just as long as he continued to smile at her in that deliciously peculiar way. As usual, he had assumed command. But she could hardly argue with the efficient way he had got rid of Edward Buchanan. In the circumstances, she felt she could safely leave discussion of his managing ways until they had returned to London. There was still that interview to be endured, after which they would doubtless discuss what possibilities the future held. She reminded herself she still had no unequivocal proof of the nature of his feelings for her.

Hazelmere escorted Dorothea into the taproom, closely followed by Fanshawe with Cecily. Seeing her chicks being ushered safely out, Betsy heaved a sigh of relief and came forward with Lang to hear their instructions.

Hazelmere consulted his watch. It was already close to four. In the curricle he could reach Hazelmere in just over an hour. The carriage would take closer to two. Dawn would be before six. He turned to Fanshawe with a grin. "I'll leave you with the coach and Betsy, of course."

Dorothea, who had moved with Cecily to reassure the clucking Betsy, looked up. Hazelmere smiled blandly back at her.

"Yes, I thought you would," replied Fanshawe, disgusted at the thought of two hours' frustrating travel with his love and her maid. "We'll make directly for Eglemont. Cecily can see Hazelmere Water some other time. Preferably not at dawn, what's more! To think I'm going to be saddled with this and I won't even reap the rewards!" He tried to scowl at his friend but could not resist the rueful laughter in the hazel eyes.

"Never mind," replied Hazelmere, aware that Dorothea had missed little of their exchange. "I rather think I've got more to explain than you." He moved to Dorothea's side and outlined the dispositions for the next phase of their journey. He accomplished this without explanation, and was about to lead Dorothea outside when she regained the use of her tongue.

"But there's no need for this at all! Couldn't we simply

go back to London?'' A long drive alone with Hazelmere had not figured in her plans.

Hazelmere stopped and sighed. "No."

Dorothea waited for him to explain, but when instead he took her arm she stood her ground. "I realise it would not be wise for all of us to return together, but there's no reason Cecily and I cannot go back in the carriage with Betsy, and you two can go down to your estates, then return to London later."

Hazelmere caught the grin on Fanshawe's face. It could hardly be missed; it was enormous. Noting the stubborn set of Dorothea's chin and the flash of determination in her green eyes, he silenced her in the only effective way he knew. Under the bemused gazes of the innkeeper, Betsy, Lang, an intrigued and approving Cecily and a still grinning Fanshawe, he pulled her against him and kissed her. He did not stop until he judged her incapable of finding further words to argue with.

When Dorothea's wits finally returned she was on the box-seat of Hazelmere's curricle, the Marquis by her side, smartly heading his greys out of the inn yard, setting them on the road leading south. She glanced up at his profile, clearly visible in the bright moonlight. Her determination to force a clear declaration from him grew. Aside from anything else, if what had just occurred was any indication of how he planned to settle disagreements between them in future, unless there was some balance in their relationship, she would never win any arguments at all. Her mind made up, she reviewed her options.

The road between Tadworth and Dorking was narrow but otherwise in good condition. Which, reflected Hazelmere, was just as well. The hedges on either side cast shadows over the road, and despite the silvery moonlight he could not see far ahead. And his love would not remain silent for long. One glance as they left the inn had convinced him that she was merely gathering her forces. He glanced at her now and found her looking speculatively at him. Her brows rose in mute question.

He smiled back and returned his attention to his horses. He had no intention of initiating a conversation. Let her make the first move.

This was not long in coming. ''Are you ever going to tell me just what has been going on?''

Thinking ''No' by far the safest answer, he regretfully settled for, ''It's a long story.''

''How long before we reach Hazelmere?''

''About an hour.''

''Plenty of time to explain, then. *Even* with your greys in hand.''

''But we have to reach Hazelmere Water before dawn.''

''Why?''

Glancing down at her lovely, confused countenance, he smiled reassuringly. ''Because that's the supposed reason for this midnight jaunt, and so at least one of you, having been so insistent on seeing it, had better do so. Just in case someone like Sally Jersey, who has also seen it, asks for a description.''

Raising her eyes to his face, Dorothea asked in weary resignation, ''Just what *is* this tale you've woven? You had much better tell me from the beginning if I'm supposed to convince the likes of Lady Jersey of the truth of it.''

Content to keep the conversation on relatively safe ground, Hazelmere obliged. He started by telling her what happened after she had left Merion House. ''You'll have to remember to make your peace with Ferdie.''

''Was he terribly bothered?''

"Incensed." He sketched the outline of the story, omitting to tell her that they were supposedly betrothed. He spent some minutes impressing on her the magnitude of Fanshawe's and his sacrifices in saving Cecily's and her reputations. Hearing her chuckle over Ferdie's mission to spread the tale far and wide, he hoped he had diverted her mind from what he had not explained.

Recovering from her giggles, Dorothea mentally reviewed what she had heard, her eyes fixed on the offside horse. This midnight drive was possibly the best chance she would ever have of extracting information from Hazelmere. In normal circumstances, his physical presence was so distracting that it was a constant battle of mind against body to formulate sensible questions, let alone combat his evasive answers. But, since he was now perched on the box-seat beside her, his hands occupied with the reins and his attention divided between his horses and herself, the odds were more even. She would certainly have to encourage him to take her driving more often in future. Silent, they passed through Dorking and into the country lanes leading to Hazelmere. Bringing her gaze back to his face, she said in the most non-committal of tones, "What were the other notes Mr Buchanan had sent?"

He recalled a comment of Ferdie's that she had a habit of asking questions so it was impossible to sidle out of them. Resigned to the inevitable, he answered, "He made two previous attempts to abduct you. That was something I didn't foresee when I decided to convince the ton of my interest in you."

The moonlight had completely faded and sunrise was not far off. They had crossed the Hazelmere boundary, and the look-out over the ornamental lake known as Hazelmere Water was not far ahead.

After a considerable pause while she tried to analyse his actions in all this Dorothea said, "I take it the first was the Bressington masquerade?"

"Yes. There's nothing you don't know about that, except I knew it wasn't a joke. That was why I was suddenly so ridiculously attentive, even attending that boring party that Sunday. I don't know what I would have done if I hadn't been able to learn your engagements. Did you know one of my footmen is walking out with your maid?"

Dorothea regarded him with a fascinated expression. He grinned and continued, "The second attempt was at the picnic you attended with Ferdie. He forgot to give you a note delivered while you were there. It was unaddressed, so he opened it when his man found it the next day. It was supposedly signed by me, but Ferdie knows my signature and so he brought it to me. Tony was with me at the time, so after that both of them knew."

"When did the rest of your friends find out?"

Impossible to deny it. "On Wednesday, at a luncheon. I had to leave town, and Tony and Ferdie couldn't hope to keep you in sight all the time."

"Did it never occur to you to tell me?" she asked.

"Yes. But I couldn't see what good it would do." Seeing her frown, he sighed. "Who could know if and when the next attempt might be made?"

The silence on his left was complete. After a minute he risked a glance and found she was regarding him quizzically. "You're quite abominably high-handed, you know."

He smiled sweetly and replied, "Yes, I know. But only with the best of intentions."

The curricle topped a gentle rise and just beyond the crest Hazelmere turned the horses on to the grass verge, cropped to form a look-out. "And that," he announced, "is Hazelmere Water."

With the sun breaking over the distant horizon, the scene spread beneath her feet was breathtakingly beautiful. He jumped down from the curricle and tied the reins firmly to a bush. He lifted her down and together they descended a flight of shallow steps cut into the escarpment. These led to a small plateau beneath the crest where a stone bench stood by an old oak. An uninterrupted view of the valley below unfurled at their feet. Hazelmere Water was a large ornamental lake edged by clumps of willows. There was an island in the middle with more willows, and a summer-house, painted white, showing through the lacy foliage. Swans cruised slowly on the gentle currents of the stream that fed the lake from one end and exited at the other.

As the sun climbed higher the colours of the scene changed constantly from the first cool sepia tones through the warm pink tints of early sunrise and the golden glow of increasing light, until finally, as the sun cleared the hills behind the lake and shone forth unhindered, the bright greens of the grass and willows and the deep blue of the lake showed clear and intense.

Seated on the bench, Dorothea watched in speechless delight. Hazelmere, beside her, had viewed the sight on many occasions. He still found pleasure in it, but today had eyes only for the woman beside him. Returning to London with the firm intention of settling their past and future in one fell swoop, he had found that, instead of waiting patient and secure for him to declare himself, his independent love had gone haring off in the middle of the night to do battle with Edward Buchanan. It really should not have surprised him. While he had little doubt she would have handled the matter after a fashion, her disposition to manage matters her own way had given him an irresistible opportunity to bring their frustrating courtship to its inevitable climax. But now, despite her apparent calm, she was defensive. To be trying to keep him at a distance after all that had passed between them seemed rather odd, even for his independent love. He watched her; delight in the scene before her glowed on her expressive face. Inwardly he sighed. He was going to have to find out what it was that was worrying her. The reins of this affair of theirs had continually tangled; he couldn't remember when he'd had so much difficulty with a woman. And now he had a sneaking suspicion that, while he had thought he had got the reins untangled and running free, they had somehow got snagged again.

With the sun riding the sky, Dorothea turned towards him, her eyes glowing. "That was the most beautiful sight I've ever seen! I'm afraid Lord Fanshawe will have to bring Cecily here at dawn after all."

Hazelmere had lost interest in Fanshawe and Cecily. "Just as long as it's you who tells him so. Having consigned him to two hours in that carriage with Cecily and your Betsy, I fear I'm not at present riding high in his esteem."

Dorothea, suddenly breathless, looked down and found that he had hold of her hand. She felt him move to draw her to him. Knowing that if he kissed her she would lose any chance of retaining sufficient control to force any admission, positive or negative, from him, she resisted. He immediately stopped. For a moment silence, still and deep, engulfed them. Dorothea, her eyes downcast, did not see the long lips curl into a wry smile. Hazelmere could think of only one way to precipitate matters, so he took it. "Dorothea?" His voice was entirely devoid of its usual mocking tone. "My dear, will you do me the honour of becoming my wife?"

Despite the fact that she had expected the question, for one long moment she thought the world had stopped turning. Then, her eyes still locked on his hand, gently clasping hers, she struggled to find words to extricate herself from the predicament the question had landed her in. How typical of him! If she simply said yes, she would never learn the truth.

"My lord, I am sensible...very sensible of the honour you do me. However, I... I am not convinced there is...any real...reason or...or basis for marriage between us." In the circumstances, Dorothea felt quite pleased with the outcome. Nicely vague.

Although not surprised, Hazelmere still felt as if he had been winded. How on earth had she come to that wonderful conclusion? Clearly he was going to have to explain a few things to his beloved. Assuming it was his motives she questioned, he went directly to that issue. "Why do you imagine I want to marry you?"

Hearing the sincerity in his voice, she felt forced to reply truthfully. Now was no time for missish sentiment. "You have to marry. I gather you want a conformable wife, to give you heirs and manage your households." She paused, then added, "Someone who would not interfere with your present lifestyle."

For once, he missed the oblique allusion. "There's nothing in my present lifestyle that marriage to you would disrupt." For some reason, far from reassuring her, the statement seemed to have the opposite effect.

Dorothea gulped. For one instant she almost convinced herself that she didn't want to know. Then she shook her head. "In that case, I really don't think we...would suit."

Hazelmere was entirely at sea. He had no idea what she

was talking about, but he heard the catch in her voice. Foreseeing an unprofitable and probably distressing time ahead if they continued in this roundabout fashion, he decided to gamble all on one throw. Cutting tangled reins was the fastest way, after all. Provided you could hold the horses afterwards. Possessing himself of both her hands, he drew her around to face him. "If you're adamant that is true, then of course I'll not press you. But, if you wish to convince me what you say is so, you'll have to look at me, my love, and tell me you don't love me."

Her heart had sunk like lead at his first sentence. The second threw her into total disarray. *How could she do that?* In the long silence that ensued she could feel his eyes on her, still warm. If she looked up she would lose.

"Dorothea?"

Mute, all she could do was shake her head.

"Why? My dear, you'll have to give me some explanation." His voice, unbearably gentle and stripped of its usual lightness, brought her close to tears. She tried to look up and failed. Wrenching her hands free, she stood and took a few agitated steps, stopping beside the trunk of the oak. Her scheming was turning this into a nightmare. Heavens! What on earth had she started?

Hazelmere watched her. Clearly she was struggling with some imagined demon, but he could hardly deal with it unless she told him what it was. Calmly he stood and strolled to stand behind her. Taking her by the shoulders, he firmly turned her to face him. One hand at her waist held her lightly while the other gently tilted her face up. She stubbornly kept her lovely and far too revealing eyes lowered. "Dorothea, why won't you marry me?"

Impossible not to answer. In the end, in a voice so small that she could hardly recognise it as her own, she said, "Because you don't love me."

For nearly a minute Hazelmere, dazed, remained perfectly still. Then enlightenment dawned, and with it came relief. Dorothea, equally immobile, suddenly felt his hands shake. Startled, she looked up and saw, to her disbelieving fury, that he was laughing! Really laughing! Outraged, she flung away. Or tried to, but he had seen her intention in those beautiful eyes and held on to her, pulling her roughly into his arms and holding her, hard, against him. Rage seared through her, leaving her strangely wan. Then his voice, muffled as he spoke against her hair and still shaking with suppressed laughter, reached her. "Oh, sweetheart! What a gem you are! Here I went to the most extraordinary lengths to convince the entire ton, or at least all those who mattered, that I was *irrevocably* in love with you and the only person who didn't notice was *you!*"

Already stiff and unyielding, she went rigid. She looked up. "You *don't* love me!"

The dark brows rose. The hazel eyes, still laughing, gently quizzed her. "Don't I?"

She tore her eyes from that mesmeric glance. If she was ever to learn the answers she had to pose the questions. "What about that bet?" she asked, trying to sound scornful and not succeeding in the least.

He propped his shoulders against the oak, still holding her against him. "Young men with too much money and not enough sense. There are always bets on such things. It's nothing new. There are bets on Fanshawe and Cecily, and Julia Bressington and Harcourt, and a few other couples, too."

Her eyes had returned to his during this explanation. "Really?"

He nodded, smiling. She dropped her eyes to his shoulder while she considered that. Hazelmere studied her face.

When she remained silent he continued, "Furthermore, my love, I feel constrained to point out that, had I been seeking a suitable and complaisant wife, I would hardly choose a lady whom I have had to twice rescue from scandalous situations in public inns."

"But it wasn't my fault in either case!" protested Dorothea indignantly. She had glanced up into the teasing hazel eyes but quickly broke the connection. In a small voice she added, "I thought perhaps you felt being married to me would be more…comfortable than being married to Miss Buntton."

"Miss Buntton?" said Hazelmere incredulously. He shuddered. "My dear, being married to a hedgehog would be more comfortable than being married to Miss Buntton." Dorothea smothered a giggle. "Whoever put that idea…oh, Susan, I suppose?"

Dorothea nodded. Then another thought occurred. "You're not marrying me because of the…possible scandal over tonight?"

"After I've gone to such lengths to ensure there'll be no scandal? Of course not." As she persisted in keeping her eyes down, he added a clincher. "Besides, if that were so, how is it that I've already got Herbert's permission to address you?"

That brought her head up. "You *have* asked his permission!"

"My dear Dorothea, you really should strive to rid yourself of these ramshackle notions you cherish of me. I wouldn't ask you to marry me if I didn't have Herbert's permission to pay my addresses to you."

The pious tone pricked her temper. "What about your mistresses?" she asked.

The hazel eyes caught hers. "What about them?"

She was at a loss. "How should I know?" she said in exasperation.

"Precisely!" The dry tone left her in no doubt of what he meant. Their eyes held, then he sighed. "If you must know, I dismissed my last mistress when I returned to London last September, after meeting you. I've had enough mistresses for a lifetime. I want a wife."

Her gaze had drifted to his cravat and her hands, trapped between them, were apparently occupied in smoothing its folds. Hazelmere sighed. "My dear, delightful, idiotic Dorothea, *do* look at me. I am trying, apparently unsuccessfully, to convince you that I love you. The least you can do is pay attention!"

Dorothea had exhausted her questions. Obediently she looked up. When her eyes once more locked with his Hazelmere nodded approvingly. "Good! For your information, my love, I've been in love with you from, I think, the moment I first saw you picking blackberries in Moreton Park woods. What's more, my reputation notwithstanding, I am not in the habit of seducing village maids *or* débutantes."

The green eyes widened. Slightly breathless, she said, "I thought that was part of the bet."

Goaded, Hazelmere replied, "The only reason I've been seducing you, albeit in stages, is because I can't seem to keep my hands off you!" At her surprise, he continued, "Oh, yes! If you think I have power over you, you have just as much power over me."

The thoroughly feminine smile that spread across her lovely features prompted him to tighten his arms around her. "Now that I've got your full attention, my love, what *can* I do to convince you I love you?"

Assuming his question to be purely rhetorical, Dorothea lifted her face for his kiss. His lips gently brushed hers in a series of teasingly gentle kisses that satisfied her not at all. She wriggled her hands free and drew his head more firmly to her. She felt rather than heard his satisfied chuckle, then his lips settled over hers in a long engagement that, despite his intentions, drifted deeper with each passing minute. At some point he pushed her cloak back, allowing him access to her body, still clad in the thin silk evening gown of the night before. Too soon they reached the same point they had in Lady Merion's drawing-room. Hazelmere, still in control despite his raging desire, mentally cursed. He should not have let it go this far. There was no way he would even consider taking her here. Her first time she should remember with joy, not distaste. But he had already left her in this state once before. He couldn't do that again.

He raised his head to look at her. Her eyes were huge and glittering, deepest emerald under heavy lids. She moved, unconsciously seductive, pressing her body against him. With a ragged sigh he turned them around so her back was against the trunk of the oak. He bent his head and his lips burned a trail to the hollow of her throat. Expertly his long fingers undid the column of tiny buttons closing her bodice and loosened the laces beneath. As his hand gently cupped her naked breast she moaned softly. His lips found hers again, letting their passions ride. There were other ways she could be satisfied. And he knew them all.

Much later, when she was wrapped once more in her cloak and resting comfortably in his arms, he felt her draw a deep breath and sigh happily. He chuckled and dropped a kiss on the top of her head. "Does that mean you've agreed to marry me?"

Dorothea smiled dreamily. Without looking up, she asked, "Do I have any choice?"

"Not really. If you don't consent now I'll take you to Hazelmere, lock you in my apartments and keep you there until I get you with child. Then you won't have any choice at all."

At that she looked up, laughing. "Would you?"

The hazel eyes glinted. "Without hesitation."

She smiled, a slow, infinitely smug smile. She felt the arms around her tighten. "In that case, I'd better agree."

He nodded. "Very wise." His eyes searched her face for a moment, as if trying to gauge her state of mind. Then he sighed. "I suspect I should take advantage of your contented state to tell you that the notice of our betrothal will appear in today's *Gazette*."

For a moment the implication did not register. Then she asked, "How on earth...?"

"I asked Ferdie to put it in. It's wiser to keep the tabbies happy wherever possible." His arm around her, he started to move towards the steps.

Feigning anger, Dorothea stopped dead. "So *that's* why you're so insistent I marry you!"

The arm around her tightened again, drawing her to him once more. "Don't start that again. I'm marrying you, you disbelieving woman, because I love you!" He kissed her soundly, then pulled her on to the steps. "Besides which," he continued conversationally, "if I don't have you soon, I'm going to go out of my mind."

Amused, he watched his love blush delightfully.

"The house is over the next rise. Knowing my mother, the entire household has probably been waiting for hours."

Dorothea was eager to catch her first glimpse of Hazelmere, and as the curricle topped the rise she looked down on the huge sandstone mansion, honey-coloured in he sun, sprawling across the opposite side of the valley. Descending the gentle slope and crossing the bridge over the stream from the lake, the curricle swept through the gates in the low stone wall separating the formal gardens from the rest of the park. Hazelmere held the greys to a trot as they followed the winding drive through acres and acres of perfectly tended gardens and lawns, past shrubberies and fountains, until the curricle reached the broad sweep of the gravel court before the main entrance.

Jim Hitchin came running to take the reins, grinning with relief at seeing the horses in one piece. He had never doubted his master would return all right and tight with the lady beside him, so had wasted no thoughts on them.

Hazelmere jumped down and lifted Dorothea down. At the first sound of wheels on the gravel, Lady Hazelmere, who had been waiting in the morning-room since five o'clock, had come to the door to welcome them. She was agog to learn just why her usually correct son had seen fit to drive through the night, apparently alone with Miss Darent in an open curricle. One look at his face warned her not to ask.

Correctly surmising that they had been up all night, she immediately whisked Dorothea upstairs to the large chamber she had had prepared. It was only then that Dorothea removed her cloak, and as she moved towards the window the light fell full on her. Lady Hazelmere rapidly revised her assessment of her son's behaviour and, turning, shooed out her maid, who had come in to help. Instead she helped the sleepy girl to bed, lending her one of her own nightgowns and forbearing to ask any questions, even as to the whereabouts of her missing clothing. The telltale signs of her son's lovemaking, showing clearly on the perfect skin, would fade by the time she awoke. No need to further embarrass the child, or to expose her to the censorious mind of her sharp-eyed maid. Her own maid, Hazelmere had informed her, along with his valet, would arrive from London later.

Leaving Dorothea already halfway asleep, Lady Hazelmere went downstairs in search of her son. Hazelmere, aware of his mother's curiosity, knew that if she once caught him she would not let him go until she had all the story. He had therefore refused point-blank to pay any attention whatever to Liddiard and had repaired with all possible speed to his apartments before she could materialise and waylay him.

Baulked of all prey, her ladyship spent the rest of the morning in comfortable speculation on what her son and the lovely Dorothea had been up to.

Hazelmere woke to the rattle of curtains. Sunlight streamed into the large apartment. He closed his eyes again. He had left orders to be woken at one. He supposed it was one.

Then memory returned and the events of the early morning swam into focus. The severe lips curved in a smile of pure happiness. A discreet cough interrupted his recollections. He reluctantly opened his eyes and located Murgatroyd, standing by the bed, disapproval in every line.

"I wondered, my lord, what you wished me to do with these?" From finger and thumb hung suspended a garment, which, after a few moments of total bewilderment, Hazelmere recognised. "I found them in the pocket of your driving cloak, m'lord." Never, in all the years he had been valeting, had Murgatroyd had to deal with such an occurrence. He was badly discomposed.

Raising his eyes to the face of his henchman, now devoid of all expression, Hazelmere sternly repressed the urge to laugh. As soon as he could command his voice he said, somewhat breathlessly, "I suppose you had better return them to their owner."

Something very like shock infused the countenance of his imperturbable valet. "My lord?" Incredulity hung in the air.

"Miss Darent," supplied Hazelmere, sorely tried.

Murgatroyd assimilated this information, his face wooden. "Of course, my lord." He bowed and had almost reached the door before Hazelmere spoke again.

"Incidentally, Murgatroyd, Miss Darent and I are to be married in a few weeks, so I'm afraid you'll have to get used to such happenings."

"Indeed, my lord?" Murgatroyd's breast seethed with a whole range of emotions. He had never before valeted to a married gentleman, preferring the regularities of bachelor households. It was the reason he had left his last position. But he had been very comfortable in Hazelmere's employ. And Miss Darent, soon to be her ladyship, was a very lovely woman. And the Marquis was... well, Hazelmere. The rigid features relaxed into something approaching a smile. "I'm sure I wish you both very happy, my lord."

Hazelmere smiled his acknowledgement and dropped back on to his pillows as Murgatroyd left in search of Trimmer.

The next five days passed in a rush of activity. Hazelmere had decreed they were to be married at St George's in Hanover Square in just over two weeks. There was a wealth of detail to be discussed and decisions made. A constant stream of couriers passed between London and Hazelmere, carrying orders and information. On that first afternoon Tony Fanshawe and Cecily dropped by on their way back to London. On hearing the news, Cecily was ecstatic; Betsy promptly burst into tears.

From Lady Merion came the news that the whole town was a-buzz with the tale of their trip to Hazelmere Water and, far from there being any undesirable comment, everyone was describing it as the romance of the Season. As Dorothea refolded her grandmother's letter Hazelmere smiled wickedly across the breakfast table. "Just as well they'll never know what really happened at Hazelmere Water."

Dorothea gasped, then, outraged by the knowing look on his face, threw a roll at him. Ducking, he protested, "I thought only Cecily threw things!"

They decided to return to London on Monday. Hazelmere spent Sunday afternoon with Liddiard. He would only be able to spare a single day in the run-up to their wedding for dealing with any further business. Liddiard was to be in ultimate charge of all his estates until they returned from their wedding trip to Italy.

Dorothea, time hanging heavy on her hands, went to sit in the sunken rose garden. It had been five days since they had arrived; five days since that morning above Hazelmere Water. And in those five days Marc had been politely attentive but curiously distant. They had exchanged nothing but the most chastely light kisses—no passionate embraces, no delicious caresses. It was ridiculous! What on earth was the matter now?

A swish of silk skirts heralded Lady Hazelmere's approach. The two women had become firm friends. With a smile her ladyship settled herself on the stone bench beside her soon to be daughter-in-law, and, as was her habit, took the bull by the horns. "What's the matter?"

Used by now to her ways, Dorothea grimaced. "It's nothing, really."

Lady Hazelmere's shrewd eyes studied the younger woman. Then she made an educated guess. "Hasn't Marc slept with you yet?"

Dorothea blushed rosily.

Her ladyship laughed musically, then reassured her. "Don't get upset, child. I couldn't help notice you were missing a rather vital article of clothing when you arrived. I presume you didn't set out from London like that?"

In spite of herself, Dorothea grinned. "No."

"Well," said her ladyship, examining the tips of her slippers as they peeped from under the hem of her stylishly elegant gown, "Marc seems to be taking after his father in more ways than one. It's something of a shock to think you're marrying a rake and find instead that, at least before the wedding, you'd get the same treatment from the Archbishop's son."

Dorothea giggled.

"Well, maybe not quite the same," amended Lady Hazelmere. "But all the Henry men are like that—scandalous on the one hand and puritanical on the other. It's decidedly confusing. Mind you, I doubt there have been many virgin brides in the family, either."

Dorothea sat up straighter. "Oh?"

"A word of advice, my dear: if you don't wish to be forced to wait the full two weeks until your wedding, you'd better do something about it. You're leaving for London tomorrow and once there, if I know Marc, you'll have no chance to force the issue. If, on the other hand, you break his resistance now, you should have no trouble in London."

"But he seems so very distant, I wondered if perhaps he—"

"*Distant?* What on earth happened at Hazelmere Water?" exclaimed her ladyship. "That sort of thing, let me tell you, just doesn't happen if a man is 'distant'. Marc's keeping as far away from you as possible because he doesn't trust himself—he knows he's too close to the edge with you, that's all. If you want him to make love to you before your wedding you'll just have to give him a push.'

Dorothea, eyes round, regarded her soon to be mother-in-law. The novel idea of forcing such an issue with her stubborn and domineering betrothed had an attraction all its own. "How?"

Tucking her arm into Dorothea's, Lady Hazelmere smiled joyously. "Let's go and look at your wardrobe, shall we?"

That evening Hazelmere arrived in the drawing-room just ahead of Penton, as usual, to escort his betrothed and his mother into dinner. As he crossed the threshold his eyes went to Dorothea. He blinked and checked, then smoothly recovered himself.

Throughout the meal he struggled to keep his eyes away from the vision in ivory silk seated on his right. But for once his mother seemed curiously silent, leaving Dorothea and himself to carry the conversation. In the end he forced himself to keep his eyes on her face. That was bad enough, but not nearly so disturbing as the rest of her. Where in hell had she got that gown? Presumably Celestine—simplicity was her hallmark. An ivory sheath with a bodice so abbreviated that it barely passed muster, with an overdress of silk gauze so fine that it was completely transparent. The entire creation was held together by a row of tiny pearl buttons down the front. He had never been so thankful to see the end of a meal as he was that night.

He watched Dorothea and his mother retire upstairs to

he parlour. With a sigh of relief he went into the library. Half an hour later, settled in one of the huge wing chairs before the fire, a large brandy by his side, he was deep in the latest newsheet when he heard the door shut. Looking up, he stood as Dorothea came towards him, calm and serene as ever, a book in her hands. "Your mother has retired early so that she'll be able to farewell us in the morning. I thought I'd come and sit with you for a while. You don't mind, do you?"

He smiled in response to her smile and settled her in the wing chair opposite his. She opened her book and seemed to be quite content to sit quietly reading. He returned to his newsheet.

For a while only the ticking of the huge grandfather clock in the corner and the occasional crackle from the fire disturbed the peace. Glancing up, he saw she had laid aside her book and was calmly watching the leaping flames. The light from the fire flickered in a rosy glow over her still figure, striking coppery glints from her dark hair. He forced his attention back to the newsheet.

After reading the same paragraph four times, and still having no idea what it said, he gave up. He laid the paper aside. In one smooth movement he rose and, crossing to her, took her hands; raising her, he drew her into his arms. He looked down into her emerald eyes, then bent his head until his lips found hers. The room was still; only the flames rose and fell, illuminating the figures locked together before the hearth. When the kiss finally ended they were both breathing raggedly. The hazel and green eyes locked for a time in silent communion, then Hazelmere bent to lightly brush her lips with his. "I love you."

Hardly daring to speak in case the magic surrounding them shattered into a million shards, Dorothea barely breathed the words, "And I love you."

The severely sculpted lips lifted in a decidedly wicked smile. "Let's go to bed."

Many hours later Dorothea, blissfully sated, snuggled herself against the long length of her husband-to-be. They had come up to his room; her room next door was not yet refurbished. Her clothes, and his, were scattered in a trail from the door to the hearth. They had first made love exquisitely, on the huge daybed before the fire. Later they had moved to the even larger four-poster, where they now lay. With a soft, contented sigh she settled herself to sleep, one arm across his chest, his arm around her, holding her close.

Suddenly, in the darkness, Hazelmere chuckled. Then he shook with silent laughter. "Oh, God! What on earth will Murgatroyd say this time?"

Dorothea murmured sleepily and dropped a kiss on his collarbone. She had no idea who Murgatroyd was and was not particularly interested. She was too busy savouring the novel sensation of having won an argument with her arrogant Marquis. Even if she did not win another for a considerable time, she doubted it would bother her. She was bound to be far too contented to care.

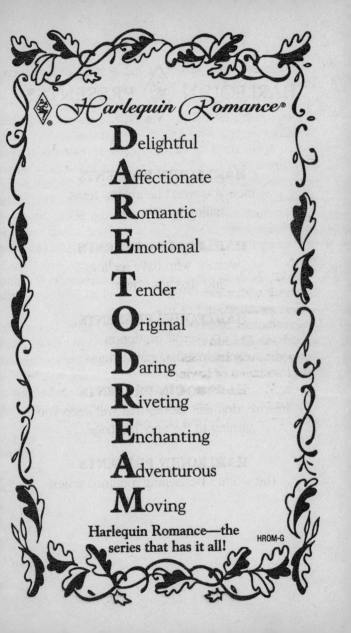

HARLEQUIN  PRESENTS®

HARLEQUIN PRESENTS
men you won't be able to resist
falling in love with...

HARLEQUIN PRESENTS
women who have feelings
just like your own...

HARLEQUIN PRESENTS
powerful passion in
exotic international settings...

HARLEQUIN PRESENTS
intense, dramatic stories that will keep you
turning to the very last page...

HARLEQUIN PRESENTS
The world's bestselling romance series!

Harlequin® Historical

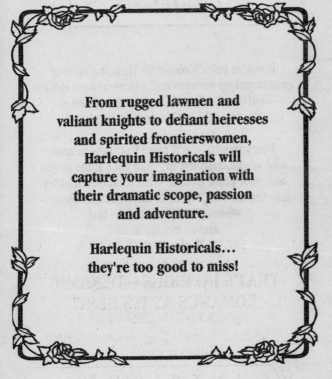

From rugged lawmen and
valiant knights to defiant heiresses
and spirited frontierswomen,
Harlequin Historicals will
capture your imagination with
their dramatic scope, passion
and adventure.

Harlequin Historicals…
they're too good to miss!

HHGENR

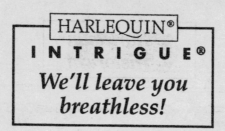

LOOK FOR OUR FOUR FABULOUS MEN!

Each month some of today's bestselling authors bring
four new fabulous men to Harlequin American Romance.
Whether they're rebel ranchers, millionaire power brokers
or sexy single dads, they're all gallant princes—and
they're all ready to sweep you into lighthearted fantasies
and contemporary fairy tales where anything is possible
and where all your dreams come true!

You don't even have to make a wish...
Harlequin American Romance will grant your every desire!

Look for Harlequin American Romance
wherever Harlequin books are sold!

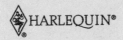

Not The Same Old Story!

 Exciting, glamorous romance stories that take readers around the world.

 Sparkling, fresh and tender love stories that bring you pure romance.

 Bold and adventurous—Temptation is strong women, bad boys, great sex!

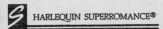 Provocative and realistic stories that celebrate life and love.

 Contemporary fairy tales—where anything is possible and where dreams come true.

 Heart-stopping, suspenseful adventures that combine the best of romance and mystery.

 Humorous and romantic stories that capture the lighter side of love.